BLINDED

AN ELKRIDGE SERIES NOVEL

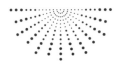

LYZ KELLEY

Belvitri
Services

BLINDED

He vowed never to return home.

His boss needs him on a critical case in Seattle, yet his honed
detective instincts tell him whoever killed his brother is part of
something more sinister than the Elkridge deputies can handle.
There's just one problem—going home means seeing Mara.
The girl he's never forgotten and the one he's loved since high
school. However, there's something he doesn't know,
something big.

Mara had big dreams. Taking over a neglected small town
flower shop wasn't one of them. Neither was losing her parents
and her independence. She's trying to make the best of life, but
weird things are happening in town, and she can't shake the
feeling of being watched. Her world tilts even more when Joey
unexpectedly arrives—her first love and the man who broke
her heart.

Why did he come back now, now when she's so broken?
How can he leave when those he loves need protecting?

PRAISE FOR LYZ KELLEY'S WRITING
AND A SPECIAL GIFT JUST FOR YOU.

I have a present for you…your very own ebook exclusive:
Regrets, the prequel to BLINDED
when you sign up for my newsletter.

Newsletter Sign Up: http://lyzkelley.net

The Molly: Award for Excellence
"A writer who will go the distance."
"Masterful dialog."
"I look forward to seeing this book on the bookshelves."

The Sheila: Finalist
"The story has great bones! The plot is interesting, the characters are unique…there are so many things to love about this story."

"H & H are both very appealing and certainly not cookie cutter characters."

"Your opening is a grabber."

"This is one of the best books I've read in a good long while. CONGRATULATIONS."

"Prose is sleek, polished and smooth, a near frictionless read."

The Marlene: Finalist
"You have a lovely writing style with dialogue and scene setting."

"The sensory details are rich, and I was able to visualize the scenes. I chuckled several times at your turn of phrase and thought they were very sassy and smart."

"The plot seems to have it all: conflict, a mystery and a romance. So kudos for creating an interesting story."

The Golden Network: Finalist
"The setting is painted well and the characters are engaging with very different voices."

"The manuscript is clean and tightly written."

"The manuscript reflects beautiful writing."

CHAPTER ONE

Elkridge, Colorado

Joey Gaccione glared at the window display of heart-shaped Mylar balloons, pink and white teddy bears, and an assortment of floral arrangements. If the obligation to get his mom flowers didn't sit across his shoulders like a three-hundred-pound weight, he'd have climbed right back in his rental car and left.

He'd forgotten today was Valentine's Day. He'd forgotten a lot of things lately. Maybe because he just didn't want to remember.

Reaching for the flower shop's door, Joey forced his feet to move forward, like he'd forced himself to board a plane in Seattle, forced himself to rent a car in Denver, then forced himself to drive to the little town of Elkridge, Colorado. His home. A place he'd avoided for more than ten years.

Entering Elkridge Blooms, he took a shallow breath. The pungent smell of the shop's pollens triggered an urgent need to sneeze, and wreaked havoc with his dutiful determination to buy something for his mother. Before he could exhale, a flash of gold captured his attention, and he turned, instantly recognizing the woman behind the counter.

"Be with you in a minute," Mara called out, a sweet melody that briefly eased the turmoil plaguing him for the past several days. She gently presented a bouquet to her customer. "Here you go, Mr. Walters. Thank you for coming in today. Tell Mrs. Walters I hope she feels better soon."

A stirring of first-crush memories helped his lungs expand, providing a much-needed pump of fresh oxygen.

Mara Dijocomo hadn't changed much. In fact, the light dusting of freckles across her nose, the way her chin thrust forward when she wanted to make a point, and her dancing eyebrows with a multitude of expressions, could still make him forget what he was thinking. At eighteen, he could sit for hours listening to the lyrical tone of her voice, or watching her gentle, yet sometimes determined movements.

She swatted at a tendril of midnight-black hair that gently curved around the edge of her chin, one of many long strands falling from the haphazardly tied knot at the base of her neck. Peaceful contentment mellowed her memorable face. Her sunflower-strewn apron furnished the splash of color that had caught his eye. Like a feather, she floated through her daily routine.

Seeing the youngest Dijocomo family member behind the counter made sense.

Joey idly inspected the older man, tallying the visual clues— retired military. He traded nods with the man before he turned back to his high school buddy's younger sister.

Mara rotated slightly. "May I help you?"

Help sounded great, especially hers, but highly unlikely. Her beautiful smile greeted him, while her ice-blue eyes stared past him, oddly off-target, just enough to notice. Her body swayed while she shifted from foot to foot, giving him the impression she had a very long list of to-dos that contradicted her serene expression.

He watched. He measured.

A pure yet raw understanding and quiet respect formed. The car accident had taken more than her family. The tragedy had also left her less than whole—a damn shame.

He'd thought about her over the years, although a little less often after he heard she was engaged.

"May I help you with something?" she asked again, this time with anxiousness fraying the edges of her question.

"Mara, it's me, Joey. Joey Gaccione."

"Joey?"

The instant joy on her face made his ears buzz. "You remember me?" Energy zinged up and down his spine, and sizzled out to his fingers and toes.

"Of course I remember you. How could I forget? You spent an entire year tutoring me, helping me ace my math and science classes." She clutched the counter. "I'm so sorry about your brother. Do they know who shot him? I heard someone say it was a poacher."

"That's what I've been told," he choked out, while at the same time working to tamp down his grief. He efficiently compartmentalized the surge of emotion and put his brother's death neatly into an imaginary box. He'd deal with his feelings another time, when he was alone...just not now.

Mara's face softened. "The town feels your loss." Her voice brimmed with compassion. "Sam was well respected. Especially since he grew up here..." Mara bit her lip, and the thoughtful expression crossing her face drew his attention.

"How come I get the feeling there's something else you want to add?"

"It's nothing. Well, it's not nothing, it's just..."

"Mara?"

A yellow lab followed her from behind the counter and

leaned in for a scratch behind the ears. Her fingers grazed the top of the dog's head, threading through the thick fur. The bliss on the pooch's face made Joey pause, while her inquisitive, off-center gaze gave his lungs a high-voltage kick-start.

"Last week, Sam stopped me while I was walking home from the grocery store and asked if I wanted a ride home."

A ping of jealousy whacked him on the chest. After all this time, she could still get his heart to beat a bit faster. "That was nice of my brother. You're a beautiful woman, Mara, and I can see why he made the offer."

She reached for the counter. "No. You misunderstand me. It wasn't like that." Her grip tightened to the point her knuckles turned white.

"Okay…then why did he stop?"

"That's just it. I'm not sure. Sam knows Buddy's afraid of riding in cars, and I only had a few more blocks to go until I was home, but he insisted. In fact, he was very insistent, and almost forced Buddy and me into his SUV. Even after I was inside the store, I heard him re-check the front and back doors to make sure the store was locked up tight. I remember thinking at the time the extra security measures were odd."

He rested his fist on his hip, feeling the absence of the service revolver that usually tugged at his waist. "Did you ask him why he was so insistent?"

"No. But I kept running into him—more than usual—and now I get the feeling I'm being watched. Maybe I'm just being paranoid, but I keep wondering if that night didn't have something to do with his death."

A murder? Now a stalker?

Anger, trepidation, and frustration all combined to create a nasty knot in his gut. With a deep swallow, he recalled his boss's voice of reason. *Don't get caught up in the anger. Let the deputies do their jobs. Trust in the system. They'll catch the shooter. Just be there for your family. Attend the funeral. Nothing more.* He'd promised his boss he'd be back in Seattle in a week or less. *Serial killers don't wait for detectives to attend funerals*, his boss's last words reminded him.

"I'm sorry," Mara said, a light pink staining her cheeks. "I'm sure you didn't come in here to talk about your brother. I bet you came in to buy some flowers. Am I right?"

"Nice change of subject." The warmth returning to her eyes ignited a similar feeling in his heart. "And, you're right, I need a thing of flowers for my mom."

"For Valentine's Day?"

"No, just something to cheer her up. And, maybe a couple of roses for my sisters and niece."

"Do you know what kind of flowers or plants your mom likes?"

He scanned the thirty- by forty-foot store. Plants in decorative containers surrounded tables crammed with small pots of flowering plants. Flowers delicately arranged in heart-shaped jars and glass vases lined every shelf of the refrigerated case, and cards, candles, and specialty gifts occupied the remaining crevices. The cozy store might have created a sense of well-being if not for the fact that he didn't have a clue what type of flowers his mom liked.

Frustration and that old sense of not living up to expectations crept back in. "Sorry. I don't have a clue."

"No worries. We'll figure something out." The oh-how-sweet way she made him feel urged him to pick her up and sweep her out the door.

Instead of spending the next several hours hearing about his failure as a son, brother, and uncle, he'd rather be taking a girl like Mara to his favorite Seattle restaurant overlooking the Sound, ordering up some fresh Pacific Coast halibut, maybe grilled asparagus, and finishing off with a dark chocolate mousse for two. If he got lucky, she would invite him to her place or accompany him home. Then again, who was he kidding? The case he'd been trying to solve for the past eight months took every waking hour. He didn't have time to even think about women, dating, or sex.

He wished now he'd taken the time to text his sister for his mother's favorite flower, but he hadn't. "Maybe this wasn't such a good idea."

"Taking flowers to a woman is always a good idea. Don't give up yet. We'll figure this out." Mara dropped her chin in concentration. The cute crinkling of her forehead and scrunched nose made him smile. "How about some red carnations with purple iris?"

Red? The image of blood pooling on the ground flashed through his mind. "I'm thinking red might remind Ma of Sam's death, so I'm not sure that will work."

"Right. That won't do. Hmmm." Mara doodled small, complex circles and curves on the counter with her delicate fingers. He tried imagining what the picture would look like if she used a pencil. The intricate pattern swirled left, then right into a tight curl, then spun out like a ballerina.

"I put an arrangement together this morning that might work," she said, interrupting his study of her dancing fingers. "It's bright and cheerful, with pink carnations, green hydrangea, stargazer lilies, and Alstroemeria to make the arrangement kind of fun. It's over here in the case."

The description didn't help, since carnations, roses, and daisies nearly exceeded the upper limits of his flower knowledge. She moved to the refrigerated cabinet and pulled a cellophane-wrapped arrangement out of a bucket of water. "What do you think? I can put the flowers in a pretty vase, or tie a soft green ribbon around the bouquet if you prefer."

He had no idea if the clumps of green and pink would work for his mom. "I don't want to trouble you. It's the thought that counts, right?"

"It's no trouble."

Before he could respond, the shop door banged open and a gust of cold wind blew in.

"Mara, I'm back," a loud baritone voice blasted through the shop. "All the arrangements are delivered, and Mrs. Newhall said she's throwing a party for her sister's birthday. She'll call tomorrow to give us specifics."

The oversized hulk hadn't bothered to look up while stomping snow off his boots and scattering ice crystals left and right. Wrapped in a worn, thick ski jacket, he lifted fingers scarlet from Colorado's abnormally cold winter to his mouth and blew air into his cupped hands. Dark hair, worn jeans, and the crisp jawline triggered a flashback.

"Tony D-Jock." Warm memories of playing ball with his high school buddy surfaced.

Startled eyes connected with his, then softened.

"Joey Catchy-Monkey." Tony extended his hand for a quick shake. "How ya doin'? I heard you were coming back for a visit. Sorry about your brother, man. But, hey. What's it been? Four, five years?"

"Ten." The weight of ten-plus years hung like a cement slab around his neck. "Four years at college. Six years working my way up to detective grade in the Seattle/Tacoma area."

"No kidding." Tony gave him an up-and-down assessment. "You've gotten a bit taller. Still playin' soccer?"

"No time. I played in the minor leagues out of college, but then decided I'd better get busy making a living. Didn't you get a football scholarship or something? University of Colorado, wasn't it?"

Tony's eyes flicked to his sister. She'd suddenly taken an interest in the flowers on the counter. The thickening silence made Joey's careless mistake even more stupid. His mother told him about the college game, the icy roads, and the drunk driver. In a flash—three-fifths of the Dijocomo family gone.

"Hey, man, I—"

"Football's not for everyone." Tony's casual tone didn't quite manage to translate into his eyes. "Besides, my grades weren't great, so I decided to come home. Good thing I did, or I wouldn't have been able to convince Gina not to marry that schmo from the Springs and marry me instead."

"Gina Martinez? You mean that cute cheerleader you couldn't untwist your tongue enough to say hi to? She finally got you to pop the question? Congratulations." Joey's smile deflated slowly. "Dude, you do remember she's got brothers built like buffalos."

"And all four brothers-in-law flex their muscles every chance they get." Tony laughed. "Sisters. Gotta protect 'em, ya know?"

"Maybe us sisters don't want to be smothered by all that brotherly macho-ness. The interference can be rather irritating, and often inconvenient."

Interesting. Still headstrong and independent as ever.

Mara began drawing those intricate circles again. "Speaking of sisters, isn't my sister-in-law waiting for you at home? You should get going."

"Crap, I'm late." Tony kissed his sister's cheek. "I got some supplies to unload, then I want to do a quick rinse and change before I go. You still okay with me cutting out early? I'm worried about last-minute orders."

"Go, already. And don't forget to take Gina the flower arrangement, or you just might not get dinner. And if you're going to use my shower, don't leave the towel on the floor for me to trip over this time."

"See how they nag? One's bad enough. I don't envy you having three." Tony reached behind his sister, yanked loose an apron string, then took two precautionary steps out of arm's reach.

Mara's instant swing-and-miss crooked Tony's mouth into

that naughty-little-boy grin understood by all men, no matter their age. Joey, however, wasn't impressed.

"Joey, my man, glad to see you. We should catch up over a beer or watch a game while you're here."

"Find me on Facebook and message me a place and time, and I'll be there." *And perhaps you'll bring your sister along.*

"Listen to this guy. He's gone all city on us."

"Would you just go? And stop harassing the customers," Mara chastised, even though her pure exasperation over being teased didn't mar her pretty face.

Joey couldn't tell whether the pink in her cheeks was from wanting to strangle her brother or embarrassment. One thing he knew for sure—Tony could mess with Mara, but if anyone *else* messed with the younger Dijocomo, even hell wouldn't be a safe place to hide. Pictures of both her brother and her late father could be found in the dictionary next to the definition of overprotective.

Back then Joey's adolescent hormones hadn't been strong enough to overpower his survival instincts. He studied her left hand. No ring. No indent. How odd.

Patiently, she retied the strings of her apron and returned to adjusting the green bow on the bouquet for his mom. "How many long-stemmed roses would you like?"

"Five."

"Okay. Pick out the ones you like." She pointed to a white bucket filled with a variety of pink, white and red roses. "Will that be debit or credit?" Mara asked.

"Credit." He flipped open his oiled leather wallet to pull out a plastic card. "You still writing songs?"

She paused and pushed another tendril of hair behind her ear. "Wow, you have a good memory."

"When we studied together, you used to talk about your writing sometimes. I remember you won the talent contest my senior year, and managed to piss off Rachelle Clairemont. She was certain her free-dance routine would take home the trophy."

"Don't say that too loud. She might hear you."

Joey remembered the blonde who'd acted like the school's halls were her private fashion runway. Remembering the way she wore designer clothing and pushed her shoulders back to highlight her...assets... made him laugh. She even had that full, pouty-lip thing down.

"Is Rachelle still in town?" he asked. "I would have wagered she'd take off for LA or New York the first chance she got."

"I think her dad likes to keep her close to home."

"Mr. Clairemont does like to be the big man in town."

Her mouth tightened, as if she had something else to say, but decided not to say it out loud. Her sour expression gave him a twinge of amusement, something absent from his life for quite a while.

She nodded before pushing the flowers in his direction and handing him his credit card. "So how long will you be in town?"

"Don't know yet. I have five days of bereavement leave."

"That's it? You haven't been home in ten years, and that's all you get?"

"No. I have twenty-six days of accumulated leave racked up, but I promised my boss I'd get back as soon as I can. The case I'm working on can't wait."

"What about your brother's case? The community is spooked that there's a murderer on the loose, and I'd think your family would want you to help. The deputies sure could use some outside expertise." Her fingers stopped swirling and began to tap. "Rumors have it you're brilliant when it comes to solving murders."

A tension strap wrapped around his chest and squeezed. His mother was famous for her colorful exaggerations. "The Elkridge rumor mill is obviously still great at distorting the facts. I don't have jurisdiction here. I'm sure the department's doing what they can to find whoever fired that shot. Homicide cases like this take way more time to solve than people think. It's not like on TV where crimes are solved in an hour."

"I imagine it must be hard, coming home after being gone for so long, especially for a funeral. But I'm sure your parents appreciate the effort."

Mom, maybe. Dad, definitely not. "It's not like I haven't wanted to come back. It's just…life has a way of getting busy."

"Life also has a way of creating opportunities. Everyone is going to be happy to see you."

Opportunities. He assumed she meant his coming home. Her optimism amazed him, considering what she'd been through. Life had a way of destroying one's innocent expectations, but even with Mara's unique challenges, she seemed grounded, with a genuine, upbeat confidence. He couldn't say that about most of the women he knew. He wished he could find a woman like Mara in Washington. Heck, he wished Mara would move to Seattle, but he could tell she was happy in Elkridge. Story of his life. Wrong place. Wrong time.

He checked his watch. "Maybe I'll see you around."

"Most likely. Oh, and Joey? Please don't say anything to Tony about…well you know. He worries about me enough."

"I won't say anything, but promise me you'll be extra vigilant and report anything odd."

"I will." Mara reached for her dog's ear to give it a good rub. "I hope the flowers make your mom feel better."

"Thanks. This rose is for you." He pushed a long-stemmed rose toward her. "Happy Valentine's Day, Mara." The splash of pink appeared again. "Take care."

He picked up the flower bundles and lifted his hand in a goodbye salute, but then remembered Mara probably couldn't see the gesture. As far as he could tell, Mara was completely blind.

CHAPTER TWO

"Don't forget the flowers," Mara called over her shoulder when she heard her brother's heavy thump-itty-thump-thumps heading down the back stairs from her small apartment above the store. "And don't forget to ask Gina what dates she wants for her baby shower. She's going to pop any day, so we need to start planning. And please quit worrying about me." She paused to smell the rose Joey had given her before washing her hands at the back room's utility sink.

Warm lips planted a smacking kiss on her cheek. "Stop nagging. I won't forget. Also notice I didn't say a word about falling down the stairs or being in the store all alone."

Very slick, bro. You nag even while claiming you're not. So typical.

The rustling of a plastic bag followed by a crisp crunch meant her brother had taken the last apple from the store's mini-fridge…again. She swore under her breath, wondering how she was going to pay the past due bills or buy groceries.

"Your thoughts are mighty loud these days." She selected a rose stem and trimmed the end to keep Tony's nagging from ruining her practiced, cheerful mood. "I don't want to hear about the stair incident again. I just tripped on Buddy's leash, that's all."

"And went flying down the stairs. You could have broken your neck." He attempted to cover his concern with a jesting voice, but failed.

"Don't blow things out of proportion."

"If you could see the bruises on your arms and legs, you would know I'm not."

She turned and pointed the floral scissors in his general direction. "You can't be running over here every five minutes. You need to focus on Gina. It's not every day a girl steals a boy's peanut butter sandwich in kindergarten and then gets to marry him twenty years later. Besides, the baby will be here soon, and you don't have the nursery set up yet."

"Yeah, I still need to do that, and get our website on-line."

"I keep telling you we can't afford a website."

"We can't afford *not* to have a website."

Mara blew out a frustrated breath and opened the flower storage refrigerator, leaning in to run her fingers over the raised-letter labels on the buckets. Finding the correct container, she selected some leather leaf ferns and another bunch of yellow daisies. "Gina should be your primary focus. Family first, business second, remember?"

"Yeah, family first. That's why I want you to take more time for yourself. You can't spend all your time stuck here. Go out on a date, or something."

"Like that's ever going to happen," she mumbled, then gritted her teeth, wishing she'd been able to keep her gloom from leaking into her comment.

"If you're thinking about Mark, don't. I'll break that guy's face if he ever shows those dimples in this town again. He's an ass for leaving you like he did, and always treating you like his personal bank account. You need to find someone decent, like Joey. I saw him checking you out earlier, so I know he's still interested. Bet he'll ask you out on a date this time."

This time? "What do you mean, this time?"

"Give me a break. No way was I going to let an eighteen-year-old date my fifteen-year-old little sister."

She aligned the bottoms of the flower stems and considered how everything in her life had changed. Losing both parents and Sarah had created obligations that shouldn't have been Tony's responsibility. She didn't like being someone's obligation, and she absolutely refused to be a burden.

"Since when did you appoint yourself my decision-maker?" Mara challenged.

"Since Dad pulled me aside when I was fourteen and told me to look out for you."

Well, crap. She let the annoyance shrink into a minor irritation. "Fact is, I'm no longer fifteen, so you can stop with the fussing. Joey's a sweet guy, but he's just visiting for the funeral." She picked up the rose he'd given her to take in the aroma that reminded her of love, mostly because her mom arranged a new bouquet of roses for her father's office each week. "Joey's made a bigger life for himself. This town will be way too small for him now."

"You never know. He might decide to come back. Maybe he'll take over Sam's job."

"Can you see him wanting it? I can't. He was always in his brother's shadow before he moved away. He resented Sam in many ways."

The contrasts between the Gaccione brothers could span the Royal Gorge. Sam was loud, always seeking praise, projecting the image of a tough guy when he wasn't. He'd had the looks for politics—trim build, friendly smile, and empathetic eyes—and those traits were most likely the reasons he was voted in as Sheriff. Mara skimmed her fingers over the shelf of vases until she found the shape she wanted. "Tony, before you leave, would you mind putting these pink carnations in the refrigerator?"

"Maybe you should have asked Gaccione to help before he left. The way he looked at you, I'm sure he would have done anything you asked."

She launched a wet rag in her brother's direction. "Would you stop? He's just a customer. I don't need or want someone to feel sorry for me."

"Close, but you missed—nice try." The rag landed on the counter beside her. "Joey might feel a lot of things for you, but sorry isn't one of them. Want to wager on how long it takes Detective Gaccione to come back for more flowers? I wasn't kidding about him checking you out. I considered ramming his head into the snowdrift outside, but let the looks slide since he might be able to have me arrested."

"Stop it." Irritation over the teasing made her want to ram her brother's head into something, and a snowdrift wasn't her first choice. "He came in to buy flowers for his mother, and he'll be gone in a few days. End of story."

"Do you think he'll help with the investigation?"

"I doubt it. He said something about not having jurisdiction. I overheard Deputy Ernie say they didn't have any solid leads, so it's too bad he won't be allowed to help."

"And you wonder why I worry about you being alone in the store. Everyone's wigged out."

That's why I didn't tell you about Sam bringing me home, or following me everywhere.

"I'm fine," she said carefully...carefully, because if she sounded too confident, stubborn, or appeared fragile, her brother would be over every night to check on her, and that was the last thing she needed. "Buddy will protect me," she offered as a compromise.

"Don't overrate Buddy's abilities. He's a good mutt, but he's no attack dog. Although he is smart. Who knows? He just might invite a stranger in, help them pick out some nice flowers, maybe even create an arrangement."

Hearing his name, Buddy lifted his head from Mara's foot. Deciding no one had issued a command or was offering dinner or treats, he laid his paw on top of her shoe again and resettled until the rear shop entrance door opened, his head popping up again.

"Just me," Kym Zhang said. "Hey, Tony. I figured you'd be home by now. It's Valentine's Day."

The smell of nail polish mixed with cherry blossom lotion meant her best friend had just repainted her nails for the third time that week. According to Kym, maintaining the nail salon's image was a must. Mara imagined her wearing iridescent purple polish with tiny pink flowers, or neon blue with white polka dots, or sassy red with glitter. The clunk of cans on the counter meant dinner had also arrived.

"Yeah. I'm late," Tony grumbled before perking up. "What did you bring for dinner?"

"Stuff to make burritos."

The sound of a paper bag rustling made Mara turn. "Tony, stay out of our food. Gina cooked your favorite meal, so don't go poking your nose into ours." She pointed in the direction of the mini-refrigerator. "If you're hungry, your lasagna leftovers from last week's lunch are still taking up precious space. Why don't you take the box with you or flush the contents, one of the two?"

"Gross." Disgust saturated Kym's comment. "I bet there's slimy green mold growing on it."

The thought of mold made Mara want to gag. "Tell Gina she needs to teach you how to cook. You would eat better. Besides, ordering out several days a week is expensive."

"How is she going to teach me to cook when she can't even bend over to get to the pots and pans?" His back-off irritation underlined his question. "The extra jobs I'm picking up in town will cover the costs."

The muscles in Mara's neck and shoulders tightened. "Some, but not all the costs. Have you checked out the prices of diapers lately?"

"Maybe you could install a storage system like Mara's so everything is within reach," Kym suggested.

"Here's an idea," Tony grumbled at Kym. "Why don't you go over and hand Gina the pans? That way I don't have to spend my time buying and installing racks. Besides, why cook? That's what sisters, wives, and delivery are for."

"Don't start, you two," Mara warned, her temper more fragile than the bunch of baby's breath in her hand. She rubbed her temple to ease the ache. "Would you just go, Tony? Us girls have plans. Also, don't forget to be here early tomorrow to do the inventory and accept the flower delivery. I ordered some white roses and a variety of gerberas that will need new bucket labels. I don't want to mix up the colors. Plus, you have four fax orders to deliver before noon, and I'm sure there will be some last minute Valentine's oops-orders. There always are. Promise me you'll be here at six."

Tony groaned. "You know I hate mornings. How about seven? And don't forget to lock the door."

Mara opened her mouth to say something but the click of the rear door made her pause. *So typical.*

At least he might make dinner on time before Gina decided to give up and freeze the entire meatloaf. Now if she could only convince Kym that DVDs without dreamy images of Viggo or Orlando were worth consideration, the evening might end up bearable.

"Your brother's bossy," Kym said with a fair amount of disgust. "Was that Joey Gaccione I saw getting out of a rental car this afternoon?"

Leave it to Kym to be the first to spot an attractive male. "Yep. He was buying flowers for his mom."

"That woman scares me. I think I'd try buying her off with flowers, too. Did he buy something for his dad?"

"No, why?"

"Because that guy is downright hostile, especially if he's been drinking. Best bet is to avoid him if you want to stay beyond the reach of his backhand."

"I think Mr. Gaccione is the reason Joey never came home."

"I bet you're right. Mrs. Gaccione's not so bad, although she did demand perfect grades and college scholarships."

"She's strict, but who could blame her with so many kids to manage, feed, clothe, and educate? I bet if everyone didn't get scholarships the family's educational fund—times five—could have rivaled the national debt."

"My mom didn't care what my grades were as long as I kept my knees locked together."

Kym's high school "uniform" of short skirts and low-cut tops made Mara smile. "You were a rebel back then." She turned to push a rose stem into the green floral foam. "Isn't Anna Gaccione four years behind us? She's the youngest, right?"

"Yep. She'll finish college this spring."

The disappointment tugged at Mara's heart. At eighteen, she'd had big and somewhat naïve dreams of getting her degree, then a high-profile career, a house in suburbia with a three-car garage, and, eventually, a large enough family to fill an oversized corner lot. Now she was stuck in the real world with the harsh truth.

"At least Tony and I got my freshman college debt paid off, as well as his student loans. I can't imagine us having to make that loan payment each month on top of everything else."

"I wouldn't want that giant wad of debt. Besides, with your smarts and looks, you don't need a degree," Kym concluded.

"So you keep telling me. But I'm not as smart as Joey. He must have a high triple-digit IQ."

"Yah, uber-smart, but bless my G-string, the guy looks yummy-hot. With those tight-fitting jeans all snug around that cute, round butt. Mm-mm-mm."

"Quit." Heat brushed Mara's cheeks as she imagined all that yumminess.

"So what's he up to these days?"

"He's a detective in Seattle."

"Does that mean he has a set of handcuffs? *Oh, baby.* He can play the lead role in my fantasies anytime he wants."

"Kym Li Zhang, what would your mother think if she heard you talk like that?" Mara scolded, ruining the seriousness of the statement by laughing halfway through.

"I wanted to come over, but I had four mani-pedi's and two wax appointments scheduled. From what I saw, he's better looking now than before. That's just mind-boggling." Her best friend grabbed her arms and rattled her entire body. "You have to tell me every single word he said. Tell me. Tell me. Tell me."

By *tell me*, Kym meant, was he seeing anyone? And how could she accidently bump into him?

Even if Mara could answer her friend's questions, nothing would come of it. Kym attracted men who were betta fish, those colorful little creatures that look gorgeous, but lived alone because they tended to be territorial, aggressive, and pick fights with anything walking by their fish bowl.

Mara shrugged and stripped damaged leaves from the flower stems. "There's not much to tell."

"Okay, don't tell me. Keep him all to yourself." Kym released her arms. "You look cute, by the way. That cream sweater with your jeans looks fabulous."

"Thanks."

She'd considered her usual: black socks, jeans, and a black shirt uniform. "It's weird. Since I can't see, you'd think I wouldn't get tired of wearing the same stuff day after day, but I do. I guess I miss those days of shopping for clothes and shoes."

"You get to shop."

"Yeah, while you and Gwen select my clothes. It doesn't matter. You both have better fashion sense than I ever had."

"We make sure you have your own unique style. I should bring over the dress Gwen found for me on her last trip to Denver so you can feel it. She must spend hours scouring those secondhand stores. Did you know she goes to the high-class neighborhoods to find the best quality deals? That's good business, and why her consignment store does so well."

"I could still hug her for those embroidered labels she made to help me figure out what color I'm wearing."

"You were a bit colorful there for a while." Kym couldn't hide her giggle.

"Go ahead and laugh. I feel like a clown some days. The worst is when I wear something backward or inside out, and then someone finally mentions it late in the day."

"Well, you look fabulous today. Did Joey ask about your accident?"

Her chest tightened and closed inward. "Surprisingly, no. Then again, he probably just felt sorry for me."

"Stop with the negativity. Did you tell him you were singing at Mad Jack's next Saturday?"

"No, of course not. He'll most likely be gone by then." A snort and rattling of bags caused her to re-examine the instant panic that clogged her throat every time she thought about locals hearing her sing. What if she forgot the words? What if she sucked? "Z…you know how it is."

"I don't know why you turned Jack down for a weekly gig. Singing in front of all those people is gonna be awesome advertising for the store. Three-percent of the bar tab could make some nice coin."

"You know I don't have enough material. I'm scrambling to come up with something for this week."

"You're just making excuses and scared. What did your parents always say?"

"That I can't grow if I'm too scared to succeed."

"They were right. You have a gift and should share it."

Another twinge of anxiety made her eyelid muscles flicker uncontrollably. Kym didn't understand that singing in public was like putting your heart on a dartboard and inviting people to use it for target practice. "Maybe I shouldn't be so nervous. I'll be singing to you, Tony, and Gina, and possibly three other people who bother to show."

"There you go again." A warm hand tugged on her wrist. "Where's that go-get-'em confidence of yours?"

"You know Valentine's Day is not my favorite holiday. Besides, I've been on my feet all day, and I'm tired."

"I know you don't like V-Day." Kym moved beside Mara to hug her waist. "That flower arrangement is beautiful. Who's the lucky recipient?"

"I wouldn't use the word, lucky. It's for Mrs. Gordon. Her husband's liver cancer returned. He died last night."

"Wow. That's sad. Gone so fast." Kym laid her head on Mara's shoulder, and then let go, started rustling things and thumping cans again. "I'll start dinner so we can watch a movie. Does Buddy need to be fed?"

The whack-whack-whack of the dog's tail against the counter made Mara brush her fingertips over her wristwatch face. "I missed your dinnertime again," she told him. "Maybe I should get a watch that chimes. What do you think?" Buddy gave her a high-pitched whine. "Follow Kym. I'll feed you in a minute. Go home," she gave the command.

Both Buddy and Kym walked the eighteen steps to the back stairwell and began the steep thirteen-stair climb to Mara's apartment. The click of claws across the tiled floor and wooden steps accompanied her thoughts, while she stored her tools in their designated spots. After carefully placing the arrangement in the refrigerated case, she followed. When she reached the upper level, she grabbed a can of dog food off the shelf just to the left of the door, and took a couple steps toward the counter. With Kym preparing food, the kitchen felt cramped.

"Smells good." Mara enjoyed a long, satisfying sniff.

"I'll slide the burritos into the oven. Twenty minutes and we should be eating."

Onions, avocados and green chili sauce were quite a way down the culinary ladder from crab cakes and filet mignon—the meal her mom had so carefully selected for Mara's Valentine's Day wedding—which would have been as perfect as her mother wanted, if not for a drunk driver and a spineless fiancé. She tried hard not to blame Mark for being scared and taking off. But she did. He deserted her when she needed him most.

Mara opened the cabinet and removed two plates. "What movie are we going to watch…or, in my case, listen to?"

"Since it is Valentine's Day, I figured a good cry never hurt a girl, and you said your favorite movie of all time is *The Vow*."

"You remembered."

"Of course I remembered. It would be sacrilege for your best friend to forget. I figured our favorite comfort meal, a box of tissues, and a gallon of cookie dough ice cream should get us through the evening. If not, the twelve-pack of beer I put in the fridge should push us over the edge."

Mara opened her arms, and Kym moved in for a hug. "I appreciate you."

"Yeah, I know."

"I wish…"

"What do you wish?" Kym stepped out of her embrace.

"Sometimes I pretend there's someone out there who doesn't mind that I'm blind or can barely walk some days.

Someone who would love me as much as Leo vows to love Paige in the movie."

"My mom said love's not a romance movie. That life's messy," Kym sighed. "But what does she know? I bet there's someone out there for each of us. We just have to be strong enough, courageous enough and patient enough to grab him when he comes along."

"Well then, let the waiting begin. But I get first dibs on the chips and salsa. And please tell me you got the spicy black bean kind, not that wimpy sugary mild."

"I got both. So don't go opening jars if you don't know which is what this time. Or if you do, sniff before tasting. You can smell the heat in that black bean salsa from across the room."

"Burritos, beer, beans…I'll be smelling something all right." Mara grunted with a thick layer of chagrin on top. If she couldn't see to open a stupid jar, how could she nab Mr. Perfect when he walked by?

Kym suggested patience and courage.

She didn't need any stinking patience or courage.

What she needed was a miracle.

CHAPTER THREE

Uneasiness settled in Joey's gut. Facing his family after all this time made him uncomfortable. Truth was, there hadn't been a reason to return until now.

Joey stared through the windshield, squeezing the car keys in his hand, trying to convince himself to put the keys in his pocket instead of back in the ignition. He took a deep breath, grabbed the flowers, climbed out of the car and popped the trunk to grab the kids' gifts. As soon as he did, the family and his oldest sister's ancient black lab, now gone white around the muzzle, poured out the front door.

First through the gate, his mom rushed forward, her arms spread wide. "Joey, my baby boy."

His ma's arms encircled his waist, her head barely reached mid-chest. He smirked. *Twenty-eight and still a baby.* Yet a good few inches taller, or his ma had shrunk.

"Hey, mom," he leaned down to brush a kiss across her cheek.

Pia, Joey's oldest sister, and her husband, Franco, came first, carrying the newest addition—Divo, aged two, according to last month's Facebook post. Eight-year-old Sophia held back, hovering on the porch. Joey's younger sister Camilla came next, holding Luca's hand. Luca, Pia's middle child, tugged on his aunt's arm, and the angry face implied his stubborn nephew was a clone of him at that age. He searched for Anna, his youngest sister and brat extraordinaire, but she hadn't put in an appearance. His dad was also missing, but that wasn't surprising.

Relief over his father's absence opened the pressure valve a little, but again reminded him nothing had changed. Every house on his childhood block looked like some contractor had plopped down Monopoly pieces in even rows, then painted them different colors to create the illusion of diversity. Uneven brick pavers led to the front door of his parents' house. A chain link fence, originally intended to keep in the family dog, still surrounded the yard. Cars that should have been consigned to a junkyard were lined up one behind the other on the long concrete driveway at the side of the house. A single black mailbox stood sentry, albeit askew, at the end of the drive.

"Here you go, Ma." He transferred the flowers into her hands, before distributing the roses to his sisters.

"Oh. What beautiful flowers."

"How are you holding up, Ma?"

"Fine. Fine. We're not going to be talking about your brother today. Maybe later. Not today. It's your first day home. You're a good boy to bring gifts, and look you've put on weight." She patted his belly as if time hadn't passed, and a tragedy hadn't struck. He understood, and decided it best to play along, ignoring what everyone had on their minds but didn't want to discuss.

With a suitcase in one hand and a bag of gifts for the kids in the other, he could do nothing but follow the rest back inside the house.

"I'll feed you more vegetables and salad," she continued. "Do you have a girlfriend yet?"

Meaning *why aren't you married yet, and when am I going to be a grandmother?* The muscles between his shoulder blades locked and bunched into a wadded mess. "No, Ma. No girlfriend. Can we go in? It's kinda cold out here."

"Of course. Everyone inside," his mother said, shooing her ducklings into the house. Five seconds later, she forgot all about babies and rattled on about who was divorced, pregnant, ill. Things he had no desire to know, but pretended to be interested in for his mother's sake. On the way past Sophia, he handed his niece a rose and winked, then paused for a second to appreciate the flustered blush.

The first step into the house time-warped him back ten years. The forest green carpet still clashed with the burgundy couch covers and the white lace covering vintage end tables. His paternal grandmother's teal, pink and brown afghan still hung over the back of his father's recliner. His maternal grandmother's little glass and porcelain trinkets still crowded the shelves, tables and every other flat surface. The mismatched objects reminded him of a garage sale table cluttered with stuff that was of little value to anyone except the owner.

In the kitchen, white cabinets and countertops held two generations of kitchenware. The "new" gas stove his dad installed when Joey was five still leaned along the far wall. Freshly washed dishes, pots and pans were stacked in a drainer for lack of a dishwasher.

He dropped the paper bag full of gifts on his great-grandparents' ten-foot, oak dining room table, which was still surrounded by a conglomeration of chairs in various shapes and sizes, enough to provide seating for everyone. The orange tablecloth was new...new, as in the plastic eyesore hadn't been there when he left for college. "Where's Dad?"

"Working," Pia said while shoving a straw into a juice box for her youngest. "He called to say he'd be here soon."

He called? That's new.

The man worked dawn till dusk. Eating, sleeping, and severe disciplinary measures were about the only reasons he showed up, and when he did, the family stayed out of his way... like Deogie, Pia's dog, now collapsed in the corner, well away from busy little feet.

A dense layer of melancholy hovered just below the hum of voices. Everyone seemed busy doing the mundane to avoid thinking too much. Thinking, especially about Sam. At least, that's what Joey was trying to do.

Camilla's face suddenly appeared inches from his nose. "You made me lose a bet. I bet Pia five bucks you wouldn't show for the funeral. Thanks a bunch for costing me money."

Typical Camilla, always in his face or, on his case, about something. "I told you when I called I'd be here, so it's not my problem you bet against me." The sentiment to express how much he'd missed her brusque attitude got stuck in his throat. Punching her, like the fourteen-year-old Joey used to do no longer seemed right, so he added, "Mom tells me you've taken over the office at the restaurant."

"Taken over? Not likely. I'm managing the best I can," she said quietly. "You know Mom. It would take a power wrench to get her to let go of anything."

More Than Meatballs—his mom's pride and joy—had been his family's second home. Before he turned eight, he bussed tables, washed dishes, sliced foodstuffs and anything else required to keep the place open.

"Yep. I know how Mom operates. She never says a thing to you, but she tells me you're doing an excellent job making sure the business stays profitable."

"Typical." Camilla rolled her eyes. "You hungry?"

"Let me guess—penne, spaghetti, or lasagna."

His sister snorted a shallow laugh. "Pretty much. I'm going to make a salad. Let me fix you a plate."

A salad would suit him just fine. Contrary to his mother's

earlier assumption, the bulkier body of a cross-trained triathlete had replaced the lankiness of the teenage soccer player.

Hearing a commotion down the hall, he went to investigate and found his brother-in-law hovering over the half-bath's pink toilet.

"Need some help?" Joey asked, assuming there wasn't much he could do to help with a thirty-plus-year-old commode.

Franco glanced up with a wrench in hand. "Yeah, talk your father into letting me buy him a new toilet. This one's been leaking for three years. I'm tired of fixing the damn thing. There's enough pipe tape, duct tape and sealant on this thing to mummify it."

Joey snorted a laugh. "I'll try, but you know how cheap he can be. Why buy new or even used, if the old one isn't ready to be taken behind the shed and shot?"

"That's my point. This thing *should* be shot. The toilet clogs every other day and has a constant leak."

"Which of course probably increases their water bill by more than what dad thinks he's saving by not buying a replacement." For eighteen years, day in, day out, Joey lived with the same type of frustration and it was one of the reasons he hopped a bus to California to take advantage of a full-ride scholarship. "I'll see what I can do. No promises. You know Dad."

His parents hated change. And with Sam's death came change. Big change. A dynamic shift, guaranteed to set off a family upheaval. An upheaval that had the potential to trigger more changes than some of the family members could handle.

Pounding footsteps came charging down the hall. Joey stepped out of the bathroom just in time to snag little Divo, toss the giggling boy into the air and then pull him in for a quick snuggle. Decked out in a cowboy costume complete with chaps, holster and a hat, the youngster fit in his arms snugly, and surprised Joey with the yearning it created.

"Where are you going in such a hurry, cowboy?"

The broad, infectious, peanut-butter-smeared grin made the tension in Joey's shoulders ease.

The little tyke's face turned serious. "Unck Dooey?"

"Yes, I'm your Uncle Joey."

A chubby fist holding a cracker spread with peanut butter, hovered two inches from his nose. "Kwacker?"

"No, thanks. You eat it."

The two-year-old giggled and pushed Joey with a fist. "Down. Want down."

Pia appeared in the hall just when Divo started to kick. Moving instinctively to protect his privates, Joey shifted the little boy before setting him on the floor and turning him toward the kitchen.

"I bet he's a handful." The two-year-old barreled around the corner toward the kitchen and then disappeared. Joey studied his older sister. "He's got your eyes."

Pia's tired eyes sparkled with pride. "Yes, but he's as stubborn as his father and curious as his uncle. He found a wasp nest last month and naturally got stung. Thank God he wasn't allergic. Remember when you were sprayed by that skunk?"

"Yeah, and you thought the tomato sauce bath Mom gave me to ease the smell was hilarious."

"You looked miserable."

"The same way you looked when you snuck out to meet Tyler Meher and ended up getting Dad's truck stuck in the mud out on Lonely Ridge. It took Sam and me two hours to dig you out."

She deserved pushback and flush of red sliding across her cheeks for bringing up one of the most agonizing months of his life.

Her eyes filled with bitterness. "Dad beat my butt so hard I could barely sit down for a week. I got grounded for two months and had to wash the truck all summer. On top of that, Tyler started dating Patty Scholler."

Patty, a busty redhead with an IQ of ten, had made quite an impression on the neighborhood and not in a positive way. "You're better off. Tyler switched girlfriends as often as he changed television channels. Are you and Franco doing better?"

"Better now that finances aren't so tight. I still intend to pay you back that loan."

"When you can," he offered quietly, though never expecting the money back, not that Pia wasn't good for repayment. "How are you holding up?"

"Some days are better than others. Mom seems to be in denial. Dad's on a rampage. He's down at the sheriff's office every other day trying to find answers. Camilla's burying herself in work and doing her best to make everyone miserable. I'm just barely holding everything together. I miss him."

"I can't believe he's gone." Joey wrapped his arms around his sister and pulled her closer to feel something, anything other than anger. "Do you want to talk?"

"Not yet. I can't." She took a step back and swiped her fingertips under her eyes.

"When you're ready." He rubbed a hand up and down her arm letting the comforting touch sooth his swirling emotions. "Mom wouldn't let me make hotel reservations. I saw a couple of new B and B's in town. Think I'll call and make arrangements." The hair on the back of his neck prickled when Pia shifted her weight. "Don't tell me I'm supposed to stay here."

"No, no, not here. Dad decided you should stay at Sam's place. Mom couldn't talk him out of it, so she rationalized that staying at Sam's would give you a quiet place away from the ruckus. Neither of them want you to spend money when there's a perfectly good bed available."

Sam's place. The prime property and cabin his brother somehow had managed to buy on a sheriff's salary.

His questioning instincts tightened with the same angst he'd experienced when his dad reached for the leather belt. "Don't worry." He hoped he sounded reassuring. "I'll figure something out."

"I can always blow up an air mattress so you can stay at our place."

A small pair of peek-a-boo eyes appeared between his sister's legs, then disappeared and then reappeared again.

"Naw. That's okay. I don't think I need peanut butter smeared in my hair at six o'clock in the morning." He laughed at his nephew's antics.

Pia glanced at her youngest. "They say the oil is good for the skin. At least that's what I keep telling myself."

A fresh sense of connection brought a smile. "Keep it up. You might believe it someday." He leaned over and gave her a kiss on the cheek. "Missed you."

"If you missed me so much, why haven't you come home?"

He'd been ready for the question, or, at least, he thought he'd been ready. The adolescent feelings of restlessness, the inadequacy, the longing to escape came tumbling back, as well as, the guilt. Guilt for leaving his sisters behind to deal with demanding parents and a struggling family business, both of which were enough to crush any kid's dreams. But he'd paid a price. His only close family relationship now seemed strained and foreign.

"I...ah...you know." His fingers twitched at his side before he pulled them in to fists to contain the whirling emotions. "I just got pulled into life."

"I get it. But we needed you. I needed you. I want my kids to know their uncle."

He shifted his weight from one foot to the other. "I'm sorry. I had things I needed to do."

Things to prove to himself and to his parents. Maybe he should have come home, at least for the summer or vacation. "I called. I even offered you a place to stay in Seattle for a few weeks when you and Franco were having challenges."

"That's not the same. Besides, running away doesn't solve problems."

Running away like you did, he heard. "You're right. I should have come home more."

"Wait!" His sister's eyes opened wider, and her jaw dropped. "Did I just hear you say I'm right? Frame this day on the calendar with a big, red Sharpie." She turned to include all her siblings and kids, exclaiming, "Joey Gaccione said his sister was right."

"Funny." Why was it siblings always reverted to their teenage behavior? "Is the funeral still scheduled for Wednesday?"

The question hung in the air unanswered when the front door opened, causing heads to turn and conversations to stall.

Adolescent fears made him watch and assess his father. The man's first few steps into the house were like a barometer. If his feet shuffled, he'd been out drinking with the construction crews, and the family would spend the evening trying to remain small and quiet. If his feet dragged in pain, the family would retreat to the kitchen, and abandon the living room to give his father space. If his feet clicked along at a brisk pace, the family would breathe a sigh of relief.

Today the man's gaze connected with Joey's, returning his son's assessment. His feet stilled.

His father hadn't changed much. Tall, built like a steam-roller, a scowl permanently embedded in his face, only this time a quiet rage simmered beneath the surface.

"Joey."

"Dad."

His father turned, hung his work coat on one of the hooks

by the front door, then handed his lunch pail to his niece, who managed to lug the large black metal box into the kitchen. "You here to help catch your brother's killer?"

Ten years ago the gruff question would have made Joey cringe, but police work and barking sergeants had helped him grow a thicker hide. "That's what the sheriff's department is for, Dad. I highly doubt the deputies will share any critical information with the family until the investigation is complete. I don't have jurisdiction here."

"Don't give me any of your damned excuses. Those idiots at the station can't find their asses in the dark with both hands. Poacher, my ass. Incompetent, I tell you." Each emphasized syllable seemed louder than the last.

Don't get involved. Let the deputies do their job.

"I'm not giving you an excuse. I came to say good-bye to my brother and support the family, but then I have to go back to work."

"Your job is here, helping to protect this family."

"I've been assigned to a team working on a big case, the biggest of my career. If all goes well, I'll get the promotion I've worked hard to deserve." *And, maybe, for once, you'll be proud of me.* "People are counting on me, Dad."

"Are you telling me your job is more important than finding your brother's killer?"

"What am I supposed to tell the six families whose daughters have gone missing or turned up in pieces? Aren't they important? Huh, Dad? What do you want me to do?"

"I want you to find your brother's killer."

Pia reached for Joey's hand to silently beg him not to cause a stir. Joey studied the family's expressions. Every one of them wanted him to defuse the bomb his father had placed in the center of the room. Now Joey understood the pressure an Olympic athlete faced when going for the gold. The expectations. The burden. The self-doubt.

"I thought Sam's death was an accident. A poacher. What am I missing?" He kept his tone and body language neutral.

His father moved closer. Joey fought the urge to take an automatic step out of arm's reach, but stifled his instinctive reaction. He couldn't smell peppermint, which meant his father hadn't stopped at the bar or liquor store on his way home.

"Anybody worth a damn would know no poacher would be anywhere near Sleeping Bear Trail," his father spit out into the living room. "It's too close to that old mine. The waters are contaminated. There's no deer, elk or moose living within three miles of the place. Plus, add .223 ammo, and you got someone who ain't from anywhere near here. Go and take a look. There's trees. Lots of them. And a wide road. No way was this an accident." His father shoved past him to the kitchen, grumbling under his breath, "Someone's got to light a fire under those deputies' butts. There's a killer out there. I figured, with your fancy college degree, you'd want to find out who killed your brother."

Joey's gut crimped into a complicated knot. Sure, he wanted to investigate his brother's death, but he wasn't about to crash into the sheriff's department with the equivalent of a Dodge 4X4. Forcing his way in would generate zero information. He'd learned that lesson the hard way. Politics, personalities and invisible procedures were involved, and the reason why he agreed with his boss to let the local department—at least on the surface—handle the investigation.

"If it'll make you happy, I'll stop by the station tomorrow and see if they'll let me look at the file. But I can't promise anything. I have no authority here."

His dad glanced up from scrubbing twelve hours of construction dirt off his hands. "Mighty generous of ya, son," he sneered.

The sarcastic tone hadn't changed. This time, however, the fear of disappointing one or both of his parents didn't automatically follow his dad's caustic statement. This time Joey didn't have anything to prove. Or anything to lose. For ten years, he'd lived on his own never asking anything of his family. Never needing anything from them. But the binding tie of obligation still existed.

He turned to Pia. "When is the funeral?"

"One on Wednesday. Tomorrow and Tuesday Dad's working, and Mom's cooking at the restaurant for the memorial service and doesn't want to be disturbed. Wednesday, Dad most likely will work until the last minute." His sister's intent stare and brow lift meant *don't ask.*

"Then I guess I'll be at the station seeing if I can't get my hands on some investigation files."

"We need you here at eleven on Wednesday so we can figure out how we're getting everyone to the church and cemetery."

"I'll be here by eleven. Anything else?"

"Nope. We've got the rest covered."

An emptiness closed in, followed by remorse for not having done something sooner about the absence of family in his life. He'd barely spoken to Sam this past year. Maybe on his birthday and a text or phone call now and then. He hadn't realized how much time had passed. Too busy working. Paying bills. Focused on promotions. But as his father had accused, they were excuses. Every one.

The image of his brother bleeding and dying in the mud on a backcountry road flashed across his mind.

"You should know…" Pia's tentative hesitation grabbed his attention. "Since Dad's been all over town raising a stink, the mayor might be expecting you." The sadness in her eyes jacked up the guilt-o-meter another notch. "Joey, I know coming home after all this time, especially because of Sam, must be hard. Just know that you being here…helps."

Oh, man. Regret, shame, remorse closed in. While he tried to think of something to say, his mom popped her head around the corner. "Come eat, you two, while the food is hot." She disappeared into the kitchen. *Saved by dinner.*

Pia rolled her eyes and headed for the kitchen. "I'm going to end up fifteen pounds heavier if Mom doesn't stop trying to shove food down our throats every ten minutes."

Joey looped an arm around his sister's shoulder. "Food is Mom's way of keeping the family together."

Pia gave him a speculative glance. "Seems you've gotten a bit wiser while you've been away."

"That or my psychology classes in college helped put things into perspective."

"You think you can use your profiling skills to figure out why my eight-year-old has decided to stop talking to everyone?"

He'd noticed Sophia standing apart from the group. Later, he'd observed her curled in the corner with her nose in a book, the rose he'd given her nestled close to her side. She did seem to isolate herself, but she hadn't gone to hide in a room, either. "It might just be that she's an introvert. I know in a family of extroverts that's difficult to accept. But being an introvert is not a fatal flaw."

"Takes one to know one."

"Know one what?" his mother demanded, placing plates on the table while Camilla set a large salad and several types of dressing in the center.

"That some people don't like to be the center of attention," Joey responded.

"Bah. How you ever going to get ahead in life if you don't stand out?"

Camilla gave her older brother the familiar raised-eyebrow, don't-stir-up-trouble look. He said nothing. Instead he took the silverware from his mother's hands to help set the table. Then Joey selected a seat at the end, as far away from his father as he could manage, to avoid triggering the man's explosive disposition.

Pia lifted her youngest toward the kitchen sink to wash his hands. The other children lined the hall outside the bathroom to do the same. Franco kissed his wife and then took Divo from her arms to set him in a high chair.

During the family chaos, the little boy studied Joey with an air of concern as if he couldn't quite figure out how his uncle fit in. Joey stuck his tongue out. The little boy kicked his feet delightedly and then released a prize-winning, three-second fart.

The kitchen went quiet. The faces in the room leisurely smiled until the baby stink reached them. Then hands waved vigorously while feet backed away in a hurry.

"Divo!" Pia scolded.

Joey started to laugh, then Camilla, then the whole kitchen filled with laughter. Even his crusty dad managed to crack a smile.

Leave it to a two-year-old to provide enough levity to help the family relax a bit and bond.

"Joey, stop reinforcing my grandson's bad habits." The light layer of humor in his mother's eyes disguised the warning.

The pride in Franco and Pia's eyes said they didn't mind.

Family. The heartbeat of life.

He hadn't realized how much he missed being a part of something bigger.

Sophia walked the length of the table to squeeze into the chair next to him, then placed a napkin and the rose he'd given her in her lap. He observed his niece while the family settled around the massive table. From the changes in her facial expression, he could tell she was listening to every conversation and had opinions about the exchanges circling the table, even though she chose not to participate.

He leaned a bit closer to her ear. "I saw you with an ereader. Are you working on school stuff?" he asked, softly enough to prevent others from jumping in to answer the question for her.

Sophia stared at her plate to fend off his scrutiny. "Just a story for fun. I like to read."

"I used to read a lot, too. Now I don't seem to have time. Can you recommend a good book?"

For the first time, his niece's eyes met his directly, then she quickly looked away. "The Chronicles of Narnia are good, but old people might not want to read them."

Old people seemed a little harsh, but fit from his niece's perspective. Time had disappeared so quickly. He again studied the top of her head.

"Oh, I don't know. Sometimes I wish I could step into a closet and disappear into another world."

Her head whipped his way, and her gaze finally, fully connected. "You've read them?" Her question came out more as an amazed statement than a query.

"Yep. I've read every one in the series. I bet Grandma has my old set in the attic somewhere. They were her favorites, too."

The spark in her eye filled him with gratification because he could relate to wanting to step into another world, a created world, a world without the pressure to be something other than what he could manage. The rebelliousness in his niece's eyes also reminded him of Mara's determination. Mara was resolved to make the best life possible, and he believed she possessed the faith she could master whatever she set out to achieve.

He'd felt that way once.

Somehow his youthful boldness had dissipated over the years.

His father glared at him from the other end of the table. "Let's say grace."

Joey placed his hands in his niece's and sister's, but he continued to process the day's events. Bumping into Mara had been an unexpected bonus. He pondered how Mara could be so optimistic after all she'd been through. The last six years of police work had ground away his idealistic edges, making room for skepticism to take hold.

Life experience had proven that working harder had nothing to do with a positive outcome. Cases went unsolved. Violent incidents increased. Bad things happened to good people—like Sam.

His niece and sister squeezed, then released his hands when the prayer ended.

And keep this family safe. Let me make it through this week. Oh, and please keep me from locking my father in handcuffs and showing him what his leather belt felt like.

Amen.

CHAPTER FOUR

"Good morning," Joey greeted the freckled-faced redhead sitting behind the sheriff department's reception counter. She didn't bother looking up, her thumbs too busy moving forty miles an hour across her smartphone's keypad, most likely texting another teen who had no idea how to have an ordinary conversation.

When Joey cleared his throat, she unglued her attention from her phone, annoyance clearly the cause of her squinty-eyed stare.

"I'm here to see someone in charge of the Gaccione homicide," he said drumming his fingers on the counter.

Before the teenager could respond, a jovial, "Joey Catchy-Monkey," came from the man rounding the corner. The teen's cell quickly disappeared into a pocket. "It's Ernie. Ernie Barker. We've been expecting you."

I bet you have. Better me than my dad, right?

The man continued forward, his hand outstretched. Joey accepted the deputy's overly enthusiastic handshake.

"Ernie. Nice seeing you again." Joey quickly released his

hand because shaking it was as unpleasant as squeezing an overripe banana.

If he remembered correctly, Barker was a year older, but always hung out with kids a year or two younger. Growing up, he'd lived with his dad and grandmother, although his long-haul-trucker father was never home. Ernie had been the guy who liked reading comic books, gawking at girls, playing sports, mostly football, only because his dad demanded he play the manly game. Odd he wound up a deputy. The man's intense vibe gave the impression Ernie did more ass-kissing than working, which lit up Joey's caution sign.

"Is there someone who'd be willing to fill me in on my brother's investigation?"

"Sure. Sure. Not a problem. There's a break room just down the hall."

He followed the deputy down a carpeted hallway plastered with award placards and framed photos of people in uniforms and then into a small room, while working hard to keep his embittered emotions in check. Three round tables, a coffee bar, a standard-sized refrigerator and a couple uniformed deputies filled the space.

"I'll be right back," Barker explained, "I need to get the case file."

You can do this. Don't think of Sam. It's just another case file. Just another set of data. Just another crime to be solved.

Joey took a seat while the deputy made a quick detour. The smell of overcooked coffee and the conversations of other department staff engaged in local town gossip wafted around the cold and unwelcoming room. Since jobs were scarce, Joey figured he'd recognize a few people, but the faces were as unfamiliar as a three-dollar bill.

Ernie returned and dropped a file on the table before taking a seat across from Joey. He crossed his arms over his light gray button-down shirt, which looked like it had been washed and then slept in. His unkempt appearance spoke of Ernie's apathy. No starch or iron had come anywhere close to the fabric. The boyhood athlete had morphed into an overweight football dad engaged in lifting too many Coors on the weekends. Joey speculated the deputy could hit a trashcan at twenty paces with an aluminum can better than he could hit a target with his sidearm.

"So what do we have?" Joey asked, the patience he'd sworn to exhibit already beginning to slip.

"We've put the evidence together, but I'm warning you, we don't have much. Basically, Deputy Sanders found Sam next to his car at 16:52, out on Sleeping Bear Trail, with a .223 caliber rifle shot to his chest. The coroner said he died from the wound. That's pretty much what we have."

That's it? The lack of data quickly diminished any assurances the sheriff's department had a tight control over the case. Joey shifted, took a long deep breath, and leaned in to open the investigation file. "Did you look at the dash cam video from Sam's car?"

The flicker of the deputy's eyes and sudden movement of facial muscles couldn't be good. "All we have are the photos from the scene. The city's budget has been mighty tight, and some of the repairs on the patrol cars haven't been completed due to lack of funds."

"Okay." *Stay calm. Don't react.* "Did he fire his weapon?"

"Don't think so. His gun was still in his holster when we found him. Dispatch said Sam called in to say he noticed one of the logging gates had been opened. No one had been issued a permit lately, so he went to check it out. The dispatcher received a non-verbal distress call seventeen minutes later."

Don't think so? Whether he discharged a weapon or not, required a simple yes or no answer.

"So, if I'm understanding correctly, there is no video, just these photographs." Joey flipped through the papers in the file.

"And from the looks of it, a basic search was conducted, but the results are not enclosed. Did you canvas the area for additional clues, like footprints, tire marks, or shell casings?"

"The scene was pretty straightforward. Besides, the sun had almost set by the time we got there. Like I said, we're short-staffed with a lot going on. That's why the sheriff was out patrolling in the first place."

You're short on something, all right. And training, protocol and common sense are at the top of the list. An uneasy tension pinched his neck nerves and rolled down his spine. "And no one went back the next morning?"

"No need. Besides, we couldn't. Overnight, some kid got separated from his family. We got the call to help search because the weather channel forecasted a foot of snow."

Snow wasn't a valid reason for not completing a thorough investigation. Ever. Especially not when the sheriff was murdered. Barker apparently believed his lack of action justified.

Every hair on Joey's forearms shivered with fury. His dad's tirade about incompetence seemed to have merit.

"I have some crime scene software on my computer," Joey said. "Do you mind if I enter this data, see if I can come up with something to help?"

"You can do that?" Barker's eyes reminded him of a startled owl, round and big. "Must be nice working in a big city with a large budget."

Joey's jaw clenched to the point his teeth ached. "I can run the simulation, but the quality of the output can only be based on how many data points are entered. Are the coroner or lab reports back yet?"

"They should be here somewhere." Barker flipped the file around and rummaged through the pages. "Doesn't look like the information's in the file."

"When you find the reports, would you mind if I take a

look?" He managed to don a pleasant mask even though he wanted to strangle the guy for his shoddy work.

His brother had been one of the department's own. Had, in fact, been the boss. Joey had expected to encounter an intense energy and expediency around finding the shooter. What he saw made him sick.

"We'll find the guy who shot him," Barker said. "Don't you worry. It's just a matter of time."

No, you won't. You won't find a damn thing. Not with this staggering lack of evidence. The fake-cheerful determination in the deputy's tone generated a bellyful of fervor. Who was Barker trying to kid? Determination didn't bring people to justice. The department had not done a thorough investigation in the first forty-eight-hour window. Critical evidence was easily erased. Weather elements. Critters. Even perpetrators could carry off evidence.

Joey didn't like this guy. Not in high school, and not now. Ernie reminded him of a fruit fly, always flying around, clinging to things. He scanned the break room, a total contrast to his office in Seattle. No one looked in much of a hurry. A few people looked his way and then quickly averted their eyes. Maybe because they didn't know what to say. Or because they didn't care. Or because they did a crap job and knew it.

Standing around chattering like a flock of geese didn't get the job done. *Short-handed, my ass.* His thoughts drifted to his brother's home. "I'm not seeing the paperwork here indicating a search of Sam's home."

"That's because there wasn't a search."

"Really? That's interesting, because I stayed in his place last night and from the looks of things his home was searched. From the tracks in the area, someone recently came poking around the outside of his house, I'd say in the last couple of days. There were fresh tracks this morning." A suffocating feeling started in Joey's chest and moved to his throat, threatening his air supply and his tenuous hold on his temper. "Considering the time I got to Sam's and the snowfall patterns, I suspect the new tracks were made sometime between eleven last night and five this morning. I checked the entry and exit points. Whoever visited was on foot."

"You do know Sleeping Bear Trail runs behind Sam's home."

Joey's breath stalled. "Good to know. I hadn't realized his place was that close."

"Several acres behind the house bumped up against the logging road."

His mind reran the video of the morning's events.

Standing at Sam's kitchen sink, looking out at the snow falling in clumps from the evergreens and contemplating his dad's words, Joey had finally taken a more detached, critical look at his brother's place. The interior of the house, framed in log beams, included an open room for both kitchen and living room, with two bedrooms, a full and a partial bathroom, and a laundry room, all on a single floor. Sam's entire life sat within those log walls and hardwood floors.

While Joey scanned the room, he had noticed more and more irregularities, while the uneasy feeling intensified.

It seemed trouble had followed his brother home, but for the life of him, Joey couldn't figure out what they might be searching for.

He had poked through the contents of a copy paper box full of his brother's things sitting on the kitchen table. Keys, a wallet, individually wrapped Life Savers, gym clothes, a water bottle, a fresh uniform...then he hit gold at the bottom. His brother's cell phone. Waving his thumb over the glass surface of the smartphone, he studied the number pad, considered possible combinations, and pressed in four digits—Sam's high school locker combination—the phone blinked to life.

Things never changed. You always bragged about being untouch-

able. Probably the reason you wound up with a bullet in your chest, eh, Bro?

The muscles in his jaw ticked while he returned his attention to the arid break room and once again swallowed his ire enough to address Barker in a reasonable tone. "You might want to dust his house for prints. Someone's been looking for something, and I'm not sure, but I think his computer is missing. Has anyone been reviewing his old case files to see if there are any clues there?"

The blank look made him want to throttle the guy.

"We, ah…we've been short-staffed for a while now."

Short of staff. Short of common sense. Short of a lot of things. Seems like there's a theme here.

"Do you mind if I take a look at the files? I might be able to find a new thread."

"Not at all." Ernie lit up like a kid who'd just been offered candy. "In fact, we were hoping you might be interested. We downloaded six months' worth of his emails yesterday, just in case you wanted to look at those as well."

Ernie left and returned moments later with a two-foot stack of files.

Joey groaned inwardly and picked up the first file.

"I'll ask the receptionist to make a fresh pot of coffee." Barker's smug tone as much as said, *poor bastard, going to be here awhile.*

Joey cringed, doubting the redhead had mastered the art of coffee making, or much of anything else for that matter. She certainly hadn't figured out how to be a receptionist. He opened the case file with the most recent date. A break-in. The next fell into the break-in category as well. Joey scanned the map plastered to the bulletin board behind him. Both cases led to a hunting lodge on the outer edge of town.

When the deputy returned from somewhere with a mug of brew, Joey glanced at the coffee maker in the break room, shrugged and then pushed the smaller stack of files in the deputy's direction. "Can you tell me more about these robbery cases? There have been six break-ins on the ridge in the past seven months."

"Just kids going up to the ridge to get drunk and hang out."

"It's winter and below freezing most nights. Seems odd it would be kids. Any arrests?"

"Naw. You know how it is. The kids are long gone before the incident is reported."

Kids? He'd gone with friends plenty of times into the woods to camp and escape the general doldrums of Elkridge, but not once did he ever have the balls to break into someone's property. Quite a few dads in the area worked the mines, were fire jumpers or loggers. There wasn't a father within fifty square miles who would tolerate vandalism. Not unless the town had significantly changed in ten years, which he was beginning to suspect might be the case. "Anything missing?"

"Nope, nothing. Burned half a cord of firewood, used the gas generator and left trash laying around. That's about it."

Firewood? Odd. Most old hunting lodges had days, if not weeks, worth of wood stacked for use. An overnighter wouldn't use a stack of pine. Ernie hadn't clued in to that, and Joey didn't feel like enlightening the guy. Not yet, anyhow.

"Did you have someone check for prints, collect the trash for leads as to who might be breaking in?"

Being questioned about standard protocols made Ernie's face tighten and cloud over. "Like I said, just kids." His tightened jaw could have cracked open a few nuts.

"Right. Kids. Do you mind if I borrow these? I can return them on Thursday after the funeral."

"Nope, no can do. Files need to stay here, but I can get you a password, and you can look at the information online."

Online? Wow, that's progressive. "That will work."

He had to swallow twice to get the sour taste of bitterness down.

The department could afford to get the files indexed and scanned but couldn't manage to buy or fix protective equipment for the deputies. Great. Just fucking great.

Good thing Ernie had left the room, because Joey wanted to punch something, and the deputy was starting to look mighty handy.

Five seconds later, the Elkridge mayor walked in the door, and the rest of the personnel in the break room decided to act busy.

Out of habit, Joey stood. "Mayor Maxwell."

"Sit. Sit. No need to stand." The mayor gave him the signal to take a seat. "Good to see you, Joey. Been a while."

Ben Maxwell qualified as an Elkridge fixture, just like the war plaques hanging on the courthouse walls. He'd been Mayor for so long, no one bothered to run against him. The small man, rounded on all corners, had a winning personality and could talk a squirrel out of its last nut.

"Yes, sir. Ten years." Joey sat back down.

"Is that right? I hear you've been living in Seattle and working as a detective. That's a big promotion for such a short period of time."

"Yes, sir. I'm lucky to be working with some of the finest in the city."

The tickly sense, the one cautioning him a bushwhack might be imminent, made Joey a bit cautious. "Word travels fast," he said, not wanting to confirm or deny anything else until he could figure out where the conversation might be heading. He didn't like to answer personal questions. Exposed too much. Almost as much as when Billy Covington stole his clothes in eleventh grade, forcing him to walk home in nothing but a towel.

"Are you going to stay for a while? Visit family?"

"Can't. The job calls. I've only got a few days before I head back. Something seems to be on your mind, Mayor. What's this impromptu visit about?"

"Just being friendly, that's all."

Joey took a deep breath. Even he wasn't dumb enough to think the mayor's questions were just friendly. The leads on his brother's shooting had grown so stagnant they smelled like sewage water.

Joey leaned in a bit, taking a bold risk. "You sure you're not here to ask my help in finding Sam's killer?"

"Now, I always did think you were a smart boy."

The pressure thumping at Joey's temples doubled. "Yep. Pretty good at reading between the lines."

"Good. Glad to know you don't have wax in those ears, either. Seems your hearing is just fine."

Joey turned and caught a glimpse of Ernie's pockmarked face staring at him from the hall. The inexperienced man again reminded him of a fruit fly, hovering and buzzing around. An irritant. In his opinion, flyswatters were invented for a good reason.

The rapid-fire click of high heels drew his attention.

"Mayor. Gaccione." Stella, the county administrator, greeted from the doorway. "Mayor, when you're done with Joey, would you send him my way?"

Stella King lived just down the block from Joey's parents. The forty-something single mother of three had a pretty, yet serious, face. Back in high school, he remembered she ran her household like a military training camp, and he figured she ran city hall much the same way. She was most likely the reason the case records had been scanned.

Ben Maxwell unfolded from his chair. "I think we're done here for today. Just wanted to say hello."

Joey stood, trailed the mayor out of the break room and then followed Stella into her office before shutting the door.

"Are you part of the greeting committee as well, or are you going to tell me what's up?"

She took a seat behind a small oak desk with pictures of her kids on every surface not covered by files and paper. "Always did like you, Joey. I did a little checking into your background."

Interesting. "And?"

Joey relaxed into one of the two guest chairs opposite the administrator, more worried about where her inquiry might be headed than the aforementioned background check. Everyone in town had heard he'd gotten kicked off the school bus in sixth grade for tossing Jared Winner out the exit door, and for burning *bite me* into the high school stadium grass with gasoline when he didn't make captain of the soccer team. Both times, his dad's belt hurt far more than detention. Other than those two incidents, his background was squeaky clean. A high-level federal security clearance letter indicated as much.

Mrs. King clasped her hands on top of a pile of paper and leaned forward in her high-back chair. "Your mother tells me you graduated with a criminology degree with a concentration in sociology."

"Psychology, actually."

"Psychology." Her brows arced a bit higher. "Even better. I'm going to be straight with you. Sam left a hole to fill, and no one in Elkridge can step into his shoes. Sure, we can bring someone in from out of town, but no one who knows this place. We need someone local, someone that knows these mountains, someone like you. I might be able to find some relocation money in the budget if you're willing to transfer and take the sheriff's position."

The acid in his stomach decided to burn a hole in his relaxed demeanor. "Mrs. King."

"Stella."

"Stella, I think you forget the sheriff's position is elected. A person can't just walk into the job. Plus, the position would be a significant cut in pay."

"But the cost of living here is lower. And you've been around this town long enough to know that those who show up to vote are over sixty, need glasses to read and only believe what's written in the paper. Getting the residents to vote you in wouldn't take much effort."

Entitled attitudes like hers were what got politicians thrown in jail, but he managed not to say so. Out loud, anyway.

"What about the under-sheriff or the sergeant? Surely whoever holds those positions will want to run for sheriff."

The rolling of the eyes and the snort provided a warning. "The Under-Sheriff's a drunk and is currently under suspension, and you've met Barker. The man couldn't even direct traffic without being told what to do."

Joey nodded. "I see your point. I'll consider your offer," he said to be politically correct, knowing he wouldn't give the position a second thought. He already had a job, and he didn't want to follow his brother's path, constantly being measured against his brother's yardstick, always coming up an inch or two short.

His face must have given away his reluctance, because a mulish resolve entered Stella's eyes. "Joey, please think about it. I know your mom wants you home."

Yeah, I bet she does. To set me up on dates so she can get more grandbabies.

"I will." *Not. Interested.* "Speaking of my mom, I'd better check in. See if the family needs anything. Will I see you at the funeral on Wednesday?"

"I'll be there." She rose from her black mesh chair and took a step around the desk corner. "One more thing."

Joey turned, wondering what her angle was going to be now.

"Sam was a good and devoted man, but he didn't have your smarts or eye for detail."

Devoted? Maybe devoted to using his good looks and bright smile to sneak by. But then the utter hollowness that had plagued him for days reminded him that Sam's guile didn't matter anymore. Nothing mattered anymore, except one thing —putting the facts together as quickly as possible so he could provide his family some assurances.

A vibration at his hip made him pause and slip the phone from his coat pocket.

"I'll let you take that." Stella pointed to his phone before slipping out of her office and closing the door, allowing him some privacy.

"Gaccione," he answered while studying the framed certificates behind her desk, working to put a lid on the heightened sense of righteousness. *Let the legal system work.* That's what his boss had preached constantly.

"Joey, it's Pia. Where are you?"

"At the sheriff's office looking over Sam's file."

The uneasy silence made him cringe. He should have given a more mundane answer. He was so used to talking to detectives and other first responders, he wasn't thinking about how his answer might affect his sister.

"Pia? Are you okay?"

"I know Dad wants you to investigate Sam's death, but until now I didn't think about what that would mean for you. If something happens to—"

"It won't." He cut her off with a quick, confident reply. "Why don't you tell me why you called?"

"It's just Sophia. It's not important."

Joey began counting to stall his impulse to give his sister crap for thinking her oldest child's needs weren't important. However, he wasn't one to talk. He hadn't been around, but suspected his niece had grown so quiet that overlooking her needs had become easy. He could relate.

"Why don't you tell me, and let me decide what's important?"

He could hear his frazzled sister talking to her two boys, telling the oldest to go in the living room and watch TV. His nephew's "no" could be heard clearly, and Joey would have laughed if his sister hadn't been so on edge.

"Sorry, Luca is being a pill today. I called because Sophia said you might have some books you could recommend. I wouldn't normally bother you with this, but she rarely talks, and she never asks for anything."

He paused to study a draft of Elkridge's financial report teetering on top of a foot-high stack of papers on the corner of Stella's desk.

"Understood. There are a couple of authors I would recommend, but the names of the books escape me at the moment. In the meantime, ask Ma if she still has my box of books. Sophia can have any of those she wants."

"Your books? As in the books you threatened to break anyone's fingers if they touched? You do realize my child is eight."

"You mean, eight going on thirty. From what I observed, Sophia respects her possessions. She'll take care of them, and if she doesn't, it won't be the end of the world."

"You've changed." Pia couldn't hide the tender emotion in her voice.

"I hope that's a good thing."

"A very good thing. According to Franco, I don't excel at communicating, but I just want you to know before it's too late that I love you. After you left for California, I was angry. Selfishly, I didn't want you to leave. Now I think I understand why you had to go. But I've missed you. I've missed our friendship. A lot."

Joey's heartbeat slowed. He hung his head. "I've missed you too, Sis. I didn't realize how much until I saw you yesterday. I promise from now on I'll come home and call more."

"I just want you to find happiness. I think Ma does as well. Will I see you tonight?" Pia asked with a frail thread of tension weaving through her question.

"I had planned on going through the investigation files and mapping out an event timeline leading to Sam's homicide, but if you want, I'll meet you for dinner."

"It's okay. Do your thing. I'm going to try to get everyone to bed early tonight. The next couple days are going to be long."

The funeral. The fifty-pound ball of dread he'd been carrying around the past few days suddenly became too heavy. Since he had no one to pass the burden to, exhaustion set in. "If you need anything call. Wednesday, I'll be at the house by eleven. And Pia? I love you, too."

"Be careful." The call ended, but not before the trembling sniffle in her voice gave his gut a squeeze.

The emotional pinch reminded him that even while dealing with the events of the past, he needed also to focus on the living. Living, as in having a life—a full life—not just a job.

At least he knew how to do his job.

Something was going on in Elkridge.

He could sense a dangerous undercurrent. Whatever was happening would leave a scar on this town. If he could, he'd like to flush out the cause before the knife cut too deep. Again, he needed facts. Facts the deputies had not been trained to find.

He tapped on the city's budget and the line showing a large number in excess funds.

Patrol cars to properly equip.

A staff shortage.

Incomplete investigations.

What is going on? Were the department's personnel utterly incompetent, or could something else be happening?

Something Sam discovered.

Something somebody didn't want known.

Something that got his brother killed.

CHAPTER FIVE

"Buddy? Let's go get some groceries?" Mara checked the dog's halter to make sure it wasn't rubbing.

Her constant companion brushed up against her leg showing his excitement to get outside. She adjusted her winter scarf, opened and closed the storefront door, then double-checked to make sure it was locked.

While inhaling to fill her body with clean, crisp winter air, the noxious odor of cigarette smoke made her want to gag. She rubbed her nose, the wool from her mitten scraping across her skin. The laws against people smoking outside of businesses never seemed to stop anyone. Last month, Kym had written a letter to the city council to complain, but nothing came of it.

Buddy's harness bumped against her leg and she grabbed the stiff leather lead, while adjusting her mostly empty, fifty-pound-capacity backpack, a.k.a. her combined oversized grocery bag and necessity pack for the dog.

"Easy. It's still icy." She tightened her grip. "Okay. Buddy, forward."

The dog's unusual restless movements caused her chest to tighten. "What is it, boy?"

She held her breath and checked for an odd sound, or movement. Buddy nudged up against her leg, moving her a bit to the right, then stopped at the edge of the curb.

"Good boy." She produced a treat from her pocket. A car drove by before Buddy moved. "Forward. Find the grocery store. Good boy."

I need to chill.

Thoughts of someone stalking her had made her jumpy and scatterbrained. She needed to focus on her business. Just that morning, she had to start an arrangement over twice because she'd forgotten what flowers she'd put in the vase. She couldn't afford a complaint. Heck, she couldn't afford to pay next months' rent, even with her disability checks. She forced the remaining tension to ease from her shoulders.

Get a grip. "Maybe after we shop, we'll swing by the park. What do you say?"

Buddy whined and gently pulled against his lead. She matched his speed, but kept focus on their destination. After a few hundred steps, the service dog seemed to settle, and she let him escort her to the corner, then to the right. The wind chimes hanging outside the hardware store the next block over provided a distant beacon. Crossing the street, she anticipated the slope of the sidewalk with its slightly increased elevation. At the next intersection, she listened for cars before crossing and making her way to Value-Shop, the local grocery store.

Buddy paused at the whoosh of the sliding glass entrance doors before proceeding.

"Hey, Mara," the storeowner, Harold Talbott, greeted from somewhere toward the back. "It'll be a few minutes. The delivery truck just got here, and we need to unload."

Harold's frenzied tone set expectations. *Busy morning. You'll have to wait.*

"No problem. I'll just start with fruits and vegetables." Mara grabbed a basket, placing her iPad on the bottom, and moved to the produce section. She reached below the counter, feeling for the plastic roll, pulled off a few bags.

"Buddy, find the apples. Good boy."

A dozen steps later, Buddy stopped. In the process of smelling a Gala apple, she detected a movement and stilled her breath. Listening for additional sound, she then moved closer to the fruit bins to get out of the way.

"Go ahead," she said to whoever waited silently. "I'm not in a hurry."

Expecting passing footsteps and a pithy greeting, she became more alert when the sounds moved closer, and the revolting smell of cigarettes and the distinct smell of licorice permeated the air. Buddy shifted uneasily and placed his body horizontally in back of her legs. Apprehension shoved her senses into overdrive.

"Am I in your way?" she asked, trying to elicit a response.

A hot breath on her cheek and the smell of hard liquor made her choke and use her grocery basket as a barrier.

Her breath shortened. Her heart hammered against her chest wall. She fisted the only weapon she had—an apple.

It's okay. It's okay. It's okay—don't panic.

An amused cackle, the kind a hyena makes when stalking its prey, turned her adrenaline spigot on full blast.

Not okay. Not okay. Not okay.

Fear pumped a gush of anxiety through her, and her mouth went dry as a saltine-cracker. She tried to take a step back, but bumped into the edge of the produce stand. The thread of panic continued to pull tighter and tighter, yanking on her nerves.

Another set of footsteps approached, and she grasped the edge of an apple basket until she heard the slight squeak of rubber accompanying every second step. Suddenly, the ashtray stench disappeared, replaced by fresh air sweetened by the fragrance of fruit and veggies. The sinister footsteps rounded the corner of the aisle, while the other set stopped a few feet away.

"Hey, Mara. I figured you for a Red Delicious, not a Gala type." That rich tone she recognized—the low F-note, with a melodic timbre, and a confident focused emphasis on each syllable.

A happy-joy-joy heat spread across her face, neck and shoulders, sending tingles to her fingers. "Joey. Thank God. Did you see a guy standing here a moment ago?"

"Only briefly. Why?"

"Because I think it might have been him. The guy I told you about." *Stay calm. Breathe.*

"You're shaking." His concern eased her trepidation and provided much-needed reassurance. "Did he hurt you?"

"No, but I still believe there's a connection to your brother's murder. You might want to see if you can get a better look."

Mara waited, listening for clues, becoming more and more discouraged as moments ticked by.

"He's gone," Joey said next to her elbow, a bit out of breath. "Maybe the store owner has security tapes I can check."

"Toto, you're not in Seattle anymore."

"Okay, so no video." A gentle hand slipped under her elbow. "Let's find you somewhere to sit down. Better yet, let me take you home."

"I'm fine. Really. I'm not going to live scared." She gently shrugged out of his grasp, then lowered the basket to ease the tension in her shoulders. "I just remembered something." The pressure in her chest returned.

"What's that?"

"Smelling stale cigarettes, alcohol and the heavy scent of licorice. I connect smell, sounds and places to people. I'm guessing, but maybe Sam noticed a guy following me and wanted to make sure I made it home. I know it sounds like I might be exaggerating, or that this is just a coincidence, but I really don't think it is.

"Coincidence? I've solved cases on less. Although, I have to tell you, the connection between Sam's murder and your stalker isn't clear. Not yet, anyhow. However, I would like to discuss your ability to identify people. It's impressive."

"My nose is telling me there's a connection."

"You think you can teach me that trick?"

"It's no trick. Recognizing people when you can't see is complicated and takes practice. It's like putting a flower arrangement together, piece by piece, but sensory visualization can be learned. For example, you pronounce my name like 'more.' The way you say it makes me smile, because I think you're going to ask for more-a-spaghetti. Then there's the Old Spice. I love the smell. My father used to wear it, and I caught a sniff yesterday. For some reason, one of your shoes squeaks— maybe unevenly worn rubber, I'm not sure. It's the only thing I can come up with that would make a similar sound. As I said, it's complicated. All the different pieces fit together to create a picture in my mind."

"I injured my left knee playing soccer, and do tend to favor the leg a bit," he offered with an intrigued yet cheerful under-tone. "You'd make a good detective. Maybe you should take on Sam's case."

His praise sprinkled a tingle of satisfaction across her skin, and more importantly eased her continuing anxiety. "Are you going to investigate after all?" she asked, curious why he'd changed his mind.

"My parents asked me to meet with the deputies—which I did. There isn't a lot to work with. Maybe I'm being too criti-cal, or I'm too close to this one and I can't be impartial, but the investigation work was crap. I'd be surprised if they have enough to arrest anyone."

"No arrest? Ever? That doesn't sound good." His reasoning

sounded perfectly logical, but below the surface, she speculated there might be other reasons causing the reluctance. "Why do you say you can't be impartial? Because he's your brother, or because you're angry?"

"Possibly both. Maybe I'm reading too much into trivial things."

"Like what?"

"I don't know. Things at Sam's place seem off or out of character. Since I know my brother and his behaviors, I could be reading into things, pushing too hard for answers."

"When you say off, do you mean like odd?"

"Off, like in off-center picture frames, slightly opened drawers, papers spread across the desk, not in a neat stack the way Sam most likely would have done it. Sam's a bit OCD. I mean, was." He paused. "Maybe he'd changed over the years. Maybe there's an inconsequential answer as to why things have been moved." His rushed inhale signaled frustration.

Mara shifted her grocery basket in her arms. "Maybe you should trust your instincts. Being blind, I learned those instincts are really important."

"You're right. Following my gut instinct is what helped me get promoted to detective grade." *That and living and breathing my work twenty-four, seven.* "Sam hasn't changed his eating habits. That much I know. His refrigerator contains beer, cartons of green, moldy food too far gone to identify, and condiments."

"Your brother is a lot like Tony. Sam ate out a lot. I can't believe he's gone." She let the thought trail off. Dismay for bringing up such a touchy subject turned her stomach sour, and she had to swallow to stave off the queasiness. "Have you ever considered that maybe you're the best person to look for Sam's killer?"

"That's crossed my mind as well. Back in Seattle, I'd be

benched if I even considered getting involved. Here, people seem to want me to take a front row seat."

She wished there were some way of easing his pain. Losing family sucked—especially suddenly—she could relate. An idea struck. *Food.* "If you're hungry, you should stop at the café. They have a new menu and Jenna makes the best caramel rolls."

"Who's Jenna?"

"You might not have met her yet. She's the baker over at River Creek Café. Her pies are wonderful, and her rosemary bread is amazing. When she bakes, you can't miss the smell. Just follow your nose. The rest of your body will automatically follow."

Just like his spicy, masculine scent. He smelled heavenly. The combination of aftershave, deodorant, and a bit of wintergreen toothpaste gave him a crisp, clean smell. She would have liked to run her hand across his freshly shaven jaw to get a better physical image. Possibly lean in for a better sniff. If she could only come up with a good excuse or a way to inconspicuously manage a feel and sniff she would.

The silence expanded, and she shifted uneasily. "I should let you get your shopping done. Sounds like you have a busy day."

"I'm not sure what I need to buy, since I don't know how long I'll be able to stay. I asked for a leave extension to see if I can help give my family some assurance about Sam's case, but I haven't received confirmation yet."

"That would make shopping difficult. But I'm sure one of your sisters will be glad to take anything you don't use."

"You're smart. You made a list."

She reached for the iPad she'd placed in the bottom of the plastic carrier. "Harold likes lists. He says it's easier to help me shop."

"Harold, as in Harold Talbott, the store owner?"

"One and the same. If the store looks different, it's because Claudia Talbott changed the layout to make shopping easier.

Somewhere near the front, she's created space to carry local produce and goods." She pointed over her shoulder. "Harold is out back unloading a delivery truck. I should just pick up a few things now, then come back when he's not so busy." She tried keeping the irritation out of her voice, but the frustration of waiting must have oozed out just enough because she felt Joey lean in to look at the list.

"May I help you shop?"

"That's okay. I was just getting the ingredients to make my mom's Swedish meatballs. Tony's been craving a batch, but I can make them some other time."

"Tony always bragged about your mama's cooking. Tell you what...I'll help you shop, if you save me some."

"Men. Always trying to get their hands on my meatballs. It's just plain sexy." *Wow. That came out of nowhere, and my flirting skills suck.*

Joey choked out a contagious laugh. Within seconds, both of them were guffawing over her major- league slip. Rather than letting her apologize, Joey gave her a friendly nudge. "I haven't laughed that hard in weeks." He released a slow, easy breath. "I sure needed it."

"You have a gentle laugh," Mara admitted, for lack of anything better to say. The easy turned into awkward, punctuated by the sound of rattling keys.

"How about we get our shopping done." His lighthearted tone turned playful. "You mentioned the café, and I sure wouldn't mind some company. What do you say?"

"Is this your way of making sure I get home safely?"

"Maybe. Would that bother you?"

Habitual stubbornness tightened her shoulders, but the desire to hold his interest urged her to hand over the electronic device. "No...I um...well, I just need to get a few apples, then if you could help me with the rest, I'd appreciate it." She lifted an apple and smelled the aroma. The bitterness had her returning the fruit to select another one. "I bet you don't have much to laugh about in your line of work."

"You're right. I was in the middle of investigating a string of brutal murder cases in Seattle when Pia called to tell me about Sam."

"Do some of the cases you investigate stay with you awhile?" she asked, while placing the bag of apples in the basket, and moving on to find an onion.

"Longer than I would like them to."

"I guess no one is immune to trauma. My father always told me it's how we deal with the bad stuff that counts." Her thoughts automatically time-warped back to her trauma. The car accident. Her parents in the front seat, the blood. Not being able to find Sarah. The panic. The familiar emptiness returned, hollowing out her chest.

"Seems we both could use a day off." He said gently sliding a hand under her elbow. "Let's get this shopping done, so we can have some fun. Sound good?"

His firm, yet gentle touch produced a giddy, almost euphoric sensation. "Sounds good."

Whoa. Did she just blow off work?

If she opened her electronic calendar, a list of past due tasks would start chirping at her, but she didn't want to think about chores, or Tony harping at her for not taking down the Valentine decorations or counting the inventory.

Didn't she deserve time off?

The last time she took off, was like…never. Didn't a girl deserve to go out with a boy she once had a crush on?

She squared her shoulders with conviction, and turned back to Joey.

"What's next on the list?"

CHAPTER SIX

T rauma. Death. Blood. All inevitable elements of Joey's
daily life, but not hers.

From her frown, he guessed Mara was thinking about the
guy who scared her. She didn't need to have any more stress in
her life. He wished there was something he could do to change
her situation, and grew curious.

"I heard about your parents and sister." His newly formed
empathy contributed to the need to connect, gain an understanding of what had happened. "The adjustment you had to go
through must have been rough."

She cocked her head to the left. "You're so refreshing. Most
people skirt around the topic. Very few are willing to talk to
me about my accident. I hate hearing the sympathy. Thank you
for not feeling sorry for me."

"Sorry? Sorry for what happened, sure, but I admire you.
Not once have you played the victim card—not growing up or
now—and I respect your courage."

"Thanks." Her arms folded inward. Disbelief underlined her
words and pinched her lips together.

The need to erase the skepticism grew. "Honest. You've

always been strong and determined. You have a solid sense of what you want, and I know you'll work until you get it perfect. I also know, you don't like anyone's help, and that is why you're going to try to argue with me over carrying this basket." Joey slid the shopping container from Mara's arm and placed a pound of chuck and pork in the bottom. "So, please don't."

Mara stuck out her perfect chin. "Why thank you, sir, for being so kind."

"You're welcome, madam."

There it was. That smile she always managed, no matter the circumstances. Turning, she lifted her hand as if searching. He guided her fingers to his arm and leaned in to get another whiff of her shampoo. That was a bad, bad, bad idea. Now, all he wanted to do was nuzzle that soft spot below her ear and make her giggle. He proceeded toward the soup aisle for some broth, before the temptation became unmanageable.

Her steps suddenly became sluggish. "Wait…did you just call me a perfectionist?"

"Among other things." His sudden apprehension turned into delight, and he placed a hand over hers to stop her from pulling away. "It was meant as a compliment. Take the way you tackled math and science, practiced your cheerleading jumps, rehearsed lines for school plays, or planned homecoming dances. Watching you in the flower shop showed me you haven't changed in that respect. I have no doubt you're going to make life what you want it to be. You're focused. Maybe that's what attracts us men, your can-do attitude, not your mother's meatball recipe."

He liked the way her fingers played with her scarf's fringe and the way she tucked her nose inside her jacket to hide her flustered reaction.

"I doubt that."

"You're a stunning woman, Mara."

"Says you. I can't see it. Literally. Half the time I wonder if

I've smudged my makeup or have a stain on my shirt." If her skin hadn't deepened to the sweetest shade of red to match the buttons on her coat, he might have thought she'd blown off his comment. But she hadn't, and he enjoyed learning he could still make her blush.

He placed a can of beef broth in the basket and headed toward the dairy section. "From where I'm standing, it wouldn't matter if your makeup was smudged or you had a stain on your shirt because the only thing a guy with any intelligence would be looking at is your smile. It's riveting."

"Riveting. Now, there's a two-dollar word."

That feather-light feeling drifted through him again. Open. Unguarded. Casual. Damn, she was addicting.

"Do you miss your brother?"

"And you say I'm refreshing. Touché, Miss Dijocomo."

He studied her face.

Sam left a vacancy in his soul, but did he miss him? The crevice Sam's death had forged in his chest grew wider.

His brother had a way about him that created snapshots in time. Playing hockey together. Rafting down the river. Hunting big game. But did he actually miss him? The answer to that question seemed elusive, and caused a heaping dose of remorse to curdle in his stomach. Why had he become so disconnected from his family? He definitely felt something. The intense, bottled-up outrage over his brother's senseless death seemed to overshadow all other emotions.

"Did I ask the question too early?" Worry lines creased her beautiful eyes and mouth, emphasizing her awareness of human tragedy.

"No, I was just thinking. Sure, I miss him." He tried infusing honesty into his politically correct statement, but knew he sounded flat and insincere, most likely because he felt something different. Enraged. Resentful. Resolved.

"But?"

The simple question opened up a few possibilities. Could he admit what he'd been feeling? Would she judge him for the distance and resentment that had grown between him and his sibling? She waited patiently. Her unseeing eyes stared directly into his soul, studying, considering, maybe even judging a little.

He rubbed his sweaty palm against his pants. "The past few days, I've felt lost. Like I've lost a part of me I'll never get back. Early on, I just wanted to be Sam's mirror image. Then, as I got older, I did everything I could to be nothing like him. Now that he's gone, I feel selfish for begrudging his influence, and now I have no one to compete with...or resent. If that makes any sense."

"It's only natural to be angry. You two were always together. In high school, everyone knew where there was one Gaccione, others were sure to be nearby. I think that's why a lot of people were surprised when you left. Well, at least, I was...surprised, that is."

"Really? You barely knew I existed, and you resented being tutored."

A puff of air lifted her bangs off her forehead. "I resented my parents for thinking a B wasn't good enough. And everyone knew you existed. You had a way of standing out. The soccer captain. The class president. Head of the chess club. Do I need to continue?"

But I just wanted to be invisible.

He placed a small carton of cream in the basket and reached for a gallon of whole milk. "My parents made sure all the kids got involved and stayed active. Sticking with soccer would have been enough for me."

"Your family was involved in a lot of stuff. I always got the feeling, though, that you never received your due. Sam seemed to snatch other people's spotlights. Especially yours."

A slideshow of memories supporting her point flashed through his mind, instance after instance when Sam swooped in at the last minute to get the applause. A bitter acid pooled in his mouth and burned the back of his throat. "He never did like to share."

"But he did watch out for all of you." Mara placed her palm on his chest, then moved her hand over a little, pausing over his heart. "Trust me. If you ever need him, he's here, in your heart. Talk to him. Listen. One day, when you least expect it, he'll be the special little voice in your head encouraging you, maybe even taunting you in that smack down, brotherly kind of way."

He liked the way her smile infected him and infused a bit of heat into his cold bones—a warmth missing until he'd opened the door to her flower shop. "Do your parents and sister give you advice?"

Mara pulled her hand back. "My sister, not so much. More my mom, and sometimes my dad." Her unseeing eyes seemed to freeze on a distant memory. "When I woke up in the hospital and learned everyone had died but me, I thought my life would end. To be honest, I hoped it would. My legs had been crushed, and I was fighting an infection. I worked hard to convince myself things would get better. Then I got the news that the blurred vision I was experiencing would get worse. I felt abandoned. I was learning to walk again while Tony was working hard to finish school. I was left to deal with hospital bills, the drunk driver case and the flower shop. I was angry. Actually, angry is kind of a mild word for what I was feeling."

Mara's hand dropped to fondle her dog's ears. "One night, after I got home from the doctor's office, I was lying in my bed, and I heard my mother's voice so near, it was like she was sitting on the bed next to me. The voice told me I had a choice. To be miserable. Or live happy. If I wanted to find contentment, I needed to live the best life I could. The next day, Tony finished his college final exams, and I got approval for a service dog. Every day since, I've been living one day at a time."

"Sounds like good advice for me, too."

"I bet you'll get a lot of advice in the next few weeks. It's important to listen only to the opinions that feel right for you."

He tucked the ideas into the back of his mind to simmer, not wanting to deal with the newly formed ache his brother's absence caused. "Let's get checked out. My rental car's parked outside. It's cold enough, I don't think the food will spoil, and it's only a short drive to the café."

"If you have the time, I'd prefer to walk. Buddy gets a bit nervous in cars, and he's still a bit agitated from that guy. He's very protective."

"Walking sounds perfect. Personally, I'd rather spend time with you than hours going through case files. We can even drop the groceries off at the store, if you'd like. That way, you can check on things."

She reached for Buddy and ran her fingers through his fur. "Like you said it's cold enough outside, so the food will be fine, and Tony can handle things at the store."

"Sounds like we have a plan."

At the cash register, he bagged the few grocery items he'd picked up. She insisted on bagging hers, which she said allowed her to memorize the position of each item so she wouldn't mistake the can of minestrone soup for beef broth.

Joey carried both sets of groceries to his rental car and stored them in the trunk. "You ready?"

"Yep. Can we walk the long way around, past the park and grade school?"

"Sure."

Absolutely. Anywhere. Just name it. He would welcome any reason to procrastinate—plain and simple. His boss had specifically warned him against investigating his brother's homicide, and to focus only on taking a break from the horrific crime spree he'd been working the last few months. Maybe all the justifications for his procrastination were excuses. That's what his dad called his reluctance. *Perspective* is what his boss would call it. *Self-preservation* is what he called it.

Childlike anticipation danced on her face, creating an eagerness in him to discover why she chose to walk in the park on a day barely above freezing. Walking a few blocks or miles didn't make a difference to him, but obviously to her it mattered—so it mattered to him. Buddy seemed to know the way, so he let the dog and Mara set the pace to simply enjoy the company.

"What's going on with you?" Mara asked. "You could be knocking on any girl's door, so why are you helping me grocery shop and asking me to breakfast? Are you trying to avoid your family? Or is it the case you're avoiding?"

A kaleidoscope of thoughts formed and reformed. Somehow he sensed that the next few words he spoke might be profoundly important, so he took his time. Drawing in a long, nervous breath, he then pushed the air and trepidation out of his body. "Maybe I asked you to breakfast because I've always found you intriguing." *And, I should have asked you out a long time ago.*

"Intriguing? Why? Because I arrange flowers for people? Or because I'm blind?"

The bold question proved his point. "I've always found you intriguing, and your blindness is only a part of who you are. What I find fascinating is your confidence, the way you delight in helping others, and your relationship with Buddy."

Upon hearing his name, Buddy glanced back at him.

"He's easy to love. All animals are." She stated simply, then walked along in silence, but her facial expressions created a symphony of reflections.

"What are you thinking?"

"How time changes people." She inclined her head his way. "It seems the last ten years have changed you. You're less intense and seem more comfortable with life. So, who is Joey Gaccione now? What's he like?"

"It's a long story."

"Well, that's convenient. I have time to listen."

Joey swallowed another semi-flippant response when her curious brow lifted, waiting for him to say something—something honest. "I'm not sure. After college, I focused on putting food on the table, paying bills, working hard, taking and making opportunities for advancement. Then, one day, I got called to a horrific scene. The father had lost his job. With no way to make a living, he took the lives of his wife and six children, then killed himself. The youngest was just six months old. The case made me stop and think. Honestly, some days I wonder if detective work is what I want to do. I studied and worked hard because I wanted to make my parents proud. Now, I'm wondering if I can continue doing the intensive work I do long-term, because I've come to realize I can never satisfy my parents."

The frigid wind whipped Mara's hair against her face. Joey stopped to tuck the stray strands into her wool cap.

"Your mom is very proud of you, Joey. You should hear her brag about her son—how smart and handsome. You're a catch. Don't you know?"

"A catch?" *Typical ma.* "She makes me sound like a piece of salmon." Yet pride still warmed his core.

"You know a good paying job isn't what makes a parent proud, right?"

That's the only thing that makes my parents proud...wasn't it? "For a man, it's different."

"I wouldn't think so. Every parent wants their child to grow up happy, be independent, and to be a kind and caring person. Your parents seem proud of you not for the position or the title of your job, but the fact that you are helping protect your community."

"I hadn't thought of it that way."

"It's odd to hear that you don't like your job. It seems you work hard at something you don't want to do."

You understand too much for someone who can't see.

"Joey, if you and Sam hadn't been so competitive and worked so hard to out-do each other, what would you have done with your life?"

"That's too hard to answer. There's never been a life without Sam until now." He pulled closer, to keep her warm, at least that was the excuse. "What about you? Who is Mara Dijocomo?"

"Oh, I don't know. I'm pretty much the same girl. Maybe a little wiser. Less naïve. More prepared. Doing what I need to do to survive. When life puts you on a train to hell, you get to know what's important, who your real friends are and who's there to help you find your way back."

"True friends. A person doesn't get many in their lifetime." A nostalgic smile tugged at his mouth. "I had good friends in college. Jobs scattered us across three continents. Then careers and commitments started interfering with regular communication. When you find good people, you hold on. Maybe we can try it. Friendship, that is."

Or something more. Being her friend would be hard, especially since he had the constant urge to kiss her and feel her soft skin beneath the palm of his hand.

"Not many people want to befriend a blind person. We have our limitations." Mara shrugged her shoulders dismissively, and he detested the careless gesture.

"That's the problem with this world. Plastic people. People who only want to associate with those who dress like them, think like them...clones. I prefer hanging with people who think independently, are confident in who they are, and don't feel the need to shrink to fit in."

"I haven't shrunk, but my world seems to have gotten a bit smaller. Blindness does that to a person."

They walked several blocks in silence. The shining sun doing little to warm his fingers. He cherished the fact she didn't need to fill the minutes with senseless chatter. She reminded him of a butterfly, capturing his attention to make him pause and reflect on the beauty of the moment.

When they neared the park, she picked up her pace.

"Do you see any snowmen?" she asked, childlike excitement glowing on her face. "The children at the elementary school were going to make some yesterday."

Joey gazed over the landscape of snow and tree skeletons dormant for winter until he found several stacked mounds. "I see them. They're by the playground to the right of the slides."

"So there was enough snow. One of the teachers stopped by yesterday morning for some willow branches. Supposedly, the children are studying the British monarchy and wanted to build the royal family."

Royal family snow people. "This should be interesting."

Buddy followed the path. A few dozen feet from the historical site, Joey started to laugh. "Yep, that's the royal court, all right. Complete with crown, scepter and what I think are supposed to be the royal medals constructed with ribbon and glitter."

"Gwen, the owner of Second Time Around, the thrift store here in town, provided the costumes. I wish I could see them."

"Maybe you can." Joey stood behind her and directed her shoulders. "In front of you is Queen Elizabeth. Take a bow." Joey placed his arms around her waist and leaned forward over her back, creating a double-person bow. He expected her to laugh, but she became still. Her free hand remained on his arm.

"What else?" she asked on a whispered breath.

She smelled of vanilla creamer, and the cozy scent brought a sense of calm. He liked the way she fit in his arms, especially the way she eased back, folding into his frame. One by one, he described each snowperson in detail, from the white gloves and hats to the ribbon sashes, to the dollar-store crowns, never letting her go. Standing together, her in his arms, he could stay that way forever, but he caught the shiver that ran the length of her body.

"You're getting cold. We should move on."

A pair of mothers, out for their early morning exercise, moved along the park's path, pushing strollers, with toddlers in tow. The soft yet insistent wail of an infant and a toddler refusing to put on his hat created a distraction.

Mara turned slightly. "Sounds like someone is cranky and someone else wants breakfast."

"I suspect the one who wants breakfast is the little girl in the stroller. She's bundled in one of those head-to-toe snow-suits." His hot breath crystallized and swirled around them. "She's wearing one of those knitted strawberry hats, complete with a green stem."

A little boy spotted Buddy and darted toward them. "Can I pet your dog?" a small, bold voice asked.

Joey took a half step forward. "I don't think—"

"It's okay." Mara leaned toward Buddy, rubbing his chest, and aimed her voice toward the little boy. "Sure you can pet the dog, but please be gentle. Buddy likes to be petted only behind his ears. He's on duty and likes to see and hear what's going on. What's your name?"

"Bradley. I'm four."

"Nice to meet you, Bradley-I'm-four. Meet Buddy. He just turned five."

"Bradley!" yelled a tired and riled woman wearing no makeup and black circles under her eyes. "I'm sorry, ma'am. Bradley, you're not supposed to approach strange dogs." The woman pulled the boy away from the dog. "What's with you today?" she demanded as the boy let out a sniffled wail.

Jealousy. Sibling rivalry. The fact that Bradley's new little sister got the majority of Mom's attention. All of which, he figured, made the little guy darn-right cranky.

Joey whispered, "From the look on the mom's face, Bradley's been pushing the right irritation buttons this morning. It's got to be tough being the only one, then, *wham*, you have to share everything."

Mara tilted her head to the left. "The way you phrased your sentence makes me think you're talking about your brother."

"Sam used to get mad when I played with his toys. I would sneak them out of his room. I remember the day I broke his favorite fire engine. The truck was this two-foot metal jobber complete with an extended ladder and an unwinding hose. I'm not sure he ever forgave me."

The mellow expression on her face morphed into something brittle and somber. "I always thought I would have kids."

His heart *kerplunked*. There was something misguided about her statement. The sentence was past tense, like Mara never having children was written in a book somewhere and couldn't be changed.

How could that be?

CHAPTER SEVEN

Joey refused to believe she didn't want to have a family of her own. Surely she considered herself capable. That preposterous thought pummeled his heart.

"You don't want kids?"

"Before the accident, I wanted a houseful, but some days I struggle just taking care of Buddy and the store. Plus, I'm not sure how I would feel, knowing I'd never be able to see my children's faces, or their drawings, or watch them cross the stage to graduate. Besides, what guy is going to sign up to date a lifetime member of the American Disability Association?"

"The right guy, that's who." Joey hoped she heard and believed his conviction.

The family moved along, the little boy waving at Buddy as he passed. Unfortunately, Mara didn't see the child's wave or how his downright crankiness had turned bright and cheerful —driving her point home.

Oblivious, she took a step in the opposite direction. An understanding of how much the accident had truly taken from her sliced a chunk out of his heart.

"Don't worry." She gave him a soft nudge and grinned. "There are about twenty thousand people in this town. Assuming half are men, I have a one-in-ten-thousand chance to find the right guy. Maybe I should start hanging out at Mad Jack's pub to increase my chances. Or hey, I'll win the lottery, and men will be falling over themselves to get a piece of my winnings."

Irritation flared in his gut like a bowl of spicy green chili sitting on an ulcer. She didn't need to win lotteries or pick up guys in bars. She deserved better.

She reached out and touched his arm. "What just happened? You went quiet on me."

"A bar isn't the best place to start a relationship. The guys there have two things in mind: one, to get drunk, and two, to get laid."

"Wonderful. I'll put on my skimpy skirt and slide on up to the bar, see if I can up my chances."

Really? Maybe I don't know you after all.

"That was a joke, Joey. I don't have time between my work and volunteering at the animal shelter, and you know I'm not the promiscuous type. Besides, with Gina being pregnant, Tony is a bit distracted these days, and there's no one else to run the flower shop. It's busy this time of year, so I don't get out much. Today's a nice exception."

Relief doused his irritation. Still, the idea of her having to search for dates didn't sit quite right. Guys were plain stupid if they couldn't see what she had to offer.

Maybe it was men who were blind.

Mara could see what mattered just fine.

The rest of their walk to the little restaurant on Main Street took just under ten minutes. Joey opened the heavy glass door, taking a few seconds to scan the vehicles and license plates of the cars parked in the front before entering. None were from out of state.

Mara moved to the "Please wait to be seated" sign.

A platinum blonde who hadn't updated her hairstyle since the Sixties, and most likely wore her grandmother's pearls, approached them with a bubblegum-pink smile. "Mara, darling. Where have you been?"

Mara nudged Buddy's rump to make him sit and then straightened. "Hey, Sheila. I've been boxing flowers for half of the male population this side of the ridge. Yesterday was Valentine's Day, remember?"

"Girl, your fingers must be raw."

"I don't mind the cuts. Especially since we need the rent money. I just hope Mother's Day goes as well."

The sincerity and concern in her voice communicated more than Mara probably wanted him or other people to know. He guessed concerns about bills and cash flow to run a business never let up, at least not for long.

Her head turned slightly toward the dining area. "Is my table open?"

"That table has your name on it, honey. Right this way," Sheila said before Joey could find a way to broach the subject of cash flow.

Assisted by Buddy, Mara followed Sheila, maneuvering around tables and chairs like a dog running an agility track.

"Here's a menu for your friend," Sheila said, dropping a laminated list on the table.

Mara turned toward the voice. "Sheila, this is Joey Gaccione. He went to high school here and came home for a brief visit."

He noticed Mara didn't mention the connection with his brother, but he could see Sheila connecting the dots.

"Nice to meet you, Joey. Sure love your momma's lasagna. Best in town. Heard you were going to help with your brother's case."

He cringed. "I'll do what I can."

He scanned the café and sure enough people were looking at him with a hopefulness he dreaded. He remained silent until Sheila disappeared, then stepped forward to help Mara with her coat.

She shrugged out of his grasp. "Thanks, but I can manage."

Noticing the irritation in her tone, he placed a hand on her woolen sleeve. "I know you can manage, but if my mother walked in and saw I wasn't doing right by you…well, let's just say I don't want that to happen. As you know, this town is very small. News travels fast. I would appreciate it if you would help me out here. I don't want my cell phone squawking in the next ten minutes."

"Thank you." Mara nodded, allowing him to help her with her coat. She slid into the booth, while Buddy found a spot on the floor beside the worn leather bench, and he hung her coat on a nearby hook.

Her index finger automatically started to draw abstract designs on the table. "I'm glad you came to my rescue today. You introducing me to the royal family also made my day special."

"Not a problem." He watched her finger spiral then loop. "May I ask what you're drawing?"

Her finger paused, and he sighed with disappointment, but then the movement started again and revitalized his delight.

"Actually, I'm not drawing so much as spelling. When I was adjusting to my blindness, the psychologist said I needed to practice writing and typing so I don't lose my skills. Thanks to Stephen Hawking, technology has advanced, but still not far enough to take away the nuances a blind person faces. The doctors, nurses and therapists all told me I needed to believe, so that's what I write, different forms of believe, like optimism and faith, to remind me."

Her explanation drifted away like an unmoored boat,

suggesting she'd said too much. Wanting insight into what made Mara Dijocomo tick, he asked, "Reminders of what?"

Her hands slowly curled into fists.

Dang it. Why do I always have to push too hard? Regret rushed in, then wavered when her hands eased flat.

"To believe. Believe I was capable of standing in order to walk. Believe I could walk, to run, and if I worked hard and accomplished running, I could do just about anything I set my mind to doing."

"Can you run, Mara?" he asked, already knowing the answer, but wanting to hear the pride in her voice, acknowledging her many accomplishments.

"Yes, but not very fast, and my muscles like to punish me for trying. That's why I like to walk. I even did a ten-kilometer walk last year to raise money for Helper Shelter, the animal adoption place where I teach classes. I'm convinced the exercises makes sure my rods and pins get lubricated, even though the doctors tell me it's more about muscles and tendons."

"That's awesome."

The pride on her face slowly morphed into a look of determination—the familiar expression he'd noticed when she was trying to solve a tough math problem. His phone rang and the temptation not to answer grew.

"If that's your mom, tell her it's my fault I resisted help." Mara's smile filled him with joy until he scanned the number displayed. He instantly swiped his thumb across the pad.

"Gaccione." He listened, his whole body sparking with a sudden anger. "When?" A swoosh of disappointment quickly followed. An awareness he was clenching his phone so hard he just might crack the casing filtered in. "The funeral's tomorrow. Yep. Understood. Yes, sir. I'll be home as soon as possible."

He ended the call and shoved the phone in his pocket.

"Is everything all right?"

Hell, no. "It was my boss calling to say another body's been found."

"I'm so, so sorry."

"I should have been there. I should have been working to help stop this lunatic. I need to do something."

"You *are* doing something. You're trying to find your brother's killer." Mara reached her hand out to connect and provide comfort.

He didn't want human touch. He wanted to get up, fly back to Seattle and get back to work. Yet, he found himself reaching across the table instead.

"You also helped me this morning by scaring that guy away."

How could he make her understand? Yes, Sam's killer needed to be found, and the deputies should catch the guy before long, if they could figure out how to do their jobs. And, if the guy, whoever he was, wanted to hurt Mara, the profile he'd been starting to compile in his head indicated Mara wasn't in immediate danger.

In either his brother's or Mara's case, there wasn't some whack-job brutally killing women every ten days or so. The serial killer would strike again—soon. The sociopath liked playing games. He liked the chase, and Joey wanted that bastard behind bars for life.

"I can tell you're upset." She tapped her finger on the table. "Since you are here, and there is little you can do about what's going on in Seattle, do you mind if I change the subject? Or would you like to talk about your case."

"I can't discuss the details of my cases. What I just told you has already hit the news outlets. So, it might be a good idea if we talk about something else."

"Okay, then. Listen up. I think you're up for a challenge. Being friends depends on how you answer the next question."

Her eyebrows moved with the inflection of each word. Her earnest attempt at light humor created an appreciation.

Cautiously, he took a breath, released it slowly, ready to answer any question she asked. "A test. All right. Lay it on me."

"Would you be willing to share a slice of banana cream pie with me?"

"For breakfast?"

"Yep."

That unfamiliar rumble of laughter erupted from his chest. Unbelievable. Twice in one day, she'd made him laugh. The stress knot at the base of his neck began to unravel. "A woman after my own heart."

He never shared food. Ever.

Maybe because he never found someone he wanted to share with.

However, with her, he'd share.

Sheila appeared when Mara raised her hand.

"Banana cream with extra whip, please." Mara paused, before adding, "I would like coffee as well. How about you, Joey?"

"Coffee, black."

Mara took a deep inhale, soaking in the melodic tones of his voice, wishing the phone call hadn't caused his mood to turn dark. However, the return of his boyhood moodiness drew some comfort. He hadn't changed that much.

When a girl had a crush on a boy who happened to be the school's star athlete and nominated three years in a row for prom king, she figured the heavens would need to open and grant her a lifetime of wishes to get noticed. Only by accident did her parents thrust her in his path when she came home with a "C" average in Math and Science. Even with that cosmic event, not surprisingly, the stars didn't suddenly shift and realign in the sky, causing all her dreams to come true.

So why was her fantasy man sitting in front of her now... now, when she couldn't even see his gentle, handsome face?

If she ever met the faerie named Fate, she'd kick her in the shins for being so cruel.

"Here's your coffee." A mug clunked on the table, followed by a liquid glug-glug-glug, slightly rising in pitch with each glug, until each cup measured three-quarters full. "Your pie will be up in a minute."

"Thanks, Sheila."

Mara reached for the wall, skimming her fingers along the table's edge until she found the individually wrapped creamer cups, and then curled her fingers around the spoon Joey nudged toward her hand.

His offer of guarded chivalry sent sprinkles of happiness throughout her system. He protected, yet supported. He'd helped her shop, pointing out sale items, yet didn't demand to play the hero when she wanted to bag her own groceries. Even her father might have approved. Kym would be envious. Her older sister would be jealous, because Sarah had tried every-thing to get Joey's attention in high school, short of crawling naked into his bed.

"Here's the pie. Extra whip." Sheila slid the plate to the middle of the table. "Anything else, just call."

In the process of taking a sip of coffee, Mara gave Sheila a thumbs-up and swallowed. She placed her cup on the table, flattened her hands, thumbs together moving them forward until connecting with the plate, nudging the pie toward the man. "Go ahead, you have the first bite," she offered, although perhaps a bit reluctantly.

"Ladies first. I insist."

My prince.

What girl didn't dream of taking the first fork of Banana

Cream Delight, rather than the guy eat half the pie in two bites and then shoving the plate across the table for her to finish off the scrounged scraps? Tony would have eaten two-thirds before passing the plate to her.

"Since we can't talk about my cases, do you mind if we talk about your accident?" he asked.

She choked on the cream in her mouth and worked to swallow both the food and the emotions clogging her throat. The noise from the kitchen, the constantly swinging door, and the servers' chatter at the cook's window could have served as an excuse to ignore his inquisitiveness, but she heard the question.

Still pushing for answers, eh, Joey? "No, I don't mind, but it's somewhat of a downer subject."

"Yeah, you're right. Never mind."

"It's not that. Over the years, customers sometimes asked about my parents or the accident, but I learned most people only wanted enough details to satisfy their curiosity. Somehow I don't think the minimum would be enough for you." *In fact I know it won't.*

No, Joey liked to push—like at math. He'd push until she gave him the correct answer. He'd push until there was no place left to hide.

"I guess maybe I'm guilty of being curious as well. When I started on the force, I worked all types of scenes. Domestics. Robbery. Homicide. I saw a lot of people at their worst. I often wondered what happened after...I mean, how a person picked up the pieces and moved on."

A long, slow inhale and exhale helped her find equilibrium, a place that allowed her to revisit the past without reliving the accident, a place where details could flow without the emotional baggage being lugged along behind.

Joey's safe. You can do this. He won't second-guess or judge like the others.

She wrapped her hand around her fork twisting the metal in her palm. "We were on a snow-packed road and running late." The words came out slightly louder than a whisper. "Dad decided to take one of the back roads to avoid traffic. From the pieces I can put together, an intoxicated mother of two took a curve too fast, overcorrected, and her car fishtailed. I don't think my dad saw the car coming until the last minute, then he swerved."

"Did the car go off the road?"

"We ended up going down a steep ravine. One minute I was sitting in the backseat talking to Sarah, and the next minute I was waking up unable to move my legs. My head felt like someone had dropped me headfirst onto the pavement. Things get a little blurry from there. I remember drifting in and out of consciousness, and at one point searching for my sister. I guess it took the medics a while to get to me."

Joey's warm hand covered hers. "Were you scared? What am I saying? Of course you were."

"Actually, no, not at first. I was pretty out of it. As soon as I got to the hospital, the doctors pumped me full of meds to fight off the brain swelling and infection. Several days passed before I learned my sister was thrown from the car because she'd removed her seatbelt to get something out of her purse. The police working the scene told me the car rolled several times, but all I remember is feeling disoriented, like I was floating."

"I'm told that's a normal sensation."

"The most vivid memories are of voices telling me to hold on, doctors asking me questions I couldn't answer and nurses explaining I was lucky. Although I'm not sure *lucky* is the term I would use to describe my situation. I underwent four surgeries and twenty-seven weeks of intense therapy learning to walk again, and a lifetime of wishing I could see another sunset...or children playing...or my family's faces."

Joey squeezed her fingers. "I shouldn't have asked. I was just curious. I know how hard it is to live with memories. There are some things you just can't un-see."

"I'm glad we can talk. I hope you know you can talk to me… anytime. So many people don't know what to say, so they ignore my blindness, or ignore me altogether. Others want to know every tiny detail so they can offer advice or compare my injuries to Uncle Harry's triple bypass or Aunt Harriett's arthritis."

She lifted her fork and aimed toward the pie. "But today, I have things to celebrate. I can walk. I have work, good friends and a brother who truly cares about me. And I have a mouth-watering banana cream pie sitting right in front of me, waiting for me to take another bite."

"You certainly can walk and do a lot of other things pretty well, I might add."

Yep. She could walk, but an antique doll with movable joints had fewer pins and screws holding different body parts together. Doctors warned her more surgeries would be required as her body continued to age. A pang of sorrow nudged its way into her chest. "I shouldn't complain. Brianne's life was destroyed. She literally has nothing."

"Do I know Brianne?"

Should I tell him? Would he get angry, like Tony?

The sting of the heartbreak made her fold protectively inward. "No. You don't know her. She doesn't live in Elkridge."

"Why do I get the sense Brianne is important to you?"

"You must be a truly excellent detective." She tapped on the table while she weighed and debated whether she should reveal the tragedy. The ache in her chest expanded. Joey turned her hand over and started drawing circles…no not circles…the word "believe," causing her body to relax and her heart to heal, at least a little.

She swallowed to clear the regrettable injustice. "The day of the accident, Brianne's mother was driving the other car. Like me, her sister was also in the car. Neither her mother, nor her sister survived. I'm not supposed to know, but a friend in Child Services told me Brianne's just been placed with a new foster family, her fourth in six years. She turned eleven last month."

"Four families? That's a bit much." The disgust in his voice reassured her.

"Not really. Brianne has severe emotional issues stemming from the accident. Nobody knows why, but she blames herself for the accident and her mother's drinking. Since that day, she hasn't spoken to anyone but me, and only once. After the nurses moved me out of the ICU, she begged to see me. Child Services arranged a visit. When she entered my room, she broke down sobbing, and all she could say was 'I'm sorry...I'm sorry...I'm sorry.' It was heart-wrenching. I tried explaining the accident wasn't her fault, but she refused to believe me. Her life's been like a puzzle that's been broken apart and jumbled, and nothing fits together anymore."

"Poor kid."

"I wanted to pick her up and hold her, but she wouldn't allow anyone near her." Mara's chest grew tight with the memory. "I can't imagine the torture of feeling responsible for such a tragedy. I wish.... Maybe we should talk about something a little less heavy."

Joey thankfully turned the conversation to safer topics, like the whereabouts of mutual friends, who stayed, who moved away. Tony came up in the context of indulging in food, and the fact he inhaled everything edible within a ten-foot radius. As the seconds ticked by, the despair lifted.

Joey turned her hand over and hugged her palm with both of his. "So, how is the flower business these days?"

Boy. Another doozy. The accident. The business. A good ol' one-two punch.

This time the way he asked the question transported her to an uncomfortable place, like an imaginary interrogation room with no windows, no artwork, no carpet, only a single table and chair and an observation mirror.

She swallowed an uneasy, queasy feeling, not wanting him to know how truly bad the business was suffering. "The flower business is doing okay. We did well over the holidays. My suppliers and I are working to come up with some Mother's Day specials." *Using less expensive flowers because that's all I can afford.* "I'm hoping to offer a couple of lower-price-point items to entice purchases."

"That sounds good." Joey's muffled voice gave her the impression he'd stuffed the remaining pie into his mouth.

She wished the slowly forming image of his cheeks stuffed with pie would make her feel better, but it didn't because her thoughts ricocheted back to her business. Most of their flower vendors were now demanding cash rather than accepting credit, the mortgage company called yesterday demanding last month's overdue payment and the international vase shipment remained stuck in customs. Somehow those realities didn't seem like a fun topic for an early morning chat. Both she and her brother had made mistakes. Lots of mistakes. But they'd learned from them. Bottom line, the flower business wasn't all daisies.

She managed to keep what she hoped was a pleasant smile glued to her face. "Speaking of the flower shop, I should get back. Tony's probably wondering where I've run off to."

Joey shifted in the booth. "I'll flag down Sheila for the check."

A few seconds later, Sheila stopped at the table, and Mara caught a whiff of her perfume and the faint smell of stale cigarettes. "Anything else I can get for you two?"

The smell stirred a memory. The flower shop. The smell of cigarette smoke. "No, we're good. Thanks, Sheila." Mara clenched her fingers into tight fists as the awareness expanded.

"You about ready?" Joey's question came to a rolling stop. "What's wrong? You look worried."

"At the shop this morning, I smelled cigarette smoke. People smoking outside of businesses irks me, but an idea just occurred to me...the smoke wasn't stale. Sheila smokes. The cigarette smell rests just beneath her perfume, and is softer, most likely because she hasn't taken a cigarette break recently. The scent this morning was strong and had a crisp edge, like someone had just lit a cigarette. I'm wondering if that guy from the store followed me from the shop."

"On the way back, we're stopping at the hardware store for some pepper spray. Promise me if *that guy* gets near you again, you'll spray him and scream one of those girly roller-coaster screams. Don't think, just trust your instincts."

"For your information, I can't do a girly scream. In fact, I can't scream, period. My dad made me take a self-defense class before I went to college, and, after three sessions, the instructor suggested I get a whistle."

"Then I'll get you a whistle. Promise me you'll spray anyone who threatens you. Pepper spray is not fatal and wears off. Maybe the guy will scream like a girl, so you won't have to."

Laughter bubbled up even as her fingertips went cold and she started to shiver. What-ifs raced through her mind like hailstones pelting a window, *ping, ping, ping.* "Let me get my wallet so we can pay the check. Sounds like you need to get home. It must be hard wanting to be in two places at one time."

"I already paid the check, and you're right, I'd love to catch the shooter before I have to leave. Here's your coat. Let me help."

She grabbed for his arm. "If I don't at least pay half, someone will start a rumor that we're on a date."

"What if I already consider this a date?" he asked, his tone soft and caressing, almost soothing. "Would you have a problem with that?"

Her unsettled mood abruptly turned the corner, and a happy excitement hip-hopped up her chest. A date. With Joey?

She liked how he rotated her fears a hundred eighty degrees in seconds. "I don't think so."

"You don't think so. Now, there's a statement that will give a man confidence."

"Sorry, it's just I haven't been on a date since college. It's a bit hard for me to get my head around." She most definitely liked the idea of a breakfast date better than pepper spray. She loathed having to carry a weapon. What was happening to Elkridge?

He gently held her jacket open for her. Warm hands brushed her neck, and her body responded. The moment felt natural, unhurried—hence the root of her uneasiness, that while everyone else might watch, judge, assess, Joey didn't care. He didn't push or seem self-conscious about her needing time to gather herself or Buddy. Maybe since he'd gotten out of Elkridge and lived in a big city, his patience and tolerance for people had matured into a genuine understanding. He never seemed to make assumptions like the other residents. If he had a question, he asked, and seemed to listen to her response.

"All set?" he asked.

All set to find out how you kiss? Absolutely. Too bad that wasn't what he meant.

"Yes. Thanks for the pie and for listening to me jabber on. Catching up was fun and a nice way to get me out of shop duty."

"I don't suppose owning your own business allows for much free time."

"No, but I do manage to take time for things I like to do."

"Such as?"

The sentiment popped up again. A genuine interest that made her feel like Taylor Swift onstage, surrounded by her adoring fans. A light shiver spread from fingertip to fingertip.

She pulled the hair out of her jacket and wrapped her scarf around her neck before leaning down to secure Buddy's lead.

"Like I said before, I volunteer at Helper Shelter once a month. They need someone to test service dogs to see if they are ready for placement. For some reason, the dog trainers think I qualify." She laughed at her joke, but noticed Joey didn't find her self-inflicted humor funny. "I also love discovering local artists who make fun gifts for the store, and, generally, making people happy."

The thought brought about a sense of empowerment until she took a step forward, and panic set in.

Confusion choked off her air.

Her mouth became dry as toast.

Crap, where's the front door?

She reached for the table to reorient, but only air moved around her fingers. Voices came from various directions. Buddy didn't have Sheila to follow, and 'exit' wasn't in his vocabulary.

Come on. Not now. Not here.

Embarrassment paraded up her face, heating her skin as it went. She stretched her arm farther, hoping to connect with something, anything.

Joey leaned closer, his hot breath on her ear, sending shivers down her spine. "Mara, you're okay. Take my arm," he murmured. "Turn ten degrees to your left, then go straight."

The uneasy, squirrelly feeling in her stomach stopped circling. A gush of relief filled her, even while a flustered residual remained. Joey gave her time to gather what remained of her dignity and take a step forward.

A kind of peace settled into place. A dreamy kind of place. A place where a woman could indulge in her fantasies of having a gorgeous hunk of a man like Joey Gaccione in her life.

That morning she'd dreaded the thought of running

errands. The hassle of getting both herself and Buddy ready, the challenge of getting from point A to B, and back.

Then that weird guy who'd scared the crap out of her.

However, the morning had blossomed into something ideal, even extraordinary—a day to record in her electronic diary.

A day marked special, with a smiley face icon.

Too bad there wouldn't be more.

CHAPTER EIGHT

Mid-afternoon on Wednesday, Tony drove Mara and Kym to the Elkridge Cemetery. Located midway up the hill, opposite Lonely Ridge, the cemetery overlooked the valley below. Mara visited the peaceful space as often as she could find someone willing to drive her up the windy dirt road.

Sliding down the icy path with one hand on Tony's arm and the other wrapped around Buddy's lead, she made her way to the wooden bridge. Kym, refusing to let Mara go to any funeral alone, followed closely behind. There were some perks to being BFFs since second grade. Kym knew her so well she could almost read her mind.

When they crossed the weathered wooden planks, Mara drew a long breath. Left, up the path at a forty-five-degree angle for thirty-eight paces, a giant blue spruce stood sentinel. Directly up the hill from there, her mother, father, and sister were buried. She turned right and followed along the path with the rest of the crowd, but her mind had turned left, thinking of the snow covering her family's burial plot.

"The temperature's dropping," Kym said, zipping her jacket.

94

"It's going to snow again. If this cold snap keeps up, I'm going to shiver off my last five pounds."

"Don't tell me you're dieting." The disbelief stumbled out of Mara's mouth so quickly she almost choked. "You don't have five pounds to lose. Why don't you break the hand warmer I gave you? The packet should last a few hours."

"Please don't tell me this service is going to last that long." Kym continued to grumble about funerals, her weight, flat butt, and anything else she could complain about while they trudged up the hill.

"You're quiet." Mara squeezed her brother's arm. "Are you okay?"

"Yeah. Gina couldn't get comfortable last night, and neither one of us got any sleep."

Mara accepted the statement, but assumed his thoughtful mood had nothing to do with lack of sleep. He didn't like visiting the cemetery, but would accompany her out of a sense of obligation. Her brother didn't believe their family was actually present, like she did, because he never saw the mangled bodies. He preferred to imagine they were on a road trip, having a great time. This place, as peaceful as it was, reminded him of things he didn't want to remember.

"Bill Mason was sweet to offer one of his tractors," Mara said. "Otherwise I don't think the ground crew could have dug a hole deep enough. The ground feels frozen solid."

"Do we have to talk?" Kym asked. "I'm huffing and puffing back here, climbing this hill. Can't we just enjoy the stupid birds chirping?"

Mara wanted to point out Kym was the one doing most of the talking, but she didn't. Mara understood what Kym's words didn't convey. No one liked funerals. No one wanted to talk about them. Call it a celebration of life. Call it a memorial. Call the event whatever was appropriate, but at the end of the day, losing a loved one sucked.

"Hold onto the back of my coat. Buddy and Tony will pull us both up the hill."

Tony snorted out a disgusted breath. "Maybe Buddy will help, but I'm no sled dog."

Mara laughed to herself while Kym snorted a similar response.

A few minutes later, they located the Gaccione family plot, where several headstones already marked graves. During her high school ditch days, the cemetery was the only place parents and teachers didn't think to look. Oddly, Mara always found the place comforting, a place to reflect and connect with complex emotions.

She squeezed Tony's arm to get his attention. "Do you see the buckets of roses?"

"Yep, but I'm not sure the Gaccione's ordered enough. We supplied three dozen white roses, but I bet there are more than forty people here. The memorial service was standing room only. You should be happy you had last minute orders to fill."

"You didn't miss anything," Kym interjected. "The service was nothing but a bunch of standing, sitting and kneeling, interspersed with praying and singing."

Mara cringed at Kym's description of a traditional Catholic ceremony. "I bet the memorial service was beautiful." She pictured Joey in a suit in the front pew with his parents. "Tony, don't forget I promised Mrs. Gaccione we'd relocate the flower arrangements to the hospice center tomorrow."

"Got it covered. However, I doubt she's thinking about flowers today."

"She better be thinking about losing weight," Kym chimed in. "Look at all those headstones. I don't think her fat butt is gonna fit."

"Kym!" Mara hissed, with a huff that was almost a laugh. Then she put her hand over her mouth to stop the giggles. The vibration in Tony's body told her he, too, had trouble not laughing out loud. "That wasn't nice."

"What? It's the truth."

"She has a point," Tony added. "Looking at the headstones, I bet the Gacciones are stacking the bodies. I wonder if they fight over who's buried next to whom?"

"Would you two stop?"

Kym snorted. "If it were me, I think I'd prefer to be cremated. I wouldn't want to deal with a mother who weighed as much as a cow lying on my chest for eternity."

"Oh. My. God. Would you just quit already? Show some respect."

"I'm showing my respect. I'm here, aren't I? It's better than I can say for Mr. Gaccione. He's MIA, again."

"Give the man a break. He just lost his son," Mara murmured, creating a reminder to spread blue flax, red fairy trumpets, and yellow lupine seeds over Sam's grave. For the last six years, she had distributed seed and planted columbines in a variety of colors closer to the headstones of those Elkridge lost. The residents often thanked her, commenting on how much the flowers brightened and beautified the area. She rubbed a mitten under her cold nose. "I'm sure he'll say his goodbyes in private."

"Maybe." Kym sounded doubtful. "I wonder if he'll be a little bit nicer now, and spend a bit more time with his grandkids."

"I don't know. Sometimes people can't or are unwilling to change. Mr. Gaccione has always seemed like a mountain to me. Unmovable. However, if Sam's death doesn't make him reflect, I doubt anything will."

Her accident sure caused her to reflect. All the little things she used to stew over no longer seemed all that relevant.

Father Sutton began the service, but she stood too far back and heard only bits and pieces. Her ability to hear the words didn't matter. Closure for the family—that's what counted.

97

Besides, Tony and Kym's constant fidgeting provided even more of a distraction. Thank goodness the service ended swiftly, because Mara could imagine that the dry humor building behind the dam wall was ready to burst from Kym and Tony's mouths. When the crowd started to disperse, she leaned in. "Tony, can you take me to the bridge and then wait in the car? I'd like to visit Mom, Dad and Sarah for a few minutes."

"Are you sure you don't want me to come with you? The path is pretty slippery." Tony sounded genuinely supportive, even though his tone conveyed he'd rather be a thousand miles from this place.

"No, I'm fine. Kym's shivering so much her teeth are about to rattle out of her head. Warm up the car, and I'll be there shortly."

"Give me the keys, and I'll get the defrosting process started," Kym said.

The jingle of keys and the crunch of rock alerted Mara to the fact that her friend had taken off quick-time toward the car's promised warmth. After several hundred steps, the terrain evened out and Mara felt the wood planks beneath her feet.

"You sure you don't want me to come with you?" Tony asked.

She wrapped an arm around his waist and gave him a squeeze. "I appreciate the offer, but I'm good." She stepped back and patted his chest. "Now go. Take care of my friend, please."

Her brother groaned. He'd never liked Kym. They had a Seinfeld sort of relationship, always finding faults in each other, but she loved them both, warts and all.

When Mara reached the blue spruce, she turned and headed up the hill, allowing Buddy to lead the way. After fifty feet or so, the dog stopped. She bent forward at the waist and reached until her hand touched the cold, engraved marble.

"There you are," she said, brushing a dusting of snow from

the top. "Just came to say hi. Nothing much has changed. Gina is due any day. Tony still hasn't gotten the nursery finished. And I'm still…"

Still what?

Blind? Lost? Figuring out how to adjust?

While she was trying to put into words her state of mind, Buddy shifted at the same moment a twig snapped behind her. She straightened and froze, listening for the clues, trying to figure out what made the sound.

"I didn't mean to startle you or intrude on your private moment with your family," the lower F-note baritone voice carried on the gentle, frosty breeze.

Joey.

"No worries. I just wanted to say hello to my family. Give everyone an update." She turned several degrees toward him. "I find it peaceful here, if a bit chilly."

"I thought I was going to overheat at the memorial service this morning. It went on and on and on."

An unexpected bubble of humor escaped as she remembered Kym's unglamorous description. "At least your family can start the healing process. Isn't there a celebration party tonight?"

"Yep. Ma's headed over there now."

"That's good. Celebrating will help later when the grief and memories take over."

The sound of shifting feet and crunching gravel made her aware Joey had become restless, and most likely didn't want to talk about his brother's passing. Like Tony, Joey hadn't actually seen the blood and broken bodies, the absence of life. Both men had only witnessed a person dressed in their best, silently resting. Then again, if one of the last things she saw hadn't been the bloodied bodies of her parents, maybe the image in her mind wouldn't be so vivid. So real. So permanent.

"Days like these are not easy. Is there anything I can do to help?" Mara asked.

"Not unless you can sniff out a killer. I thought for sure, with all my training, I'd be able to identify someone of interest. But I got nothing. Not a look of guilt, or something out of character. I was so sure the killer would be in the crowd."

"I know you want to get back to Seattle. Like you said, maybe you are trying too hard to get closure."

"Are you going to stop by the restaurant?" Joey asked. "My sisters assure me there's food enough for the whole county."

Mara shook her head as disappointment settled in her chest. "Tony needs to get home to Gina, and Kym has client appointments, so I must pass. I have some orders to prepare for delivery tomorrow."

"Maybe, I'll stop by later to say hi."

A nervous excitement shimmied up her arms and nestled into her chest. "That would be nice, but your family needs you today. You should probably see if you can find your dad. I'm sure your mom is worried."

"He's at Mad Jack's warming a bar stool and doing his best to empty a couple of whisky bottles. As far as I'm concerned, he can stay there. The family doesn't need to deal with his drunken anger today."

The raw ire oozing from his words didn't need interpretation. "I'll be around whenever you want to talk."

"Thanks. It's nice having someone I can talk to."

That banana cream pie contentment again filled her with bliss. "I like your company, too."

There was *that* hesitation again. She waited. "Is there something else you wanted to say?"

"I was wondering if you were done here. The temperature seems to have dropped several degrees in the past few minutes, and the path is getting a bit slick. I was hoping you might allow me to accompany you to the parking lot, but I don't want to rush you."

His heartfelt sentiment weakened her do-it-yourself willpower. She'd tried over and over and over again to convince herself she didn't need anyone—that the status quo fulfilled her desires.

Most days her willpower held strong as a brick wall. Some days it wobbled, but today the wall cracked straight down the middle and collapsed. The need to rely on others and her lack of complete independence stung. The reinforced realization poked at her vulnerabilities, triggering a feeling of instability she didn't like.

"I'm fine. I'll be down in a minute." *But she wasn't fine.*

He said nothing for the longest time, then his footsteps moved off into the distance.

"Mom, Dad, Sis, take care. You have my love."

A small voice came whistling through the evergreens as Mara reached for Buddy's halter.

I didn't hear you, she replied in her thoughts. *Say it again.*

Crisp wind prickled her cheeks. She waited. Then the advice came again, like a soft whisper floating on the air. *Allow yourself to trust.*

Trust. "Thanks for the suggestion, Dad, but that's a tough one. It's going to take time."

She often wondered whether the voices in her mind were from past conversations or if they truly were whispers from the other side. Either way, she recognized the advice. Her father had spoken to her often about having confidence in the choices she made, and trusting her gut. The image of sitting in his office, having one of many "intellectual discussions," as he called them, warmed her heart. Too bad the memory didn't also warm her almost-frozen fingers. "We better go, Buddy. People are waiting."

Halfway down the twenty-degree incline, she stopped. "I

know you're there. If you insist on making sure I don't slide down this hill, you might as well lend me a hand."

Footsteps ascended the path, and a hot breath caressed her cheeks.

"How about an arm?" Joey offered.

How about a kiss? She blushed. "An arm it is, then."

MARA LEANED CLOSER, possibly to soak up some of his warmth. Joey liked the closeness, and wondered what her actions and body language might mean.

All morning, Joey had surveyed the memorial and funeral service crowds and their body movements. He monitored for deception, perhaps a lack of eye contact, or nervous shifting, or an aggressive, wide-legged stance, any behavior to provide insight. In particular, he studied the mayor, the county officials, and the deputies, then prominent Elkridge citizens...anyone with something to lose. Not having a current baseline of facial expressions or body actions, he had to rely on his instincts.

He found nothing.

He hadn't been able to derive anything conclusive from his observations, which was disappointing. Actually, it was beyond disappointing.

He wanted closure.

For him.

For his family.

Interrogating people during a funeral didn't seem right. Besides, his mother could probably learn more in five minutes at the town's beauty shop than he could after spending the whole day talking to the residents.

So, he stood sentry behind his mother and sisters during

the service, feeling helpless and disoriented, like a failure, until he saw Mara. Somehow seeing her made his world stop spinning.

Joey took another step. She so easily fell into his rhythm.

"Did you learn anything new going through the investigation files?" She rotated her head in his direction.

Only that the files were full of spelling and grammatical errors, and were notably incomplete.

He studied her open, inquisitive face so full of hope. "Not really. The case documentation leads me to believe the deputies considered the case clear-cut."

"Oh?" Her tone sagged. "I'm not surprised. Some people desperately want to believe the shooting was an accident. A poacher. It's much harder to convince people there's no danger when there's been a murder just outside of town."

"Can you keep a secret?"

Her brows folded together. "Yes, better than most. When you lose one sense, people assume you're deaf, dumb, and blind. Townspeople don't share much with me, except for Kym, who does most of the talking. But because of my invisibility, I hear a lot of things I'm sure people wouldn't want me to know."

People were so very ignorant in their perceptions. "I want to keep this under wraps…"

"I understand."

"In one of the crime scene photos, I could see letters scraped into the ground. I enlarged the photos, and believe Sam tried to leave a message. There's a J, an I, and an F, followed by either a B or P, I'm not sure which."

She squeezed his arm, and he could practically feel her attention sharpen. "Interesting. If there were only three letters, I would think initials, but with the fourth letter, I'm not so sure. If I had to guess, I'm thinking he ran out of time before he could finish."

"Or his message was damaged. Another picture shows a

footprint butted against the letters. My guess is the first-responders didn't see the letters until after they removed the body and had already stepped on the evidence. I'm assuming the J is for Joey."

"It seems logical. I can't think of anyone in town with a name starting with 'I,' though."

Joey considered her grave face, and wanted to change the expression. "Nope. No Ian, Ida, or Ichabods running around."

She giggled at his feeble attempt at an English accent. He liked the way her mouth lifted into the slight curl at the corners.

"What if..." Her tone grew contemplative. "What if the 'I' isn't a letter, but a slash mark?" That would be J / FB to FP. However, I still don't know anyone with those initials."

Now why didn't I think of that? "You might be onto something."

He took in a long breath of chilly air, hoping to douse the burning frustration over the lack of professionalism that had destroyed this investigation.

The whole situation reminded him of Reba McEntire's song, "When the Lights Went Out in Georgia," only this time the case lacked a suspect, a judge, or even circumstantial evidence. Even a poacher couldn't be convicted on what the department had paper clipped together.

How ironic.

Her body suddenly tensed. "I feel pavement. Do you see our delivery van?"

He wished she'd been on the case. Her review would probably have been more thorough. "I do. Tony just waved. Would you like to ride back with me?"

"Buddy's not used to—"

"To riding in cars. You mentioned that the other day. But what happens if you have an emergency, and he's forced again to ride in a stranger's vehicle? You might want to test him, prepare him, to see how he reacts. We're not far from town."

She dropped her chin to chew on his idea. The longer she debated, the more hopeful he felt.

"You have a good point. We'll have to find a way to secure him. Riding in a car without a seatbelt makes me nervous."

"Understood. We'll figure out something."

"I'll let Tony know he and Kym don't have to wait." Mara released his arm. "Buddy. Forward. Van." She gave the command.

With her head up and shoulders back, there was a certain confidence in her stride. Joey wasn't convinced he'd be that sure of his step if their positions were reversed.

A swell of joy filled him, replacing the earlier feeling of defeat over the lack of vital clues, the inability to know who to trust, and his parents' high expectations. The tension had felt like a weight loaded bench press bar sitting on his chest.

Mara turned and pointed in his direction. The smile on her face made his heart jiggle with happiness. His obstacles were minor compared with hers. The woman continually showed him how to take one step forward with spirit and poise.

One step.

One fact.

That's all he needed, one small, critical fact to help solve his brother's murder. If he couldn't find one...solving Sam's murder might just take a lifetime.

CHAPTER NINE

Thursday morning, Mara enjoyed the warmth of the sun on her face and the bristly fur of the large German Shepherd rubbing his head against her leg.

"Gojo, you're going to make Buddy jealous," Mara said while rubbing the dog's stiff ears. "Thanks for bringing him to class, Dave. He's very sweet and will make an excellent service dog."

Dave moved closer, his tall frame suddenly blocking the sun's sensation. "The class was really full today. We didn't get much time to work together."

Thank goodness Dave wasn't a smoker. Not liking how the dog trainer invaded her space, she took a step back, putting Buddy and Gojo between them. "Gojo's almost ready for service assignment, aren't you, big boy?" She leaned in to give the dog an atta-boy rub.

"Expect so. I was wondering if you'd like to get a coffee, and talk about finding my next dog to train."

"That's nice of you to offer, but I really do need to get back to the flower shop. Karly's inside if you would like some help. She's more familiar with the dogs."

"Maybe next time." Dave's displeasure clearly outlined each word.

Not likely. "See you next month."

"I'll be here." Mara stepped back to allow Dave, the other trainers and dogs to pass. The sounds of handlers loading dogs into cars gave her a sense of satisfaction.

"Why didn't you go for coffee? Dave's a nice-looking guy." Karly, the owner of Helper Shelter, draped an arm around Mara's shoulders.

"In my case looks don't matter. Dave needs to relax a bit. He makes me nervous. A softer hand gains a dog's confidence more quickly and easily. I don't like trainers who use fear to intimidate or crush a dog's spirit." *If only Dave could learn from Joey. That man had a semi-truckload of patience, with plenty to spare.* "Guess what?"

"What?"

"Dave reminded me that next month two more service dogs will be ready to be placed. That means possibly two more fosters."

Karly's excitement made her friend wiggle with delight. "Who would've thought a year ago that we'd have a full training class schedule with a waiting list? I had two more calls this week of people asking to be put on your list. You sure you can't manage more classes? Or, better yet, take on a couple service dogs to train? It's good money. Trainers are telling me they are getting ten-thousand or more per dog."

Mara groaned, feeling the weight of an already overloaded plate. "Sorry. Once a month is as much as I can do. Tony's getting better about relieving me at the shop, but he would still rather just handle the deliveries and order the flowers. He panics a bit when someone orders an arrangement and I'm not there to help. And, that leaves no time to properly train dogs."

"I know. I just want you to be able to get out more. Not be so strapped to the store."

"Have you been talking to Kym? She said the same thing."

Like Kym, Karly had been her friend since grade school. In junior high, she'd decided she wanted to be a veterinarian, but grew up with an alcoholic mother and boomerang father. A boomerang because her mother kept tossing the drug user out of the house, and he just kept returning. Alcohol and drugs drained their bank account to the point where it couldn't cover food and rent, much less veterinary school tuition.

"You do good work here," Mara praised, squeezing her friend's waist, hoping Karly accepted the compliment this time.

Karly released a deep sigh. "Getting people to care about these abandoned animals isn't easy. However, some guy from Leadville approached me last week about hunting dog classes. I'd rather train these dogs as service or companion dogs, but working breeds need to run, so I might not have a choice. I'm determined to put every one of my dogs in a good enough home that they're never again in danger of being put down."

The number of euthanized animals in the US was what had fired Karly's zeal when she was in seventh grade. While researching a paper, she'd learned about the number of abandoned animals killed each year. Since then, Karly's sole mission in life had been figuring out ways to prevent animals from being killed for no other reason than that they didn't have a home. Her secondary goal? Finding animals a safe and healthy environment.

"I bet there's someone in town who'll teach the class so you don't have to," Mara suggested. "I don't know how you do it with all the kennels and foster families you have to coordinate."

"Don't forget the cat room. And if people don't stop dropping off their rabbits and rodents, I'm going to have to find a room for them as well. Did I tell you someone dropped off chickens last week? What am I supposed to do with chickens?"

A snicker and the familiar spicy sent of Old Spice cologne made Mara turn. A glittery happiness cascaded through her body, and she couldn't help but smile. "And just what is so funny about chickens, Detective?"

"Boy, you're good." The amazement in Joey's voice gave Mara a bit of a thrill. "You've got to teach me that sensory identification thing. Maybe I'll talk you into coming to Seattle to teach a class."

A groan started in her belly and worked its way up. "No. Absolutely not. Can you imagine me, luggage, Buddy and his kennel? Just thinking about traveling gives me the heebie-jeebies. How did you find me, anyway?"

"I stopped by the store. Kym said I'd find you here volunteering."

You came to find me. Well, crap. How am I supposed to protect my heart?

Like Dave, she'd tell him she was needed at the store, but his awkwardness made her second-guess and drew her curiosity. "Joey, do you remember Karly from school. She's Kevin's sister."

"Kevin Kane and the KK family. I remember," he said with a flicker in his voice, like a light bulb just turning on in the room. "There're a couple more brothers thrown in there somewhere."

One of the smaller dogs barked in the kennel, triggering a cascading chorus of barks in various pitches. "That would be us. It's feeding time. I'd better get started," Karly said. "Nice seeing you again, Joey."

"Karly," Joey responded, almost dismissively.

Karly squeezed her arm, and Mara turned. "I'll be in to help in a minute."

Why the squeeze? Mara pondered.

Since she'd gone blind, people had been giving her signals all the time—both verbal and physical. Without the benefit of body language, interpreting the ambiguous clues became impossible, forcing her to ignore what might have been important information.

She rotated toward Joey. "What's up? I can't imagine you want to adopt an animal."

"I was hoping to get your help."

"My help?" She couldn't imagine what assistance she could provide a gutsy, able-bodied man.

"I don't trust what I'm seeing in the investigation files. I need to recreate Sam's murder scene and need your visualization skills if you're up to it. The deputies did such a crappy job collecting the evidence, I decided it might be easier if we start from scratch."

"I still don't get how I can help."

"I'm not sure either, but my instincts tell me if we work together, we can shake something loose."

Under Joey's layer of positive certainty, she heard a stitch of desperation. He wanted answers. Since he'd asked, she couldn't refuse. "If we're going up Sleeping Bear Trail, I think we should take Gus."

"Gus? Do I know Gus?"

The slightly higher tone of voice made her wonder if he might be jealous. She sure hoped so. Her pride could use a bit of bolstering.

"I'll be back in a minute." She turned back. "Better yet, why don't you come with me?"

Mara reached for Buddy's lead, followed him inside, through a second door, down a long line of barking dogs and then stopped in front of the last kennel. The clean smell of Borax meant Karly's morning had been busy. Mara squatted and reached her fingers through the wire cage.

A sandpapery tongue licked her fingertips. "There you are. I have someone I'd like you to meet. Gus, meet Joey. Joey, Gus."

"Hey, there." Joey sounded amused. "Did you win the prize for ugly? Because you're one gnarly looking mutt."

"Awww. Don't hurt Gus's feelings. I bet you'll see him in a whole new light by the end of the day."

"I doubt it, but I'll keep an open mind."

Grabbing the Beagle-mix's halter and leash from a peg beside the door, she opened the gate and released Buddy's lead. The high-pitched, happy whine of Gus's greeting lifted her spirits, but added a tinge of sadness. "I wish I could take you home, little guy. Gus, sit." The wiggling mutt brushed his head against her leg, doing his best to be still so she could attach his halter and leash. "You smell like vanilla. You've had a bath. What a good boy."

She turned to the man waiting patiently for her. "Do you think we all can fit in your rental, or do we need to get the flower van?"

"If I put the back seats down, I think we should be good. It's only a short drive. Buddy seemed uncomfortable during the last ride, so I overnighted some equipment the Seattle K-9 unit uses to secure their dogs. I just picked it up from the house."

"That's really nice of you." A buzzing sensation made her lightheaded. There was a reason she wanted to kiss this man.

"What's nice?" Karly's footsteps grew louder, along with the rattling of a bucket. The dogs' enthusiasm meant dinner had arrived.

"Joey purchased equipment so Buddy can ride in a car safely. We're going up to Sleeping Bear Trail. Joey wants some help reconstructing Sam's crime scene. I'd like to take Gus if you don't mind."

"Absolutely. I don't know why those idiots over at the sheriff's department didn't come and get him in the first place. He could have also helped with the missing boy they found too late." The hollow sound of buckets hitting the floor spoke of irritation. "Joey, Gus may not look like much since he got caught in a fire, but he's a good scent hound."

"Can he find a shell casing or maybe a cigarette butt?"

Mara inhaled. Cigarettes and alcohol.

"Maybe," Karly said. "If you point him in the right direction.

A couple of days ago, I took him on a training run, and he had no trouble finding the objects I'd hidden. You should take his pack jacket. The flannel and canvas will help keep him warm."

"That I think I can do." For the first time since he arrived, Joey's voice sounded confident and less stifled.

"Oh, I forgot." Embarrassed heat burned Mara's ears. "I promised to help feed the dogs." *Sheesh. A friendly guy comes along and, whoosh, out go my obligations.*

"I got it," Karly said. "If you, Gus and Joey can help this town heal from such a senseless and cowardly act you should go. Take one of the extra kennels off the shelf in the storage room."

Mara moved toward her friend's voice, arms outstretched. Arms encircled her shoulders and pulled her in. "You're awesome."

A puff of air warmed her ear. "Have fun." Karly squeezed her a bit tighter before letting her go. "And don't worry about the store. Let your brother take some responsibility for once."

Oh, crap, the store. Well, maybe inventory can wait one more day. "Tony takes responsibility, just in his own way." The defensiveness skipped out of her mouth before she could trip it. Poor Tony. She wished people could see how much he'd changed in the past few years. "I should call him."

"Don't you dare," Karly grunted with a scolding undertone. "He's not expecting you for another couple of hours. Go. Help Joey with his investigation."

Buddy nudged her hand, telling her he wanted to play with his friend. She appreciated her little fuzzy toddler, who'd never grow up, was full of go-go-go, and always wanted to play. As a trainer, she shouldn't let him. He would tire easily and crash too soon, but who was she to prevent her full-time companion from having a bit of fun?

"Joey, would you like some help getting the dogs settled?" She followed the excited noise out to the parking lot.

"We're good. I appreciate your willingness to help." At least Joey hadn't lost all hope. "I need to find answers before I leave."

That's right. He needed to get back home.

"Then, let's get started."

"Mara, I..."

"It's okay. I understand. You don't want to go up to the ridge alone."

"I'm not sure you know how much I appreciate your help."

For some reason, his easy baritone made her think about a rush of water over river rock. The jingle of aspen leaves moving back and forth like gold coins in the sun. The fantasy suffused her with a peaceful contentment and filled a void, a deprivation she hadn't known existed.

She let a slow smile form. "That's what friends are for, besides it's nice to feel useful."

He closed the SUV hatch and jiggled it to make sure the door closed safely with Gus's kennel tucked in the back. "Then let's go and get this over with. I feel a craving for sweets coming on. Possibly a nice big slice of banana cream pie."

Maybe she should have just climbed up his body and given him a smack of sweetness now. A slow-glowing happiness spread through her chest.

"What were you thinking about just then?" Joey took a step closer.

"Deciding what type of pie I want." *And kissing you.*

CHAPTER TEN

Joey drove through Elkridge and up the winding valley road toward Sleeping Bear Trail. Tall pines and dormant aspens framed the road as the elevation increased. The wind whistled through the canyon, and sunbeams made the remaining snow from the last storm sparkle.

Reaching the abandoned logging road turnoff, Joey slowed and made a right onto the dirt road, stopping a few yards from the locked gate.

He shoved the car in park and cut the engine. His fingers tapped on the steering wheel to a silent tune while he debated the best approach to gathering more data. "We'll have to walk from here," he told Mara. "It's just a quarter of a mile up the hill. The road is a bit muddy in spots. Maybe this wasn't such a good idea."

"I've got my hiking boots on, and I'm warm. That's all I need." Mara zipped her jacket and wound a wool scarf around her head. "Let's go."

The mountain air, brisk against Joey's face, reminded him how much Seattle's more temperate weather differed. He pulled his wool cap low over his ears. "You sure you'll be warm enough?"

"Once we get moving, I'll warm up. What's the plan?"

He grabbed his computer tablet. "Don't tell anyone, but I downloaded the crime scene photos. Using the pictures, I want to walk through the scene to get a better understanding of event timing. Your job is to question the data and find alternative explanations. I want to poke at every piece of evidence until we have a clear picture of what might have happened."

Dozens of crime scene photos, organized in a grid, filled the computer screen. A visual, yes, but not a complete picture. The creepy-crawly sense prickling the back of his neck meant critical details were missing, specific details required in order to uncover what really happened to his brother.

"Do you think Gus will allow me to put on his coat and halter?" Joey asked with a heightened level of skepticism.

"Let's find out."

Joey pocketed the car keys and took a deep breath. For the next several minutes, he moved slowly, opening the kennel door, putting on and adjusting Gus's packs.

"You're okay, Gus. I'm not going to hurt you." The way the dog watched him with his ears down, tail tucked, gave the impression the animal was waiting for a swift kick to the ribs. Joey wanted to throttle the man who instilled this fear. Some man had abused this dog, he had no doubt, because Gus wasn't afraid of Mara or Karly. Just him.

"That's a good boy. Almost done. Just one more strap. I want to make sure your pack doesn't rub over your burn scars."

Mara leaned in and rested her hand on Gus's head. "You might be interested to know Sam arrested the dog's owner and charged him with animal cruelty. He got three months in jail and a seven thousand-dollar fine for setting Gus on fire."

Fire. Shit. His hand rested on Gus's pack and then slowly

pulled into an angry fist. "Karly said he was in a fire, not that he was the one on fire."

"She's worried if she tells people the true story, Gus won't find a good home. I believe you've already guessed he has some trust issues."

Joey slowly turned Gus around to look into the dog's eyes. Intelligence. Determination. Stubbornness. Just like the woman standing beside him. "I've got a feeling Gus is going to find a good home. Aren't you, boy? Are you ready to go?"

"Ready." Mara's courageous tone and the excitement of the dogs settled his nerves.

Past ready. More than anything, for his family, for the citizens of Elkridge, he wanted the coward who did this locked up.

"There's a gate ahead. I'll go first." He approached a metal structure. "Watch your head." He placed a hand on Mara's head, helping her visualize how far she needed to duck to avoid bonking her forehead. "The dirt road curves around to the right. After that, we should be able to see the crime scene."

After checking his phone for the time, he listened to the sounds in the woods. Birds aware of their presence flew from branch to branch, watching and waiting. He led Mara farther up the road and around the bend, anxiety made his breathing shallow.

"Let's let the dogs run. They won't go far." Mara released Buddy's collar and Joey let go of Gus's. Immediately Gus put his nose to the ground and began making a looping pattern, racing twenty yards ahead and then running back only to repeat the process.

Mara squeezed his arm. "Tell me what you're seeing."

He honed his senses into the emotionless zone and scanned the road, looking at the tree line for a moment, searching for something with a shine, anything to alert him to another presence. Rounding the bend, he saw it. The site. His blood slowed, making his fingers numb. He gripped his computer tighter and forced his body to keep a steady pace with Mara.

"The place Sam fell is just ahead. On the right, there's a twenty-degree slope with a mixture of evergreens, broad leaf trees and bushes. The vegetation is thick. Very little could get through. On the left, there's a fifteen-foot dirt clearing, before the tree line starts."

There's trees. Lots of them. And a wide road. No way was this an accident. Poacher, my ass, his dad's emotionally charged comments echoed in his head.

"The road is straight for about four hundred yards, then curves back toward the left." He checked his watch: 14:07. He noted the angle of the sun, the slope of the hill, the curve of the road, and calculated how the angle of the sun would change the scenery. Then he saw the distinct stain on the side of the road.

His brother's blood had turned black with age.

"We're almost there," he choked out to keep his bubbling fury from impacting Mara.

"Okay. I've got the general layout. Let's start with the *why*? What made your brother stop? Why here? Why not at the gate? Why not farther up the road? What could have caught his eye and made him stop?"

He crouched several feet away from the scene, imaging the events unfolding. "Good question." He communicated the placement of every critical element—the car, body, road, sun, trees—allowing Mara to place each item on her mental grid. "I wonder if he saw something up ahead."

A movie of possible events began to play in his head, fast-forwarding and rewinding as necessary to define possibilities. Alternatives.

"Based on crime scene pictures, it appears Sam had pulled to the left-hand side, his SUV pointing up the road. To your point, why didn't he drive another couple hundred yards?

From what I can see, the road opens up in about a quarter of a mile. Why did he stop here? Why not farther up the road?"

Joey studied the photograph showing the position of the patrol car. "Sam's door was left open." He moved to the left to align his sight with the body and visually traced a straight line to the ridge on the right about three hundred yards. "Sam was shot in the upper left side of the chest. The only place where someone with a rifle could miss an open car door and hit a human chest is just about fifty yards up that hill in front of us."

"If that's the case, the shooter would have had a clear view of who he was shooting. From what you told me, there are no trees blocking the view."

"Exactly." *Sam was murdered. There's the proof.*

He scanned through document images and research notes. "The day had been exceptionally warm for February—records indicated sixty-eight degrees. The heat could have been the reason Sam wasn't wearing his protective vest."

"Assuming he wore one. At the café, I overhear deputies complaining all the time about the weight and how those vests restrict movement."

Frustration burned in his throat. "True, but standard-issue equipment should be worn at all times. Period. No excuses." The policy had been drilled into him since the first day on the job. But Sam never did like rules. "Studying the pictures, my guess, based on the blood spatter and the caliber of weapon, is that the bullet hit hard enough to drop him to the ground. Once down, he tried to radio for help, but couldn't, sending only a silent signal to alert the department." Joey studied the contours of the landscape. "I wish I had those lab reports. There's a notation here that Sam had bruising along the ribs, but without the full report, I don't know whether the bruising was recent or from a prior accident."

"Joey. You mentioned you and Sam were a lot alike in some

ways. We already know Sam was trying to leave a clue, but what else might he do?"

Awareness buzzed through his mind—the Jekyll and Hyde effect of not wanting to think about Sam's death, yet being driven to find answers.

Fractions of ideas pieced together. "If it were me, I'd try leaving as many clues as possible. Something. Anything to provide information for my team." He scrolled through the pictures on the computer screen reviewing the position of his brother's body, then squinted closer.

His hand. I see it. "Mara, you're a genius. Sam's hand is gripping something, and he's pointing a finger."

Before his mind engaged, he grabbed Mara and gave her a sound kiss on the lips. In that single beat of his heart, he instantly regretted the spontaneous act. He'd been thinking about kissing her for a lifetime, and the kiss he'd just given her seemed an eternity away from his fantasy. In his dreams, the connection was tender and satisfying.

He stopped and cupped her jaw. "I'm sorry. That was inappropriate, especially here, in this place. I wasn't thinking, but I have to tell you, I've been waiting a long time to kiss you." He took a step back. "It's just this place. Sam. Wanting to spend time with you. It's a lot to deal with all at once."

"I'm sure coming back, dealing with your dad, and your own grief, it must be hard."

"It seems so surreal. Sam's gone. He's really gone."

Mara touched his chest, then slid her arm up to touch his face. "If I could take your pain away, I would."

"You can't." The sting behind his eyes intensified.

"I know."

He leaned in to capture her lips. The sweet kiss felt comfortable, like a soft summer breeze, even though the temperature hovered around freezing. When he lifted his head, he interpreted her facial expressions, and damn if he didn't see disappointment.

"Mara?"

"I'm not breakable," she whispered, then tugged him closer. "Kiss me like you mean it. Let me help ease your pain."

God, he needed this. Needed her. He dove in to ease the hurt. The edgy, hard and wet kiss inspired him to push a bit further. Her whimper filled his mouth. Caution made him want to draw back, but she sank her fingers into his hair, gripping and pulling, urging him for more. He gripped her hips hard and pulled her close, wanting to feel her press against his chest.

Finally. His brain cells stopped functioning. They gave no thought to where they were. No thought to his brother's case. No thought to him leaving. Only the woman and the man existed.

The dogs playing nearby eventually engaged his subconscious. Reluctantly, he began pulling away, her lips clinging to his for a moment longer before she released him. Desperately he worked to get his knees to lock so he wouldn't fall on his ass.

"That sucks," she breathed with a bit of a frazzled attitude.

"Excuse me?" He dropped his hands.

Her hands slowly slid down his chest. "All these years, I've wondered what it would be like to be kissed to the point I'd forget the outside world exists. Finally, you kiss me in a way I've only imagined, and it's in the middle of a crime scene. Not under mistletoe, or on New Year's Eve. Sometimes the timing in my life sucks."

She was pissed. And that was just fine, because he'd been pissed for a good long time. First about her brother warning him off, then about finding out she wasn't married after all this time. Feeling something other than hollow about the subject of Mara felt good. Actually, it felt terrific.

"Buddy, come," she called, then released a sound somewhere between irritated, euphoric, and enlightened or all at the same time. "We better stay focused. Now that we know for sure Sam was murdered, we need to find something to help the deputies find the killer."

Well, hell. She had a point. "You're right, but if there is one thing I've learned this trip it's that life is too short to ignore opportunities. I could be shot tomorrow, and if that's the case, I'm sure as hell not going to wait to get another kiss."

He took two steps and pulled her into his arms again, this time taking his time. He pressed deep, replacing his air with her fragrance. Her body tipped back and her knees unlocked, but he held her safe, just like he'd held her in his heart all these years. She tasted so damn good, he wanted to absorb her body into his. He kissed his way to her earlobe and nibbled, then licked the soft spot under her ear. She groaned and cocked her head to the side to give him access. The curve of her throat and the heat of her body made him press closer, tasting the salt of her skin. Wanting more.

When Buddy gently stepped on her foot, whimpered, then sat waiting, Joey finally called a halt to the glorious comfort he so desperately needed. Her head dropped forward, nuzzling into the crook of his neck, breathing deeply. His arms were locked, frozen, not wanting to let her go. The ache became excruciating.

He rested his chin on the top of her head.

She became so silent, he refocused. "Mara?"

"Hmmm?" A saturated sigh of contentment floated up to him.

"Did that suck?"

"No," Mara pushed the hair from her face, "I have to admit that didn't suck. In fact, it was pretty awesome. Do you feel any better?"

"I do. Thanks."

"We'd better get back to finding clues before whatever this is between us gets out of hand. You're leaving soon, and I'm sure you want to have some answers before you go home."

"Maybe, you can find some leftover mistletoe another time and we can practice."

She adjusted the scarf around her neck, tucking in the ends to block the chilling wind. Not the response he'd hoped for, but he'd take the flustered emotions rather than her turning and walking away. At least she didn't close the door completely, but maybe she should have. Pushing him away might have been easier. She wouldn't leave Elkridge, and his job was in Seattle. So, what did that leave them?

Nothing. That's what.

Working to find a distraction, and get his push-pull emotions under control, he retrieved his computer and expanded the photo images, again noting the direction of Sam's pointed finger.

The bloodstained patch of ground formed a permanent image. His lungs again burned with a wild rage while his eyes scanned every rock, muddy surface, blade of grass. He studied the natural patterns in the earth...and then there it was. An unnatural configuration.

"I think I found something." He stepped carefully around the edge of the evidence to place his body in the same direction as his brother, and leaned in.

Weather elements had deteriorated the markings. "There's another mark."

Why had these details been missed?

Mara came closer. "What do you think it is?"

"It's a bit washed out, but I think it could be an arrow pointing at the ridge behind us. It's the same ridge, based on the angle, where the shot was fired."

Frustration pulsed through his arteries. He'd looked through the documentation. Nothing in the investigation report indicated that in the last few seconds of his brother's life, he'd tried to leave clues. How could the investigative team have missed it? Or did they?

He retrieved his phone to take a video and some additional pictures. He glanced at the ridge in front of him, then at his watch.

"Tell me about the ridge." Mara encouraged. "Is there anything about it that looks off? Dead or a lack of trees? An odd color? Movement? Anything?"

"Not that I can see from here."

"I'm still thinking the J stands for Joey. If your brother used the last of his strength to tell you something, you need to follow the clues. You should take Gus to search for clues while it's still daylight."

"Good idea." He gave a shrill whistle to get the dog's attention. Buddy turned, but Gus continued to wander. "That's just great."

"What's wrong?"

"Gus. He's wandered off."

"Let me try." She lowered into a squatting position. "Buddy? Bring Gus. Go on. Bring Gus. Bring your friend."

Buddy circled wide through the trees. At first, Joey thought Buddy had ignored Mara, until he appeared just above Gus on the hill and started herding Gus back toward their position. Twice, Buddy had to circle around Gus, but eventually, the Beagle mix got the idea.

"Unbelievable," Joey released under his breath.

"I taught Buddy to find things for me. If I name something, he usually can bring the item to me. I wasn't sure he could figure out how to bring me a live object, so it was a good test."

"You're good at arranging flowers, but seriously, you should think about training dogs, and I'm not talking about a once-a-month class."

"Don't you start. I'm getting enough pressure from Karly. If she had it her way, I'd work at the kennel full-time."

Upon hearing Buddy's panting return, she stood and reached a hand toward Gus. "Good boys. Joey has a game for you to play."

Gus tilted his head at Mara working hard to translate what she was saying. Joey pulled from his pocket a pack of cigarettes and a shell casing, and held them out for Gus to sniff. The dog ignored him, and walked around Mara to hide behind her, while Buddy watched.

"This isn't going to work."

"What happened?"

"I can't get either Buddy or Gus to engage. Maybe, you should try."

Mara held out her hand to accept the items, then reached down to wrap her arm around Gus's torso. "Yes, you're a good boy." The Beagle-mix gave her a lick from chin to nose and made her sputter for a second, before he settled to take an interest in what she wanted to show him. He shoved his nose into the items and then pulled back with a heavy sneeze.

"I agree. Ucky stuff. But you need to take a good sniff. Good boy. Now, find." She released the dog and pointed.

Gus cocked his head to the side, ears lifted. "Find," Mara repeated. She showed Gus the items in her hand again. Seconds later, Gus took off, nose to the ground. "Am I aiming in the correct direction?"

"Close." Joey moved her arm ten degrees to the right. "That's closer."

She pulled her arm in and then thrust it forward as she stood and took a step in the same direction. "Go. Find," she commanded again.

"Is it working?"

Hell, yeah it's working. Note to self. Never underestimate the woman. "Buddy and Gus are making their way up the hill. Are you still warm enough?"

"I'm warm, but without Buddy, I'm not sure...I..."

"We can do this together. You've got this. Just tell me what you need."

Mara reached out a hand. He gently grabbed her fingers and brought them to his lips for a little nibble.

She squeaked out a surprise before he placed her hand on his arm. "Thank you for coming with me."

"That's what friends are for."

Reluctantly he turned to monitor Gus for any peculiar behavior, but so far, observed nothing. Mara moved along beside him, but when she tripped, he placed an arm around her back. "I've got you."

"I know."

The soft, muttered words spoken with conviction, giving his pride a pump of satisfaction.

The complete trust on her face created a bold confidence, one he often emulated on the job, but rarely ever felt when with a woman.

"There is a felled tree just ahead." He tightened his arm around her waist. "Ready? Leg up and over. That's it." She waited for him to do the same before continuing on.

"I forgot to tell you the rest of what I found this morning. I went for a long run to refresh my memory of the area. It seems there's been a lot of activity on Sleeping Bear Trail, especially for an old logging road that hasn't been used for some time. According to county records, there are seven isolated hunting lodges that have been vandalized during the off-season. The odd thing is all the thefts are within an eight-mile radius of Sam's house. The gas generators were emptied, the firewood used, large truck and small utility tire tracks were found. All the tracks heading into the woods."

"The firewood was used? That's odd. That would be weeks' worth of burning."

Well at least someone around here has a brain.

"I thought so too. I checked the locks. All expertly picked. There were efforts made to cover some of the tracks. The lack of animal droppings in the area told me there were humans present. If my dad identified all these issues, why didn't the sheriff's department?"

"Well, Ernie was sorta dim in high school, but I get a feeling that's not what you're talking about. My guess is you think someone's covering up evidence."

"You'd be right."

Mara tightened her fingers around his arm, just as Gus barked three times and started to whine. "It looks like our boy has found something. I just hope it's not a pile of bear poop."

"Or worse…a skunk."

"Or a skunk."

The way she eased his burden made him want to brace Mara against a tree and kiss her until all his obligations and anger over his brother's senseless death disappeared. But guilt made him check that urge. He shouldn't be going there. He was leaving. The last person he wanted to hurt was the beautiful and brave woman beside him. She'd had enough challenges in her life and he wouldn't complicate matters.

Halfway up the hill, he spotted Gus sitting and waiting. Joey scanned the area and approached slowly.

"Karly said you were good, but I had my doubts."

"Did he find something?"

He picked up a stick and lifted an empty shell casing Gus had his eye on. "Yes, he did. No cigarettes, but there's a marijuana roach and some footprints."

"Good boy, Gus." Intelligent eyes stared back at him. "I should get the shell casings and marijuana roach to the lab…" His gut twisted. *And have the evidence disappear? I think not.* "On second thought, I'd better hold onto this stuff for awhile." Pulling gloves and plastic bags from his pocket from an occupational habit, he collected the evidence.

Gus's ears perked and he focused at the tree line on the ridge. The feeling of being watched sent chills up Joey's arms. He stood. "Mara, you look like you're getting cold."

"I'm all right."

He shoved the evidence bag inside his coat pocket. "Just the same, I believe we found what we were looking for, let's get back to the car and get warm."

Escorting Mara down the hill, he moved a bit quicker, a disquieting feeling pushing him to move faster. When he reached the road, his phone buzzed and he groaned. *Not my boss.* The local number provided relief.

"Gaccione."

"Hey, it's Tony. Hope you don't mind. I got your number from Pia. Is Mara with you?"

"Yeah, she's here."

"Would you let her know I have a flower delivery for Lizzy Cranston, but Gina will be at the store, so she doesn't have to rush back. Or she can take the day off, if she wants."

"I'll let her know. Wait, isn't Cranston the old biddy that used to drive by the High School and give us all the finger?"

"The same. Karly said you and Mara are going over the evidence."

Joey cringed. He'd have to be more careful with his actions, especially where Mara was concerned. He ignored the comment. "I'm not sure flowers will improve that woman's temperament. Maybe a ton and a half of chocolate. Then again, cocoa might just make her more bitter." Joey laughed at his own pun, then a spark of an idea grew as Mara attached the leash to Gus's collar and called to Buddy. They continued walking side by side down the mountain road.

"Hey, Tony, you must get around town a lot."

"By getting around, I hope you mean in the flower-delivery-route sort of way."

Interesting. "Yes. I'm talking store delivery routes. Has anyone from the sheriff's office asked you if you've seen anything out of place lately? Out of state license plates? Out-of-towners at Mad Jack's? That sort of thing?"

"No, nothing, unless…"

Tony's "unless" had a mighty big anchor tied to the end. "What are you thinking?" Joey asked, waiting for the other shoe to drop.

"Gina did say something strange last night at dinner. The girls at the salon were bitching about the lack of supplies at the grocery store—you know those things gals need every month. And this morning at the café, Harold was complaining he couldn't keep enough on the shelf. Supposedly, some guy came in and bought an armful. I don't know any guy in this town who'd be caught dead buying that stuff, much less an armful. Now condoms, that might be a different story. Then Gina told me her prenatal vitamins were on back order. There can't be enough pregnant women in this town to force a prenatal vitamin outage."

A sex trafficking profile flipped through his head. He doubted Elkridge had anything to do with trafficking routes. Or did it? The FBI dealt with sex crimes.

FB as in FBI? Was that what Sam was trying to tell him? To call the FBI?

Uneasiness made him swallow the bitter taste circling in his mouth, giving him heartburn. "I'd appreciate if you kept me informed of any oddities around town."

"Okay. Maybe TMI, and probably not what you were looking for."

"Any information is good. You never know what missing piece of information will blow open a case."

"So are you going to stick around awhile?"

"Only a few more days. Why?"

"No reason."

Yet, a guy hardly ever asked a question without a reason, and he assumed the woman walking quietly beside him was the explanation.

"Tony, you have nothing to worry about. Promise."

"I told Mara you were a good man." Tony's tone softened. "I should have kept my big mouth shut in high school. I thought you just wanted to give her a bounce. Us football players can be a little slow."

"You said it. I didn't. For the record, you were wrong."

"Are you not interested anymore because she's blind?"

He stopped and covered the phone's mic. "Mara? It seems Buddy's got a good nose on the car. Go on ahead. I'll catch up."

"Take your time. Buddy, forward." She waved as Buddy and the trio made their way down the dirt road.

He turned to make sure his voice wouldn't carry. "Keep talking and you're aiming to get cracked in the mouth the next time I see you. You should know me a bit better than that. There is no way I can get out of going back to Seattle. I have obligations back home, and I'm not about to start something I can't finish."

"What's in Seattle that's not here?"

Nothing. But you need to mind your own business. "I'm part of a team. The force is like its own little community, and the guys in my unit have become like family. Plus, Seattle's got more than two dozen restaurants, and theaters by the dozens."

"Hey, Mad Jack's put in pool tables, and bands play there now. You can come back and be part of this community."

The Seattle neighborhood where he lived was within walking distance of nightlife and beaches—however nice, none of them stacked high enough to block out Mara. She still smelled like a mountain valley in springtime and made him dream of the future in a way he hadn't considered possible.

"If you're interested," Tony interrupted his swirling speculation, "Mara's singing at Mad Jack's on Saturday. Maybe we can have that beer we talked about. And, for what it's worth, I'm sorry. You and Mara would have made a good match."

What is this, apology day? "Life doesn't always work out as planned, and sometimes there's just no going back." *But there's always the future.* And, Joey was desperately trying to figure out how Mara and Elkridge fit into those plans.

"I respect that. Don't forget about Saturday."

He'd already decided to stop by. "Would you like me to have Mara give you a call?"

"No. We're good. See you, Saturday."

"I'll be there."

What-ifs buzzed around in his head. What if more was going on in Elkridge than anybody knew? What if his family and Mara were truly in danger? What if….

All questions.

He needed to stop with the questions and get some answers.

Fifty feet from the car, he caught up with Mara. A warm comfort descended through his neck, into his chest and settled in his core. When he got within a few feet of the SUV, her easy expression allowed him to release the tension spring wound too tight. With her, he didn't have to fight against the counter-clockwise motion. He could just follow the circle of time and let life tick naturally onward and watch for opportunities, because he was starting to think Elkridge might be a future possibility.

"Hey," she said with a pleasant, yet anxious, smile. "Was that your boss?"

"It was Tony. He said he had a delivery to make and that Gina was covering the store."

"Is that all he said…I mean, he wasn't mad, or anything?"

"He didn't sound mad." *Only protective.* "He said not to rush back, and take the day off if you want."

Several emotions flashed across her face simultaneously to the point he had no idea what she might be feeling. He opened the back hatch of his SUV and gently loaded Gus into his kennel and secured Buddy. "Since you don't have to work today, what about we take Gus back to the shelter, then I make you dinner? How does steak and potatoes sound?"

"What, no pasta?"

That smile of hers gets me every time.

He shouldn't find her sexy, bundled to her chin in her navy blue coat, her eyes peeking out from behind her scarf, mittened hands dangling at her sides, and clearly mocking his mother's cooking, but damn if he didn't think she was sexy as hell anyway. The smile creasing the corners of her eyes made him want to pull her into his arms again for a nibble and savor. She'd been twisting him into knots since he was a teen. "No pasta. I can't afford any more of my mother's cooking. As it is, I'll need to double my workout schedule."

"Oh. Bummer. I guess that means no dessert, either. Jenna from over at the café brought me some Bramley apples. They feel like gnarly round balls, and are best for cooking. I was hoping to have baked apples for dessert."

"I was thinking of something else sweet for dessert."

She lifted her chin, and her whole face lit like a neon sign that said, *proceed straight ahead*, and he wasn't about to slow down.

Not this time. And he angled in for a kiss.

CHAPTER ELEVEN

"I'm stuffed." Joey's tone held a satisfied warmth which resembled her mood.

Across the small table in the center of Sam's small, yet uncluttered kitchen, Mara set her spoon down next to the bowl with remains of her half of the baked apple. The smell of butter and cinnamon and vanilla ice cream still tempted her to take another bite. Or maybe, she could convince Joey to take another spoonful so she could get a no-calorie taste.

The memory of his kiss made her lips tingle.

"Steak, asparagus, potatoes, and on top of all that, dessert. I don't think I've eaten that much, ever. Where did you learn to cook?"

A snort of laughter filled the room. "Would you believe television? When I joined the force, I had to work the swing shift. Most of the time I got off work at three, sometimes four in the morning. I could never sleep when I got home, so I'd watch this cooking show. There isn't much on T.V. at that time of day."

"No, I don't suppose there would be."

"One chef liked to keep recipes simple. Three or four ingredients tops. He made it look easy, so I tried a few things. Don't get me wrong, I'm no Wolfgang Puck or anything."

Gotta love a man that cooks. "You're better than most." *Not that I've had any experience.* "Let me clean up since you did most of the work." Mara stood faster than she should have and grabbed the edge of the table, the mostly empty glass of red wine doing funny things to her sense of balance. The buzz of alcohol made her feel relaxed—possibly too relaxed.

The harsh scrape of a chair across the hardwood floor meant the brewing of an argument.

"I figured we could clean up together," Joey suggested. "Why don't I stack the dishes on the left? Dishwashing liquid is next to the faucet. You wash. I'll dry and put away. Sound good?"

No arguments. I so want to kiss this man. Together? No push or pull. Working with Joey made her think of a greeting card—she: the pretty, colored card; he: the protective envelope—complementing each other perfectly. The all-too-domestic image created a problem—a huge problem.

He was leaving. If only she could get him to see that Elkridge needed his expertise. Needed him.

"Sounds good." She focused on determining which double-bowl sink had the locking drain, then poured the liquid soap in her hand to get the right amount and to give the water time enough to heat. She reached for the first plate as the smell of the lemon and the feel of bubbles tickled her senses.

"I'm dropping the silverware in the water to soak."

The heat from Joey standing next to her rattled her nerves. How could the ordinary sound of metal clinking against metal, stir up more than just an ordinary affection for the man?

He fit too easily.

Was that the problem?

Since their heart-pumping kiss that afternoon, her body had been stuck in overdrive. Every nerve ending had flickered and come online, sending pulsating messages from node to node, reminding her that her sex drive had backed out of the storage shed and was ready to be driven. Hard.

The blame for her heightened sexual appetite was definitely hers. She'd pushed him, knowing he would respond. The moment the words, *that sucks* slipped out, she was a total goner.

Holy crap, the man could kiss.

He hadn't lingered in any one place, but instead covered the entire landscape of her skin, stimulating every centimeter, making her want to drive closer to the edge of a dangerous cliff just to experience the exhilaration of feeling sexy. Now, hours later, she still felt sexy, an odd experience after having felt simply blind for so long.

With a long exhale, she released the dish into his waiting hands.

"What are you thinking?" he asked.

Nothing I want to tell you. His deliberate and methodical movements provided comfort. The habitual, almost predictable way in which he lived also gave her an odd sense of security.

"I'm visualizing all the collective evidence you relayed in my head." The little white lie slipped from her lips and she grimaced as the sound of his dish drying paused.

"Think of anything new?" His tone sounded so hopeful, the guilt expanded.

"No, still processing."

"Ah." The dejection in his tone made her heartsick. *If only she could help...*

The heat from the open potbelly stove and the snap of tinder sparks from a fresh log added to the hot coals captured her attention. Lifting the last plate, she dunked the dish into the foamy water, letting the warmth ease her churning thoughts. He moved next to her, his scent even more devastating than his kisses. She could breathe in his essence every day and never become tired of him. The smell automatically conjured the image of the boy, even though today she'd discovered the man.

His frame had grown, strengthened and expanded to support the more masculine concerns of the adult. His broad shoulders and arms had surrounded her body and made her feel splendid things, yet provided a safe place for her to lean into. His working hands had helped, supported and never pushed. The glorious way his body expressed his wishes thrilled her. She grieved for the wasted years…and wondered what might have been.

His breath on her neck sent a frisson of heat through her. "Maybe we should save grinding through more details for another day. Sometimes new concepts can form when least expected."

"Another day? That may be a problem." The dejection from the previous minutes deepened.

"Have you booked your flight?" She chose to concentrate on washing the silverware rather than the regret squeezing her chest.

"Camilla offered to book my flight, but I haven't received a confirmation text yet. I need to get back soon." She could just kick herself for asking a question she didn't want answered. The knowing was the same as when a delicate rosebud popped off its stem, only much worse.

To avoid the inevitable, she forced herself to think of something besides how good his body felt standing next to hers. "I can't stop thinking about Sam's death and the series of bad things happening in Elkridge." Visions of the landscape and corresponding scene details swirled in her mind. "I need to do something. I want Elkridge to return to the safe, cozy town I remember. I've already received two wedding order cancelations. This town can't afford to scare more tourists away."

"Solving all of Elkridge's problems is going to be a challenge all by yourself. Are you worried about Elkridge or your business?"

"Both. Since you won't be here, I've got to at least try something."

Joey's silence made her evaluate the reason for her frustration. "I'm sorry. I'm not being fair. It's just that I wanted...I want..."

Joey took the forks and knives from her hands and turned her slowly around. "What is it that you want, Mara?"

"This town needs your skills, but I understand why you can't stay. I do. I just hoped things were different."

A calloused thumb brushed over her cheek. "If it helps any, I don't want to go, but I have people depending on me back home. The families of those women are counting on me to help bring a killer to justice. My offer is still good—come to Seattle. I'll make sure you are safe."

"That's just it. Seattle is such a big city, I might get lost. Everything would be so different. You'd be worried about me, when you should be focused on your case. I couldn't do that to you." *And I can't depend on anyone. Not in that way. Being too dependent on my parents enforced that lesson.*

His heated breath spread tingles across her face before his lips landed. The sadness of his leaving evaporated as the ache of wanting him heated her veins. She wanted this man. A moan escaped from him when their tongues touched, and he slid a hand under her butt cheek, pulling her closer. She wrapped one leg around his to anchor her body to his. Suddenly, he pulled back.

"My Mara. Always thinking of others first." He placed his forehead against hers. "Our timing always seems to suck."

"Yes. Well, I've discovered life just doesn't always allow people to stick to a plan. Fate likes to toss in a couple of grenades and blow things up every now and then."

Joey guffawed. "That's a nice way to put it."

Mara pushed out of his arms and turned back to the sink to explore the water for more dishware. Over her shoulder, he leaned to take another dish from the drying rack.

"I know you don't trust the deputies here. Do you think if you showed the FBI the evidence you found, the information would get their attention?"

"It would be nice, but I doubt it. The FBI doesn't investigate homicides unless on Indian reservations, or the homicide is linked to a bigger crime." The heat from Joey's hand moving slowly up and down her back absorbed into her skin. "The information needs to be concise and compelling and fit within their wheelhouse. Good thought, though. Let's get you situated on the couch."

"First I need to feed Buddy." As soon as the dog heard his name, he appeared and rubbed up against her side. "Did you have a nice nap by the fire?" The thump of a tail on the kitchen cabinets gave her a clue. "Bring your backpack." She gave the dog a slight shove.

Hearing Buddy's running pounce and the dragging of metal buckles along the floor increased her appreciation for the dog's abilities. "Good boy." She accepted the slobber-covered bag. "Ready for dinner?"

If the thud, thud, thud on the wood provided any indication, her boy wanted dinner immediately. Filling Buddy's travel bowls with kibble and water took only a few seconds. She placed the metal bowls in what she believed to be the corner of the kitchen, then turned and let out a slow gasp of frustration.

Blasted alcohol, or was it Joey's kiss. Something had made her brain go all fuzzy, and she couldn't remember where the couch or door was located. *What am I doing?* Joey-on-the-brain was her problem. Lack of attention to details could get her into serious trouble.

"Need some help?" Joey asked.

"I just need a minute," she responded, keeping the distress from overwhelming her outward calm.

Think. Feel. She reached and ran her fingers along the counter. The couch was located in front of the wood stove. A heat source was in front of her. She slid a foot forward with hands outstretched and ran smack into a chair. She took a long, slow pull of air into her lungs and released a breath.

"I'm being stubborn and stupid. I'm trying to avoid swallowing my pride and asking for help from the only person in the room who can make this easier. Life is ten times harder when blind." *And you want me to move to Seattle? Ha! I can't even manage to navigate a single room.*

Exasperation caused her to curl inward. Her body tightened with tension. *Just suck it up. Stop being an idiot.* "Uh, Joey?"

"I'm here. You're fine, and you're not stupid. Visualize this. You're at the kitchen table. The kitchen counter is to your immediate left, and the front door is behind you to the right. There are two bedrooms and a bathroom to your immediate right. I'm standing at the coffee table. A couch is in front of me, with a large area rug covering the floor. The potbelly stove is behind me. Do you have a visual?"

"Yes, thanks." She moved around the table with small, measured steps.

"In my line of work, I've met some amazingly strong people. You're right up there with them. You can do anything you set your mind to, Mara. And asking for help isn't a sign of weakness. It's a sign you're smarter than the rest of the population."

"Some days I don't feel very smart."

"I bet there are days you don't feel like getting out of bed. But you get on with your day anyway."

She reached her hands forward feeling the heat from the fire. One step after another, sensing with her feet and hands, she moved visualizing the space. When she connected with leather, she turned left to the end of the couch and around the edge until she found him, her hand landing on his chest.

Excitement spread slowly up her arms. Her smile widened and the pure bliss gushed from her heart.

"You're so beautiful," he said, his voice mirroring her feelings.

She lifted her fingers to his face and let them glide over his skin, stopping at the ridges of his brows, then the creases next to his eyes, then sliding down to gently glide over his lips, dipping slightly at a dimple in his chin, then to his jawline. The soft skin, the rough texture of stubble, the curves of his bone structure, told her Joey hadn't changed much. He was still the same man she'd dreamed about so long ago. She rested her hands on his chest and let out a sigh. "So are you."

He lifted her chin with a warm finger, and his lips met hers halfway. She slid her hands around his neck, pulling, wanting more. If heaven existed, she'd just found it. His earthy scent. His weathered skin. His stabilizing energy. Nothing smelled better, not even fresh bread from the oven, or a puppy or lilacs in the summer. He filled every crevice in her heart, gluing the broken pieces back together, one breath at a time.

He released her lips on a sigh and pulled her closer.

"Are you doing okay?" he hummed close to her ear, breathing heat down her neck. His hands moved up and down her sides, caressing, making her feel things she'd never experienced before.

"Not sure." She delighted in the strong, steady beat of his heart and the muscles engaging and releasing while his hands and arms comforted her. His nipples were tiny, aroused pebbles which made her realize two things. One, she wasn't the only one affected. Two, she was far, far beyond being just okay. *Incredible* came to mind.

"I think someone needs to hit the play button, because my mind has stopped working." She nuzzled closer, shivering with anticipation. "Wow. Half a glass of wine, and I can't control my mouth. Note to self. No more drinking in the presence of a sexy male. Oops. There I go again."

His chest shook with laughter.

She buried her nose in his neck and felt his pulse leap when she nibbled on the soft skin. Buddy came and brushed against her leg. Her constant companion never had reason to be jealous before, and she found his overt attempts to put his body between them irritating. She gently pushed the dog aside and gave him the silent signal to lie down.

"You're so tempting," he whispered with a rough, needy sigh.

She wanted more. Him to fill her. Yet, her mind screamed, *NO!* He wasn't going to stay, and she couldn't fathom going to a big city. But her heart still yearned for the connection.

Buddy suddenly jumped. His front paws connecting with her hip, pushing her sideways. Joey's arms kept her vertical, then his body stiffened an instant before he pushed her behind him and down to the couch. "Stay here. Keep down."

"Joey?"

"Stay down."

Quick footsteps moved toward the kitchen. A drawer opening, then a clicking noise, like a bullet being lodged into a chamber, echoed through the room.

"Joey? What's happening?"

The thumping in her ears became so loud she couldn't hear anything else.

No. Calm down. Listen.

"Mara, call Buddy to you and keep him quiet. I saw someone standing outside the kitchen window. And I see fresh footprints."

"Why would anyone be up here?"

"Exactly. No one has any business being anywhere near this place except family, and they would either walk in or knock, not peer through a window." Hurried footsteps moved toward the door. The rustling of fabric told her he'd paused long enough to peer through the front window.

"Stay here," Joey commanded before heading for the front door.

"Don't go. Let's call someone."

"Who? Those idiot deputies? I'll be fine."

No, don't go.

Her heart slammed against her chest walls when the door opened and closed.

Please, please, please! I can't lose anyone else.

I can't lose him.

CHAPTER TWELVE

Joey hugged the side of the house, steadying his breathing, listening for movement. At the corner, he took a quick peek at the tree line behind the house, pulled back, then peered around the corner again, shining the flashlight held in parallel with a Glock he'd found in his brother's closet. After the first encounter with a mystery visitor, he'd taken precautions to have a weapon ready. He wished now he hadn't left his more familiar sidearm in Seattle.

Fresh footprints disappeared into the woods on the far side of the house. He visually followed the trail of evidence back to the front window and, thankfully, toward his rental SUV, not the door. Scuffled prints wrapped around the edge of the car's shadow. No windows were broken, but then he saw the damage. Sliced tires.

He lowered the gun and let his heart rate slow. Straightening from a crouched position, he debated whether to call roadside assistance or Pia.

The front door slowly opening made his decision easy. The tires could wait for the morning.

"How am I supposed to keep you safe if you don't stay put?" The authoritative tone he used on the job came booming out.

When she squared her shoulders, he braced for excuses as to why she hadn't followed his advice, but the facial expression of a woman torn between worry and assurance made his frustration evaporate.

"What happened?" she asked.

"Someone decided to slash my tires. Not a big deal. Especially since it's a rental, and I have insurance."

"That's not funny," she said, making him realize his efforts to ease the situation for her sake didn't help.

"No, no it's not. And, it's not the first time I've had a visitor. Which leads me to think there's something in that house somebody wants, but I can't figure out what." *And that pisses me off.*

Joey walked past Mara into the house. "Looks like I have some work to do, and I should figure out a way to get you home."

"We."

The force behind the statement stopped him in the middle of gathering her backpack, emptying the water bowl and placing the empty dishes inside.

"*We* have work to do. My suggestion is you put on a pot of coffee so we can get to it." Mara allowed Buddy to lead her back to the couch. She dropped to her hands and knees and began gathering magazines and coasters that had slid to the floor when Buddy pushed her over. "When we're done, I can sleep on the couch. There's no reason to disturb anyone tonight."

"If you stay, you'll take the bedroom. No debates."

Mara popped her head above the couch back. She looked only partly mollified. "Agreed. Now tell me how I can help?"

He glanced at the window, then at the dog, who watched him closely. "Why didn't Buddy bark?"

"He's a service dog, not a guard dog. He's been trained to

react, but not bark. He communicates in his own way. If I had been paying attention, I would have realized he tried to warn us. I misinterpreted his reaction as jealousy."

"Jealousy?"

"A service dog is a one-person companion. When a new person enters the owner's life, dogs sometimes have difficulty adjusting. Like humans, they get jealous over the loss of attention. It's one of my training session topics."

That means you don't date much. He hated that a sense of satisfaction caused a smile to cross his face—but he was a man.

Joey shoved a coffee filter and scoops of coffee into the small appliance and hit go. "Then we should listen to Buddy from now on, because tonight could have ended a lot differently." *We might have caught a killer. Or gotten shot.* "Other than coffee, can I get you anything?"

"Nope, I'm good," she responded without angst. No trembling or tears in sight.

Respect replaced his concern. "Then give me a minute. I'm going to call this in."

Because, if for no other reason, he wanted the incident on record.

He scrolled through the numbers until he found one for the deputies. Joey took a few minutes to relay the events, but suggested a report be filed in the morning since there wasn't much to be done at this point. Then he dialed roadside service. The dispatcher promised to have a tow truck available first thing in the morning to assist with replacing the tires.

While holding for a confirmation number, he observed Mara. He could tell the events of the evening were closing in on her now. She straightened the pile of magazines and books on the table, then moved the items from left to right and right to left so many times, the reading material ended up right back where they started.

After conveying the necessary details, he hung up, poured

coffee and a teaspoon and a half of creamer into a pottery mug, just the way she liked it and worked to stop his hands from shaking. The reaction didn't come from the chest-pumping action of chasing a night stalker into the woods, but the knowledge that Mara would be spending the night. Here. Alone with him. Together.

His body quivered with awareness that he worked hard to turn off. But a specific part of his body had decided to engage the autopilot, and he no longer had access to the control panel.

It's not like you're going to sleep with her, he told himself, willing himself to believe his own rhetoric. The separate rooms would help. *Nothing's going to happen,* he repeated over and over in his mind. He was leaving. Going back to Seattle. Right? That was the plan...wasn't it?

"How about we start with what we know." She looked so cute and eager, he didn't have the heart to tell her his investigative training included complex diagraming tools, but the explanation wouldn't have helped her relax. Besides, he liked the pure determination on her face. She'd do whatever was necessary to save her town and help find Sam's killer.

"Here's what my gut is telling me." He poured another cup of coffee. "Sam got in over his head. Knowing him, he didn't ask for help and went barreling into something big and messy. He didn't have someone like, my boss, telling him over and over that playing the hero could get you dead." Joey braced the counter and took a step back to stretch his tight back muscles. "His computer is missing. He lives smack in the middle of crime activity. He had to know something was going on." He picked up the mugs and moved toward the couch.

"Stop!"

Joey froze. "What's wrong?"

"Take a step back."

He complied.

"Did you hear that?" Mara unfolded from the couch. "When you stepped on the floor, it sounded different."

Joey studied the wood planks disappearing under the rug. "You're right." He set the coffee cups down to shove the couch back. "A couple planks have been replaced." Joey pulled a utility knife from his pocket and pried at the corner of one of the planks until it gave way. "Well, I'll be damned."

"What did you find?" Her hand went to her chest as if trying to keep her heart from pounding through the wall.

Joey lifted a pile full of documents and a couple more evidence bags from beneath the floorboards.

Excitement, puzzlement, fury all stirred together to concoct an emotional cocktail. "Looks like we have clothing fragments, some assorted jewelry, a fingernail tip, and some Elkridge city council memos. Looks like my brother was doing some investigating, and this might be why he was murdered."

"From your voice, it sounds like you don't want to turn this evidence in either."

"There has to be a reason Sam didn't trust his department. If he didn't trust them, then neither will I."

"Do you have a way to scan the documents?"

Joey's gut wrenched and he went on alert. "Yes, why?"

"Two reasons. Having a copy wouldn't be a bad idea. And two, if you can scan the pages, I should be able to access the information on my reader."

"I don't think it's a good idea for you to get involved."

"Let me remind you, you were the one that came to find me today. I spent the day freezing up on that ridge helping you find clues, and tonight if it weren't for me, you wouldn't have discovered that hidden compartment. Besides, I'm already involved."

"You said you weren't cold."

"You're missing the point." Her scrunched facial features

looked so damn cute he almost laughed, but he managed to contain his response.

"I have a scanning app on my phone that might work. If I can't get the information in the format you can read it, promise me you'll let this drop."

"Scan the items, and if my reader can't read the documents, then maybe you can read the information to me. Besides, you might catch more information if you read the information aloud, rather than skimming."

"Has anyone ever told you that you are a pertinacious woman?"

"Well now, that's a mighty fancy word for stubborn, Detective."

For the next two hours, he scanned documents and took pictures of the evidence. Nothing glaring popped out. Mara challenged each theory and reminded him of facts he'd temporarily forgotten.

Mara included her knowledge of the local townsfolk and rumors. Since she owned a flower shop, she was the first to learn about births, weddings, and funerals. She was best friends with a nail salon owner and that added a whole new layer of details. He and Mara discussed every nuance at length before agreeing where to place the detail in the sequence. Once the pattern started to fall into place, he duplicated the information on the software program. Questions such as how the FBI and a small-town sheriff might be connected were added to the software notepad section along with the shortage of feminine products and prenatal vitamins. Both seemed like a supply problem, but then what was up with the jewelry? Years of experience caused him not to rule anything out. By the time all the details were assembled and entered into his computer, there were more questions than answers.

When Mara yawned and stretched, he gently set his

computer on the coffee table. "I think it's time to quit for today. We can look at this again in the morning."

Luckily she agreed. He wouldn't sleep. Not with her in the next room. At least he'd have something to keep his mind occupied.

"Let's find you some towels." He moved to the door of the first bedroom that had been transformed into Sam's office. "I know there's another set in here somewhere...found them." He grabbed the stack off the closet shelf before moving to the master bedroom. "I can offer you an oversized T-shirt and some sweats, but they're Sam's, so they'll be a bit big."

Her face turned a bit pale, and he pondered the reason. "Is there anything Buddy needs?"

"No, he usually sleeps on the floor next to me, so he should be fine."

"If you want to take a shower my shampoo's on the edge of the tub."

"I'm fine," she said, forcing a smile—a cheap imitation of the real deal.

She stood at the end of the bed, holding the stack of towels, her lips pressed into a tight, flat line.

He tapped on his thigh while he assessed the situation, wondering what she might be thinking. Coming up with nothing, he moved to the door. "I'm right outside if you need anything."

"Good night," she murmured, barely loud enough to hear.

He shut the door behind him, then walked to the couch where he slowly sank into the leather. Tension returned as he looked at the list of notes she'd helped him create. He had questions. Lots and lots of questions, but not about Sam's death. Mostly centered on his feelings for the woman who fascinated him. The woman he shouldn't start anything with because he had to leave, but still the woman he wanted to make love to and then wrap protectively in his arms for the rest of his life.

If he could roll back time to when he was seventeen, he'd have done a lot of things differently. He could have taken her camping or rock climbing or put her on the back of his motorcycle and taken off on a road trip, just the two of them. So many should-have regrets.

Movement behind the bedroom door made his mind wander. He closed his eyes and imagined her getting naked, her soft curves under his hands, her hair trailing across his chest.

Squeezing his eyelids tight, he tried blocking the images, but thwarting his imagination didn't work. Getting up, he completed the required activities to prepare for bed before settling in for the night. Staring at the ceiling, he watched the flicker of light from the potbelly stove dance on the open beams.

Then he heard it.

The creak of hinges that needed oil, and the soft shuffle of footsteps.

He reached for the jeans just beyond his fingertips. *Dammit.*

She appeared before him, his brother's shirt ending mid-thigh. Her face, illuminated only by the light of the stove, gave her an angelic appearance. The dark silence made everything move in slow motion, like the moon rising in the night sky. She turned to go.

"Mara?"

She turned back and pointed toward the bedroom. "There's no heat in the room. I can't get warm."

Heat. Right. "I only have the extra blankets."

"Oh, okay."

"No. Not okay. You probably won't sleep if you're cold. We have two choices. We can sleep on the floor by the fireplace, or we can share blankets and body heat in the bedroom."

Bedroom. Please pick the bedroom.

She crossed her arms, then uncrossed them. "Sleeping out here means one of us will have to stoke the fire every couple of hours, and I most likely won't be able to walk in the morning. The pins and rods in my legs don't take kindly to cold, hard floors."

Shattered legs. Right. "Then we'll share the bed. Why don't you get tucked under the covers while I grab the bedding?"

She hesitated for the longest second. He held his breath. *Don't change your mind. Please, don't.* When she turned and walked back into the room, air whooshed from his chest.

Oh, man. He rubbed his head, trying to wrap his mind around what had just happened. *You can do this. Just stay in control.*

He launched vertically and reached for his jeans, pulled them on, then gathered the bedding into his arms. The moonlight through the open bedroom drapes allowed him to see a lump on the far side of the bed. He spread the covers over her and then walked to the dresser on the opposite side of the room, letting excitement fill his limbs. Opening the first drawer, he felt the contents, then opened the next and then the next. When he closed the final drawer, he took a frustrated breath.

"Is there a problem?" A small voice came from the bed.

"Just an underwear problem." The awkwardness got stuck in his throat, and he worked to clear the uneasiness. "I haven't owned boxers or briefs since I turned twenty."

She sat up with the sheets tucked under her arms. The moon reflected off her naked skin. "Do you mind if I ask another question?"

"What's your question?"

"Is there a reason you don't want to have sex with me?"

His brain forgot to send the signal to breathe, being way too preoccupied with hoping he hadn't misheard her.

"I just figured with me leaving, you wouldn't…well, you know…that sex wasn't a possibility."

"Gaccione. When are you going to stop thinking? Seems

you've been thinking for a long time now, and your brain's conclusions don't appear to be working for you."

He choked off a laugh. "You might be right," he said, praying for two things. One, she wouldn't change her mind—because evidently—he'd turned into a dumb-ass. Two, the three-pack of condoms was still in the bottom of his shaving kit. "Question for you. Are you sure about this?" He hated asking, but he wanted to make sure she had no doubts.

"I've missed out on a lot of things in my life. Not attending a high school dance because no one asked. Not finishing college because I needed to learn to walk again. I don't want to also miss out on things because I'm afraid. You're going to leave. I get that, even though I wish you wouldn't because Elkridge could use someone with your talents. That aside, this might be our last chance. I would hate to always wonder."

"Wonder what it would have been like?" he asked, hearing the lust in his voice.

"Something like that."

Her response added heat to the room, warming the air several degrees. The strongest woman he'd ever met made him look at his life differently. Maybe she didn't put herself in front of bullets like some of the women he worked with, or compete in triathlons like others, but she could certainly bend him in half.

"I don't want to have to wonder, either. Just give me a minute." *Because I require several to screw my head on straight.*

He turned toward the bathroom to search his shaving kit. Mara's moonlit image made his testosterone levels shoot straight off the charts. He'd been dreaming about this day for years.

The air in the room crackled with excitement. After a long minute, he let out a calming whoosh of breath. She wanted him —the boy from the wrong side of the river. He didn't need to prove anything to her. Never had. Even today, the only barriers between them were ones he'd erected.

Today, all he needed to be was the guy who didn't care that she was blind.

And honestly? Her being blind didn't matter one damn bit.

CHAPTER THIRTEEN

M ara laid back and pulled the covers to her chin, the boldness from the prior moment dissipating.

What am I doing? Satisfying my curiosity? Grabbing an opportunity? Being stupid?

The ruckus coming from the bathroom gave the impression Joey was deconstructing the room in search of something. She would have laughed herself silly if the situation hadn't turned so serious.

"Sounds like you're dismantling the bathroom," she said to lighten the tension.

"I'm just looking for something," his hesitant voice responded. "Have you changed your mind?"

No. Yes. Well, maybe. "It's just that it's been a long time, and..."

"Yeah, years for me, too."

"Really?"

"I've been waiting years to make love to you." His voice was quiet, like he wanted to share a precious secret.

"Oh, God. Now I have to live up to your fantasy of what you think intimacy will be like?"

LYZ KELLEY

A shiver started at her core and moved outward. *That's just great. I'll just shiver to get warm.*

When the bed dipped, the courage she so frantically held onto slipped from her fingers. Bashfulness extended its claws and made her want to scramble out of the other side of the bed. The longing to feel a man's touch—this man's touch—made her stay. Her skin tingled with anticipation. She needed to know there was at least one man out there who still found her attractive.

Night air ran across her body as he lifted the bedcovers to slide closer. Next came the blast of his body heat.

"Come here, Mara. Let me warm you."

He touched her arm, and she moved to his side, growing more adventurous, wrapping her leg and arm around his body, snuggling as close as she could without lying on top of him.

He flinched. "Jesus, woman. Your feet and nose are like ice cubes." He quickly tucked the extra layers of bedding around them.

His nakedness set off a fresh wave of shivers. She treasured each movement of muscle, each heartbeat, the rise and fall of his chest with each breath. Just thinking about what he might do next brought her close to an orgasm—a rare treat.

But the thought of the real thing, him inside her, made her body explode with a renewed curiosity and clench with longing.

His hands moved up and down her spine, massaging and stimulating.

"I should tell you I have lots of scars," she warned.

He turned his head, his day-old beard scraping across her forehead. "Why do guys think of scars as badges of honor, and women regard them as marks of shame? That's always confused me."

Good question. Why did she?

At least she could walk, even if a bit stiffly, and she could

154

still get out of bed and function. Her doctors considered it a miracle.

"There are very few people in my life who don't make me feel like a cripple. Thank you for being one of them."

He kissed the top of her head. "Maybe you should just stop caring what other people think. Besides, they're probably jealous."

A skeptical puff of breath blew into the night air. "Jealous?"

"You're beautiful, smart, talented. Yep, jealous. You've built a life for yourself. A good life. That's more than a lot of people can say."

The thrum of his heartbeat pounded in her ear while memories of her past clicked by, a slide show of events— College...the crash...therapy—until there was only darkness. The struggle. He'd missed the journey, only seeing the end result. If that's what he saw, then possibly she hadn't done so bad.

"I've come to love my life here," she murmured. "That's why I hate this constant strain. People are starting to feel scared. Watchful. I wish Sam hadn't been elected sheriff."

A quick intake of air suggested she'd startled him. "Why? People say he was good at his job."

"He was. But if he hadn't been sheriff first, then you might not be so resistant to running for the open position. Being compared to and constantly measured against your brother must be tough. I know you have a job in Seattle, but you're not happy there. Your tone, and the words you used to describe your work gives me the impression your job is not fulfilling. You talk about people depending on you, the team, but not once have you said you like your job. People depend on you here, too. You could make a difference if you didn't look at is as taking Sam's position."

"True. But being a detective and being sheriff are two different jobs."

"Misdemeanors and felonies are different as well. I'm asking you to look at the true reason you're not considering the job."

Joey rubbed her frozen extremities with his hands and feet when she curled in to find warmth. "I'll think about it."

She relaxed her fisted fingers and let them expand over his pecs. He had a runner's body, hard and lean and gloriously perfect in almost every way. She detected the residual fragrance of baked apple. The delicious combination of apple and masculinity made her want to continue breathing in, never exhaling. Never letting the addicting smell escape.

"Are you getting warm?"

Blazing. "Yes, thank you," she gasped, insecurity making her hold her breath.

Joey released a long, shaky breath of his own and shifted slightly. "Your nose still feels like a hailstone." His fingers closed around her nose, and he gently rubbed his fingers and thumb over her skin to increase circulation.

The wind picked up outside, and the pines brushed against the window with a constant tap-tap-tap. As her limbs warmed, her body grew heavy. A screech made her flinch.

"Easy." Joey's arm instantly pulled her closer. "It was just an owl. You're safe." His quiet, whispered breath brushed like silk across her neck.

She closed her eyes to sweep away the activities of the day and let the heat emanating from Joey's inviting body cocoon her in contentment. The light touch of his hand rhythmically circling and soothing pulled her into a carefree state.

"Joey?"

"Yeah?"

"Are you ready to practice some more?"

"I'm more than ready. I'm going to show you how beautiful you are."

The breath she'd been holding slowly emptied from her

lungs. She leaned in and kissed him slowly, methodically, making sure she would remember every moment.

"Joey, I want you to know, I understand there are no certainties in life. If we do this, there will be no strings holding you here. The next few hours will be about two people indulging in a curiosity. That's all. But you need to agree. When you leave for Seattle, I don't want you looking back. You need to look forward. Toward your future."

She waited for him to say something, but he didn't. He only pulled her in closer.

"I'll accept your terms for now, but I will be coming back. Whatever this is between us will not end here, today. I want you to know that, Mara." His voice was gruff and filled with need.

"Then no regrets?"

"Only one. That I didn't come home sooner."

GOD, she was stunning. Joey kissed her, deep and hot with a passion to demonstrate she wasn't a temporary woman in his life. He wanted to make her feel what he felt. The joy. The euphoria. If he could stretch the night into eternity, he would. When he pulled back, he studied the circus of expressions dancing across her face.

"That's more like it, Gaccione." Her smile expanded. "Keep on practicing. You'll get there."

A groan and a semi-laugh escaped. He buried his nose in her hair and inhaled, lifting onto his elbow.

How was he ever going to get on that damn plane?

"Joey, why are you quiet?"

He nuzzled her neck. "I'm concentrating. I want to make sure I get this right."

Her teasing smile broadened. "I'm not looking for perfect. I told you practice is not a bad thing." There was a slight trace of humor in her voice, but he suspected she didn't find the situation amusing.

"I want to take my time," he said, lifting the edges of her t-shirt.

She made a low, incoherent sound in her throat, fluffing the covers enough to allow her hand to touch skin. When her cold fingers touched him, a shiver racked his body, not from the cold, but from the sizzling heat of her touch.

"In a hurry?" he asked, leaning closer to connect with her skin.

"Yes," she whispered, letting the word elongate into a hiss. Her exhale made his body sing.

His willpower to hold off sagged. "Slow down. We have time."

"No, we don't."

Time. She had a point. The sands of the hourglass were draining away, and he couldn't stop them. He pressed his hand against her heart to feel the beat and connect to her rhythm and her to his.

"You're so beautiful." He cupped her jaw and pulled her to him. "I need you. I need this."

Her body relaxed beneath his. Her hand rested on his hip.

Inch by inch by inch, he revealed her skin. He let his hands skim over the soft surface, feeling each muscle respond to his touch. Bunching her shirt, he indulged, scattering kisses here and there before working his way past her belly. His fingers slid over the delicate lace of her waistband. He skimmed a finger along the silky fabric, diving deeper and deeper with each caress. She shifted and reached toward the sensation. Her reaction made him search further to find every sweet spot.

"What are you waiting for?" she asked.

"You're just going to have to wait to find out," he teased.

She made a choking sound and pressed her hands against the covers, where his full erection clamored for a connection. "I can already see." she murmured.

He dropped his head, kissing and licking the skin just above her waistband.

"Patience," he admonished lightly and began working to release the barrier of her underwear, rolling the fabric down her hips. Tossing her panties to the floor, he went to work on her top, but she was already reaching for him, sliding her hand along his rigid skin.

"Teach me something new," she demanded.

"My pleasure."

Her impatient fingers reached and circled around him, stroking and pulling.

"Slow down, Mara," he gasped against the artery pounding in her neck, while he tugged her head back gently with a fistful of her hair.

She growled and centered his hips over hers, refusing to be deterred. He reached for the condoms he'd placed on her dresser, lifted to his knees, and slid the protection in place because he wanted to protect her, love her and keep her safe.

She lifted her hips to close the distance between their bodies.

"Pleeeease, Joey. Don't make me wait any longer."

He slid a thigh between hers to open her and allow her to reach him. "Then let's not wait."

The words barely left his lips before he thrust forward and filled her. She arched to meet him, and he almost let go, but squeezed hard to hold on.

His breath raced with hers, pushing harder and faster, both not wanting to cross the finish line first, but sprinting together to get to the end. With a couple of thrusts, both pushed past the peak, coming with a one-two finish, Mara just barely in the lead. He collapsed, his body and hers pressing deep into the mattress, both fighting for air.

Neither moved. His forehead rested on her pillow. Her arms were still wrapped around his back.

"That was a good warm up. Can we go again?" she murmured.

"Mara. My little minx." He rolled. "Absolutely. Like you said. We need to practice." He used a tissue to dispose of the condom, then tucked her into his side, running a finger over her breasts, playing and circling her puckered nipple. "God, you're perfect." He reached over to play with the other breast. She pushed back and rolled her hips, and, damn, if he didn't respond. He shifted to his knees and settled lower. His lips caressed and then moved between her thighs to create a distraction.

"A slower speed this time." He divided the soft folds of her skin to find her nub of pleasure. Closing his eyes, he duplicated the small circles Mara drew on the counter, circling in and out, round and round, until her breath thickened, her body vibrated and jerked.

"Joey. There! Now!"

"Not yet." He slid his body next to hers, then rolled slightly back, pulling her across his chest, to allow his other hand access to her breasts and nipples and to hold her in place.

"I need—" Her voice stopped on a whimper.

You forever, he hoped. Bending his head down, he used his teeth and facial stubble to scrape her skin lightly. The thrill of her reaction surged through him.

He concentrated on his fingers, drawing more and more intricate patterns, making her body respond. "Let go," he whispered next to her ear, and got a moan in response. "You feel wonderful." He pinched a nipple, rolling the skin between his fingers. "You like this?"

"Oh. Oh!" She let the reactions burst out on a puff of breath. The muscles in her legs strained. He shifted his hand lower and felt her wetness.

"Yes," she shrieked. "Don't stop."

She reached for him. Knowing what she wanted, he pushed her to his side, keeping her in front of him, one of her legs draped over his hip. He returned to making the tiny circles that made her purr. Rocking into her, he allowed her to climb and climb, moving ever higher. Her body responded to his touch, and, a few seconds later, jerked and clenched down around him. He kept the motion going to allow the spasms cascading across her to roll on until she crossed the apex and started the slow slide to the other side. Finally, she lay limp in his arms.

After a few minutes, her breathing returned to normal, and she leaned her head back toward him. "But what about you?"

"Don't worry about me. Like I said, we've got all night."

He lifted her face to his and gave her a long, slow kiss, and damn if her body didn't respond again, wanting more.

He wanted more. He wanted to dive into her chest, capture her heart and keep loving her forever. He didn't want to let her go, ever. He reached for another condom and slid it in place. "My turn." He pulled her on top of him.

"I like the sound of that."

She centered her hips, ever so slowly enfolded him into her. He moaned and reached for her waist. She had become his world. She rose onto her knees, and he felt her absence, but then there she was again.

He was hers. Nothing else mattered anymore. Jobs. Making his parents proud. Nothing but proving he was good enough for her. No matter what. He wanted to protect her.

She pushed down, as if wanting more. He wanted to give her everything, and when she lifted again, he thrust to meet her. She gasped his name in pleasure, and he couldn't help but touch and caress and make her part of him. He wanted their bodies to connect in such a way that he couldn't tell where she left off and he began.

He wanted to fill her completely.

He needed her.

Forever.

"Mara." The fervor of emotion caught in his throat, preventing him from telling her he loved her.

The raw look on her face made thinking and feeling while making love to her impossible. If he couldn't express his eagerness, he prayed she got the idea how much he loved her with every touch and thrust.

Just as an orgasm embraced her, he thrust harder so they could forge the peak of bliss together.

His body floated in a serene state of euphoria. The tranquil giddiness created a yearning so complete, he refused to allow another second of time to pass. The word *"love"* formed to describe the feeling.

But the word seemed too simple.

Purely inadequate.

Because sometimes love wasn't enough. Life didn't always come in neat little packages.

He groaned, not wanting to let time slip by or think about what came next.

BUDDY'S MOVEMENTS pulled Mara out of a body-numbing slumber. The kind of sleep where every muscle and tendon had been in the same position for so long, blood circulation had slowed.

The early morning light streaming through the window and the cozy warmth made her want to return to drowsy bliss.

When she attempted to roll over, a light breath whispered across her face and made her pause. Legs and sheets were entangled to the point she couldn't move. Arms held her plastered against a wall of muscle. Her mind slowly remembered. Thinking Joey was asleep, she searched for his wrist to slide out of his embrace.

"Going somewhere?" The vibration of his voice rolled through her.

His hand skimmed off her stomach, freeing her, but she didn't want to be free. She wanted to be consumed.

"Joey?" The whimpering need in her voice didn't go unanswered.

When his lips touched hers, her body melted with lust. His hand cupped the back of her neck, his thumb pressing against her jaw to get a better angle. His lips pressed deeper, his tongue caressing the edge of her lips, nudging her to let him in. On a sigh, she opened to him, letting him explore, circle in and out, out and in. When he pulled back, she followed, clinging to him.

"I'm almost ready to fall off the bed." She tightened her grip. "We need to adjust."

"Sorry. I'm not used to sleeping with anyone. I'm a sprawling bed hog." He lifted and shifted their bodies to the middle of the mattress, pulling her on top. His hands played. Her hands remained paralyzed.

She didn't have the sexual knowledge or skills to match his. Every one of his touches and caresses treated her to a unique and stimulating experience. The insecurities pounded in.

Let me just get through this without making an idiot of myself.

He reached up and coaxed her face closer to his. When their lips touched, his hands stroked over her shoulder blades to her lower back, holding her in place. His kisses traveled from jaw to neck, then to her ear. Her body sighed with pleasure.

"You're amazing," he whispered.

That did it. Her bones melted into a puddle of sensations.

Every nerve ending flashed an erotic signal from one point to the next, stimulating, creating heat and a glorious tension. His body reacted, and she allowed her weight to press in, letting a moan escape on the next kiss. His hands pulled her closer and closer. She finally found the courage to graze her fingers over his body, touching, feeling the contours, the thickness of his hair. She sank her teeth into his skin, tasting, absorbing.

"God, woman," he ground out on a slow, husky groan before diving in for another kiss.

His hand brushed her nipple and squeezed the tip. Every additional touch reminded her just how naked and vulnerable she was. Then she touched his nipple, and suddenly the urge to suckle became too intense to resist. She moved her mouth over his puckered skin, her tongue running around the edges. His chest arched to meet her caress.

She'd missed the intimate touch of another human being, but she hadn't known how amazing and powerful a connection with the right person could be. Even the couple of dates she'd accepted had felt off and left her feeling lonelier. There hadn't been any feeling of excited potential. No passion. In fact, that was the problem. Dates with the other men felt like a cookie jar without the delicious contents.

The moment Joey walked into the flower shop, the long-ago spark burst into a steady flame and opened the door to an element of knowing, of deep recognition.

Using his shoulders as leverage, she pulled her body towards his mouth. She wanted to taste the sweetness of passion. Indulge in it.

Just as her lips attached to his, a cold nose nudged her side. She wanted to ignore the dog, but then a strange sound—a human sound—accompanied another nudge. The noise must have registered with Joey as well, because he rolled her beneath him, shielding her, lifting only enough to look out the window.

"Crap. It's the tow truck." He brushed a soft kiss on her forehead. "Stay here. I'll be right back."

A flurry of activity next to the bed lasted for several seconds. Her body mourned the loss of heat and the touch of skin, but she also recognized the disruption had doused the sensual flame. She wouldn't be able to get the fire back. Reality and fear had already sneaked in the back door.

Buddy leaned against the bed, pushing harder into the mattress, trying to connect.

"I know. You need to go out. Give me a minute, 'cause I have no idea where anything is."

Reaching toward the floor and feeling around, she connected with what felt like cotton and pulled it closer. She shoved her arms and legs into clothing, hoping the garments were the right way around, then made her way to the back door. Joey had explained the door was somewhere to the left of the potbelly stove, but with no heat to guide her, she made a series of educated guesses until she reached her destination.

After Mara unlocked and opened the door, Buddy hesitated, sniffed the ground nearby, then trotted off to do his business. Standing still, she strained to hear the surrounding activity. Behind her, the front door opened.

"Yeah, I know you're short staffed and want me back," Joey said in an even tone with an unusual heaviness. "I just got my ticket confirmation. I leave Sunday."

That's tomorrow. Her breath snagged on an inhalation.

At the thought of his imminent departure, a suffocating sorrow overwhelmed her and incinerated her contentment.

"The internet signal here sucks. I'll review the new information when I get home." Joey sounded frustrated and was silent for several seconds before responding, "Yes, sir. Got it. I'll be sure to stop by your office first thing. See you then."

Home. Elkridge wasn't his home anymore. She needed to remember that.

Joey mumbled something indecipherable under his breath and then rushed toward the bedroom. His footsteps paused, then came toward the back door.

"You're up." Disappointment clearly outlined and bolded his words.

She understood. He could quadruple his disappointment. The frustration and the emotions wouldn't come anywhere close to equaling hers. "Buddy needed to go out."

"The tires should only take a minute to fix." His way of saying, *we can go back to bed and not be disturbed for the rest of the day.* Unfortunately, with daylight came responsibilities and reminders. She needed to find a chiming watch.

"I'm not sure of the time, but I need to open the shop at ten, and I most likely have arrangements to prepare for delivery. If I don't, my phone's going to start ringing, Tony is going to ask questions."

"Questions you don't want to answer, like where you spent the night."

She didn't like his admonishing tone. "It's not like that."

"Then explain it to me, because I understand about the rumor mill in this town. My mother seems to take pride in being the perpetrator of gossip."

She didn't want to care what other people thought, but darn it, she did. Soft footsteps approached and she prided herself for not flinching when he tucked a strand of hair behind her ear. With a patience that stunned her, he didn't push. Simply waited for her answer.

"I heard you on the phone," she admitted. "The trouble is I was reminded again that you're leaving, and I'm staying. You know how cruel people can be."

His swift inhale told her she'd hit her mark. She didn't like the cowardly punch, but she didn't have anything else to throw at him.

He moved even closer, close enough his heat made her skin

respond. "You can do better than that. Tell me what this is about."

Her jaw went slack. Concocting a bald-faced lie would be so easy, but she couldn't. Not to him. Not the guy who'd treated her with respect, providing a solid foundation to lean against.

Honesty soothed her and calmed in her stomach. "What we did. When you touched me, you made me feel special. And I liked it." His movements caused her hands to raise and connect with his chest. "No, please don't. The moment's gone. I thought I could do it. I thought I could have sex, but being together wouldn't be just sex for me. I wish I could be different, indulge in the spontaneous, but that's not me. I've never been that person."

"You shouldn't want to be different." A gentle hand skimmed down her cheek.

Blood tromped through her veins, attacking her resistance. Her tongue slid over her lips. God help her, she wanted him. But all of him. She didn't want just a sliver.

His scent consumed her and drove the need to wrap her body around his. "Do you mind if I take a shower while we wait?" She needed to get his scent off, although washing would only help a little.

He pulled his hand back but remained, invading her space. "Would you like some company?"

Her high school crush had just bypassed lust and gone straight to overwhelming desire. She'd gotten in way, way, way too deep, and needed to dig out fast. Only she needed a backhoe to get her out of this one.

A flutter of nerves flickered through her for an instant before she crushed the trembling need. Her chest muscles tightened, throwing up barriers to protect her heart. She wanted him so much. But once she had a real taste, not just a sample, she would want the long-term, and he couldn't provide her the solidness she wanted.

Be strong. "It's tempting," *you're tempting,* "but like I said, I had better pass."

The metaphysical step back registered. The image of a door closing, then being locked and bolted, came to mind. She wanted to reach out and confess her fears, but her practical mind wouldn't allow it.

"While you shower, I'll find us something for breakfast," he said in a monotone making his mood impossible to read.

"Great." She managed a smile even though she wanted to cry.

Making her way to the bedroom, she searched for the bathroom. Finding a doorway and a sink, she shut the door and felt her way to the toilet before collapsing. She let the memories of the previous night wash over her. The way his hands warmed her body. The way his whispered passion made her quiver. The way he made her savor the bliss of the moment. She would never be able to let him go now that their bodies had tangled together, touching, feeling, relishing. The intimacy would haunt her for the rest of her life.

In the hospital, she'd made a commitment to herself to live without regrets.

Loving Joey, fully and completely, yet not being able to hold him might just be the one regret she'd have to live with the rest of her life.

CHAPTER FOURTEEN

After dropping Mara off at Blooms, Joey visited the sheriff's office to confirm the tire slashing evidence was recorded and the deputies were acting on the information.

The discovered documents and articles remained hidden underneath Sam's living room floorboards, the photographs of each item in an encrypted folder on his computer.

Joey was certain whoever slashed his tires also killed his brother, yet the deputies acted like he'd just handed them a piece of gum. Rage in his gut burned. He treaded the thin line of politics, especially when he asked to look at a recent theft file.

"Please tell me you're trying to find the person who slashed my tires." He pushed the incident report file toward the middle of the small conference table, tapped on the file, then shook his head at Ernie. "This guy, the thief, he's not the killer. The profile indicates it's someone local. Do you know anyone needing a drug fix?"

If Ernie had common sense stored between his two ears, he'd have concluded the theft seemed too predictable. Jewelry. Small electronics. An envelope of cash stashed in a desk drawer. All missing. The envelope of cash and selected pieces of jewelry gave him the clue.

"Several. Heroin. Crack. Meth. You name it," Ernie drawled out the information. "Kids get bored, try it and before they can blink they're hooked."

"One of them is your thief. Funerals are easy pickings for lazy robbers. Drug abusers are definitely lazy and daring when they need a fix. I would look for someone who lives close by. On the same block or a family member." Joey tapped the file. "Did you get the labs back on Sam's case yet or send someone to take a mold of those tire tracks I found?"

"I assigned Deputy Cuhna to take a look at what you found this morning. Sam's lab work hasn't been processed yet. We had to send the information to the state lab, and they're pretty backed up."

Backed up, or are you stalling some more?

"You said you downloaded my brother's email history, but I never got the files or the coroners report. I'm leaving tomorrow. Would you mind checking to see if the information's been loaded to the secured drive yet?"

"I loaded the files, but you may not have permission for that folder. I'll make sure you get access." The deputy stood, walked the two steps toward the door, then stopped. Turning with a puzzled frown, he said, "Looking for something in particular?"

He wished he could say. He'd read through the city memos again. But nothing made sense, and he didn't want to accidentally set off alarms. Mara kept telling him he knew Elkridge. The truth was he'd been gone a long time, and a lot of things had changed.

"Nothing specific. I'm still throwing the net wide to see if I can't get a few pieces to connect before I leave. Do you know if he had any recent interactions with the DEA, FBI or any other agency?"

"Odd you asking about the FBI. Sam put a call into the FBI about a month ago. Not sure why"

Yes. I'm right. The initials on the ground were about the FBI.

"There might be something in his office. Want to take a look?"

No. He wanted to respect his brother's privacy. If this were anyone else, he'd be first through the door, but this was Sam's stuff. His brother never liked people messing with his things, and was the first one to throw a punch when he found someone in his room. Rummaging through his brother's personal effects was disrespectful and the reason he didn't ask to see his brother's office in the first place.

But Sam was dead.

The harsh actualization he'd never get a chance to repair the past wrongs choked off his air. Why did he think competing against Sam was necessary? All the rivalry did was rip them apart—prevent them from having a solid relationship.

Sam, bro. I'm sorry, man.

Time was running out and he didn't seem to have a choice. The trail of information had pieces missing. Which meant he had to dig deeper, then deeper, and still deeper, until he found the answer.

"Sure. I'll take a look."

The yin and yang burden of not wanting to know what Sam had gotten involved with, but being driven to find answers, made him respond, "Lead the way."

He followed Ernie down the carpeted hall to the last office, where a US flag stood proudly in the corner. The white-painted walls were covered with all the usual certificates, but a painting of Elkridge valley, just as the leaves turned gold and fiery red, captured his attention. Taking a step closer, he inspected the signature. Just as expected, his sister Anna's scrawled name painted in small black lettering sat in the bottom corner. On the desk sat a phone, pottery mug, nameplate and the usual desk items squared in perfect horizontal and perpendicular lines. Joey moved behind the desk and stood by the black leather chair. "Has anyone removed anything from the desk?"

"Your dad took his personal items last week, but no one else has been in here."

Joey scanned the neat piles of papers, unlike the scattered papers at the house, which solidified his suspicions. Someone had searched his brother's place in a hurry. Joey studied the desk, creating an inverse image. His brother being right-handed, he opened the left-hand drawer and then lifted a pile of business cards to thumb through the stack. A couple of cards down, a gold embossed FBI shield caught his attention. Special Agent Bantner. He grabbed a pen and jotted down the number.

"Mind if I stay here for a bit?"

"You have anything you want to share?"

Who could he trust?

Joey perused Ernie's body language, looking for any signal, a flicker of the eye, a tick of the jaw, a twitch of a finger—anything to indicate deceit. Good people wound up in bad situations sometimes. Small town deputies and mayors were no exception. "You know these things take time. I'm still trying to put pieces together."

"If you find something, the mayor would like to be kept in the loop."

Sam must have pushed some buttons hard enough to get noticed. Knowing his brother, he pushed harder and harder, refusing help, enjoying the thrill of single-handedly solving a big case. Joey wanted to find Sam's killer, but didn't want to make the same mistakes. He'd been trained by some of the best and wasn't about to become someone's target. He had time. The rest of his life kind of time.

"That's a good idea. When I have something worth sharing, I'll be sure to schedule a meeting."

Ernie nodded an approval. "I'll call on the lab files again, see if I can't get them expedited."

"Perfect."

Ernie disappeared through the door before Joey pulled out Sam's chair and slowly lowered his body onto the leather high-back. *Okay, bro, fess up. What were you playing at here? I'm getting closer. I can feel it. I just need a little more help.* He tapped on the piece of paper with the Special Agent's quickly scribbled number.

Why not?

He lifted the handset and dialed. "Hello, Special Agent Bant-ner? This is Detective Gaccione."

"From Denver, right?" the deep, concise voice responded.

"Actually, no. I'm Joe Gaccione from the Seattle Detective Division. I think you might have been talking to my brother, Sam Gaccione. He was killed several days ago, and I'm hoping you might be able to tell me what he was working on."

The accentuated pause on the other line made his pulse pound in his ears.

"Sorry to hear about your brother. He called about FBI activity in the area."

Odd. "Do you have agents working on the case in the area?" *Was Sam working with you?*

"I'm not at liberty to say. That's classified. But your brother had some interesting theories. If I were you, Detective, I would watch your back. Loop me in if you discover anything. Call anytime."

Joey's stomach started to churn, and he wondered if he might have to revisit his morning's granola bar. *That's just great. Everyone wants to be kept in the loop, but won't reciprocate.* "Fair enough. Thanks for the warning."

He hung up and sank farther into the chair. *Who did you trust that you shouldn't have, Bro?*

For some reason, Mara popped into his mind. He could trust her.

"I thought I heard your voice." Stella released the doorframe and walked into the office to take a seat in one of the two guest chairs. "You look good behind that desk."

An ambush. The muscles at the base of his neck and shoulders seized. "Yes, but I already have a desk in Seattle." *And, with the last name Gaccione, I don't need another desk or a target pinned to my back, and I certainly don't want Mara to be a target.*

"Your response just means we'll have to try harder to get you to stay. I found some money in the budget. Just say the word, and I'll put through the budget reallocation proposal at the next committee meeting."

"The team I'm currently working on is counting on my help. My boss wants me home. Maybe you can spend some of that newly found money to fix equipment."

Eighteen hours before Pia had called to give him the news, the stalker had taken it upon himself to hack his last victim into pieces, creating a mosaic of body parts. The sight of the walls splattered with blood and human remains haunted his dreams, and made the bile in Joey's stomach churn and pool at the back of his throat just thinking about it. His psychology degree meant he couldn't avoid envisioning the scene frame by frame by frame.

The rage of the perpetrator.

The terror of the victim.

Intuition is what made him good at his job. Damn good. It's what made his boss put him on some of the toughest cases, even if he was the youngest member of the team. It's also what made him unable to sleep at night and sometimes question what he did for a living.

During his annual assessment, he'd recently told the department psychologist that he was fine. Good thing the shrink hadn't looked too closely at Joey's definition of fine...as in, Freaked out, Insecure, Nervous and Emotional...FINE.

Yet, he *needed* to finish the job, because he just couldn't let the team down.

Stella stood and gave him a direct stare. "Just tell me we still have time to convince you otherwise."

"I'll be leaving town tomorrow, so I guess the answer has to be no."

"That's too bad. You would have made a great sheriff." She turned back at the door. "It's a glorious Colorado day outside. The sun is shining. An elk sauntered through my garden this morning. Maybe you should take a walk. Remember why the folks around here love this place. It's a great town."

"Still trying to change my mind?"

"Never hurts to try."

If she pushed any harder, she just might punch a hole straight through his willpower. He pocketed the piece of paper with the information he needed and gave some thought to his true desires. "Would you mind seeing if Ernie can forward me the lab results electronically?"

"Will do."

When Stella exited the office, his mind again turned to the business card in his hand.

FBI? Sam I got your message, but why would you be calling the FBI? And what type of activity would be classified?

Joey activated his cell phone contact list, scrolled through some names to his buddy on the Joint Task Force, and dialed.

"Chuck, hey, it's Joe Gaccione."

"Hey. It's been a while. What are you up to these days?"

"Funny you should ask. I've got a puzzle you might like to help me brainstorm."

"Yeah? Lay it on me."

"Colorado legalized marijuana. I'm trying to figure out if, or how, that might play into a small-town sheriff getting murdered for no apparent reason, and why the FBI may be involved, instead of the DEA. Got any ideas?"

"Let me do some poking around, see if I can track something down. You do know Colorado is a drug highway to Canada."

His gut tightened. "That's news to me."

"Small planes and hidden mountain runways make tracking air traffic difficult."

"Yeah, but drugs are still the DEA's problem, not an FBI issue. Maybe that's a good enough reason not to take the mayor up on his offer to become town sheriff."

"You'd get bored."

Bored? Maybe. Kidnapping, pornography, sex trafficking, tax evasion, counterfeiting, mail fraud. What else did the FBI deal in? He drummed his fingers on the desk, trying to remember. "You're probably right. I appreciate the information."

"Hey man, gotta run. I'll let you know if I find anything."

"Thanks." Joey tossed his cell on the desk and leaned back in the chair, thoughts racketing through his mind like a pinball bouncing from one place to another.

FBI. DEA. Sam's killer needed to be stopped.

If the deputies would just do their jobs, it was only a matter of time before the guy was apprehended.

Then again….

"Awesome-sauce. The parking lot's full." Kym's excitement didn't rub off.

Mara swallowed several times to keep from vomiting. A double dose of fear made her regret the day she promised Mad Jack she'd sing at the local pub. "It's just the end of the dinner crowd. Everyone will be leaving soon, before the music starts."

"I wouldn't count on it." Kym opened the pub's front door. The noise hit Mara like a blast of a jet about to take off.

Three songs. Just eleven minutes. That's all it is.

But those few short minutes generated opportunities for her to humiliate herself by forgetting lyrics or notes. Her fingers tightened around her guitar case handle. *You can do this. You've always wanted to sing for people. Now's your chance.*

"I need a drink," Mara said, stopping just inside the place.

"That's the way to do it. You *go*, girl!"

"I meant water." Mara crooked her mouth into a smile, and most likely crushed her friend's assumption she'd emerged from the safety box she'd lived in for the past six years. Risks. She needed to take more risks. Wasn't that what she'd been telling herself that past several months? Wasn't that why she'd had sex with Joey? No more regrets. "Maybe a glass of wine wouldn't kill me."

"No, a glass or two might just do you good."

Mad Jack's sounded way too crowded for a usual Saturday. Large screens televising basketball, football and hockey hung in various places, depending on a person's preference. Tony had been all excited when the pool tables and dartboards were updated a few years back, not that the games made a difference to her. The smell of buffalo burgers and garlic-seasoned fries made her mouth water. She wished now she hadn't given Buddy a night off. If she embarrassed herself, she'd want a way to get out of here, pronto.

Kym led her to the far corner where a small stage and dance floor accommodated different types of regional bluegrass, country and rock gigs throughout the week.

"Mara, you made it."

Jack's deep, gravelly voice and an emphasis on the *M* in Mara contributed to his verbal profile. Mad Jack had owned the pub for as long as she could remember. A Harley rider back in his day, rumor had it he'd ridden into Elkridge one stormy afternoon, and decided he'd had enough of the sleet, hail and rambling from job to job, dropped his kickstand and stayed.

"Hey, Jack. It's busy tonight."

"You can thank Kym for that. The fliers around town helped."

Mara yanked her arm out of Kym's grip. "You didn't."

"Now, don't be getting pissy about things already done. Who better to support you than your friends? Besides, the bigger the crowd, the bigger your three-percent paycheck."

Well, poop on a stick. She did need the money, and singing on stage had always been her dream—at least in theory. "If I suck, at least I won't have to see everyone cringe. Maybe, I should just record my songs and try to put them on YouTube."

"Would you stop! You love to sing. And you wanted to

thank the residents for supporting you and the flower shop by singing a few songs. You're going to be great. Let's get you oriented to the stage and then get some grub. I'm starved."

"There's a news flash. Where does your tiny body put all that food?"

"Action-packed days, baby. If I had one of those step-tracker thing-a-ma-jigs, I bet I'd clock ten miles easy."

Mara slid her foot forward to find the stage and set her guitar on the edge. "Why don't you go order dinner? I'm not hungry."

"Talk about yummy." The way Kym stretched the phrase like a piece of warm caramel indicated she'd suddenly become distracted by eye candy—the zero-calorie kind.

"No, you can't go there. You promised to be my escort tonight."

"No problem. I might be off duty in about thirty seconds because your yumminess is headed this way."

As Mara stood there trying to piece together what Kym meant, all possible options ceased when a familiar squeak provided the answer. She grabbed the back of the nearest barstool.

"Ladies. Rumor has it there's live music tonight. Thought I would drop by."

Drop by, my Aster. Her dry and tangled tongue prevented her from responding.

Kym grabbed her by the arm, effectively keeping her feet anchored in place. "We were just about to order some dinner. Want to join us?"

"We were?" Mara asked.

"I had dinner at my folks', but I can join you. Let me get my beer. I left it over by the pool tables. Tony and Gina are playing, and everyone's making bets."

"On who's going to win?" Mara managed to choke out, even though she knew the answer. Gina hardly ever lost.

"No. On when Gina is going to deliver. She's barely able to get that protruding belly close enough to the table to use the pool stick, so betting on the pool game wouldn't be fair."

Kym placed her dinner order with Jack and then escorted her to the pool tables, where a large number of voices laughed and taunted the players. Mara could decipher Tony and Gina's voices, as well as Jenna from the bakery, Harold and Claudia from the Value-Stop grocery store, and another female, possibly Gwen from the Second Time Around thrift store. Her frayed nerves unwound a bit more.

"She's here." Gina stopped playing to hug Mara. "Hey, Kym. Tony says you're next up."

"Who's winning?" Mara asked.

"I was until the baby got in the way. Tony's thinking he's going to kick Joey's butt next."

"He can try. But I sincerely doubt it's going to happen." Joey's smug voice gave her a triple-shot of glee. *Go, Joey.*

Tony boomed from across the room, "Want to put some money on it?"

"It would be cruel to take your money, Jock-o-boy."

The audience let out a rowdy set of jeers, hoots, hollers and the deliciousness of family and community made her smile, until the scent of a familiar aftershave pummeled her senses.

"You should smile more often," Joey whispered into her ear. The heat sent a shiver to her toes, reminding her how his naked body felt against hers.

"Do you two need somewhere private?" Tony asked in a not-so-private tone.

Heat from the social spotlight beamed down on her, and her cheeks burned.

Kym's arm, the one she'd been holding onto, disappeared when her friend marched forward. "Tony, quit being an ass, even though I know it's your natural state of being."

"Easy there, tiger." Joey's commanding tone caused conver-

BLINDED

sations to halt. "We don't need to extend those claws. Tonight's supposed to be fun."

Kym meowed, then purred like a cat, then hissed. Typical Kym.

"My beer has disappeared." Joey said above the crowd noise. I'm going to get another. You two want anything?"

"Water for me," Mara said.

"A lager would be great." Kym snuggled up to her ear. "Isn't that cute? Him being all protective."

"Please stop poking. He's leaving for Seattle tomorrow. I overheard a conversation with his boss. I think he's demanding Joey return to work. Something about being short-handed." Her statement had revealed more than was prudent, evidenced by Kym's contemplative silence. Mara didn't want to discuss Joey or the intimate deliberations still whirling a hundred miles an hour in her head, making thinking about anything else almost impossible. "I'm going to warm up and see if I can remember the words to the songs I'm supposed to sing."

"Don't sneak off to a corner. I promise to be on my best behavior."

Best behavior. Don't think so. Kym never could keep her feet going in a straight line. That was why Mara adored her friend and never wanted her to change. During the past twenty-plus years, her friend's rebelliousness had rubbed off on her in small, sometimes unpredictable ways.

Wasn't tonight her little piece of rebellion?

If her parents had still been alive, they would have found ways to talk her out of playing at the local bar, but they weren't around to direct her life. Not anymore. So their opinion didn't count. She needed to stop being so afraid. Keep taking chances. Like being with Joey. Otherwise, she'd end up living a very safe and very empty life.

Mara rallied her courage. "I want you to have fun, too.

181

Enjoy yourself. I'm going to light up that stage tonight, just for you. You'll see."

"Wow. Who kidnapped my friend and replaced her with this confident person?"

"I always have confidence. It's just when it comes to my singing, it decides to play hide-and-seek."

But that wasn't entirely true.

Somehow, over time, the unbendable steel bar of courage had slipped away into the darkness. Blindness did that to a person. However, blindness didn't equate to irreparably damaged. Tonight she would prove it. She managed to find a quiet corner to listen to the friendly game of pool until Joey beat Tony. Tony, convinced the win was a fluke, challenged Joey again with the same result.

"For those who ordered, your food's up," Jack's voice finally announced.

"Didn't you order a salad?" Mara affectionately tapped Kym's fingers when she wrapped her hand around her forearm. "Dinner can wait a bit. Go kick my brother's ass in a game of pool. Show him how it's done. I can manage."

Only a fraction of a second ticked by before Kym yelled, "Rack em' up, Tony." Kym pulled her closer to whisper in her ear. "At the end of the bar there are a couple of free stools. Go straight past the pool tables and keep on truckin'. Joey ordered onion rings, and I got you some potato skins."

"You didn't—"

"My treat. Now go have fun and stop worrying."

Mara's spirits lifted, giving her the courage to put away the self-defeating chatter tromping around in her head. She could get on that stage and sing to a crowd of people. She could do it. Now, if only she could walk to the bar without knocking someone's drink over.

Finding an empty barstool, she hopped on.

"Mind if I join you?"

Joey's question sent a waterfall of giddiness down her back. "Sure. Your onion rings should be here somewhere. It's this plate...I think." She pointed to her right.

"You and your gold-medal sniffer. Has to be the best around."

Her sniffer required intense training after her swollen and bleeding brain had stopped sending signals from the occipital lobe. Doctors focused first on physical conditioning to get her walking again. Comparably, sensory therapy was a snap. She pulled her plate closer and felt around for the silverware roll. Finding it, she unrolled the set.

"When one sense is lost the others start compensating. You should try putting on a blindfold one of these days. I bet you'll smell more than you expect."

"I still want you to teach me sensory identification." Joey reached over her shoulder to take an onion ring.

"There's not much time, since you're leaving tomorrow."

The chewing sound slowed, then stopped. A plate scraped across the counter. "Don't remind me. My boss doesn't like to take 'no' for an answer."

"I'm sure he needs your help."

"Yeah. The job commitments I can't escape, but being home —spending time with you—with family. Being in Elkridge again...isn't what I imagined."

"Why? Because you assumed time stopped when you left, and it would be the same when you returned?" she asked, already knowing that's what he assumed. His silence proved her right. "It's not like you were never coming back. Now you know it's not so bad, maybe you'll visit more often."

"I can call too, you know."

"Not if we don't have each other's phone numbers."

A tug at the back of her jeans meant her phone had been lifted with the finesse of a pickpocket. "Here, put in your passcode. I'll program my number into your phone. You can call me anytime you like."

With her finger, she drew half of a letter M to open her phone, then handed her cell off. The giddiness of a "boy" giving her his number escalated, then dissipated.

Just her bad luck.

She'd finally found a guy with a steady job, a good family, who was a virtual sexual superman in bed, and accepted her—blindness and all—yet, he was leaving. Not only was he leaving, but he also lived in a completely different state. After tomorrow, she wouldn't be able to touch those glorious muscles or smell his luscious scent. She wouldn't be able to look forward to him popping up at the grocery store or the animal shelter or along the city streets. She wouldn't be able to hear his easy laugh or his dry humor. She would miss him, the same way she missed seeing the sun rise each morning. He'd become a cherished part of her life.

"Here's your phone." He placed the iPhone in her hand. "When's the singing supposed to start?"

"Now," Jack said before she could answer. "Otherwise the next band's going to get on stage."

"Jeez, Jack." She lifted her water glass, trying to soak away her nerves.

"Don't blame me if the crowd gets hostile. People are here because of you." Jack tapped her wrist. "Performers get free food. How about I give those potato skins to Tony, and I make you a fresh burger after you sing. How's that sound?"

"Holy, crap, Jack. You sure know how to heap on the pressure."

Pressure. She didn't like pressure. She never performed well under pressure. A warm hand covered hers just as her mind began to implode.

"Relax. You got this," Joey said, releasing the emergency

valve and reminding her to be brave enough to fill the emptiness in her life with good things, positive things, fun things.

"I'd better warm up," she finally managed to squeeze out, pushing her untouched hamburger aside.

She made her way down to the end of the bar and stage. A mixture of encouraging voices, shouts, and good wishes followed her. A few hands reached out to pat her on the back as she walked by.

Opening her guitar case, she rediscovered the solid grounding music provided. Music. A place she could always go, no matter what life demanded. A quietness of mind descended. The noise of the crowd, the negative voices in her head—everything—became tranquil.

Kym appeared at her elbow. "There's a mic and a barstool on stage, just like you requested."

"Thank you."

With her guitar in hand, Mara lifted to her toes and slid onto the barstool, settled back and adjusted the mic. Strumming a few cords, she adjusted the tension on the strings, letting the remaining rigidity in her body slide away.

Relax. You can do this.

The images of her parents and sister appeared, then Joey, moody boy who didn't smile often. She wanted to sing to *that* boy, the one who'd become her friend, a kind and gracious man.

"Hi, everyone. Thanks for joining me to celebrate tonight. Most of you know about the car accident that took my parents and sister six years ago. However, five years ago today, the doctors finally released me from physical therapy. After the accident, the doctors told me I might never walk again, but here I am, walking onstage."

Whoops and hollers filled the room. Embarrassment made her blink and blush. "Thank you. I hope you like what I picked for y'all. This first one is for you."

CHAPTER SIXTEEN

orgeous. Joey couldn't be more in awe of Mara.

G   She sat onstage, spine straight, chin lifted. Right there. There was the sparkle he'd been waiting to see. That glimmer of transcendence he saw back in high school when she took the stage for the talent contest. Singing made her sparkle like the North Star.

After the first line of the song, the audience grew silent, stunned by her talent. Joey already knew how well Mara could sing, but wow, his jaw still dropped open. *Hello, lady.* Gone was the unsure adolescent voice, replaced with the rich, sexy, full range of the woman.

He loved the song choice, and obviously, so did the rest of the audience. In fact, he loved everything. The way her hair framed her face, the way her body expressed the song, the way her skin glowed in the stage lights. If she could only see the crowd, she would know her full effect. Then again, seeing all the familiar faces might make her more nervous. The song beat thrummed, bounced and weaved through the audience.

"Impressive," a familiar voice said close to his ear.

"Ma? Pia? What are you doing here?"

Pia gave him a friendly shove. "Scoot around. Franco's parking the car. One of the regulars at the restaurant said Mara would be here tonight. I figured that's why you suddenly had plans. We don't often take a night off. A night on the town sounded fun. We wanted to give Mara our support."

Maybe Sam's death provided his family a new perspective after all. Never had his family been so supportive of anything he cared about.

His mother gave him a hug around the waist. "A mother knows her son's heart."

That transparent?

"Where are the kids?" he asked.

Pia pulled out a chair when Franco arrived. "A babysitter's watching the kids. Camilla's watching the restaurant. She said to tell you she's sorry that she's been so distant lately."

A young waitress, barely keeping her tray horizontal, slid four beers onto the high-top table.

Pia tapped his forearm. "One of those is for you."

He stared at the amber-filled glass and then at his mother.

"What?" She sat up a bit taller and pushed her shoulders back. "Don't give me the hairy eyeball. After I've raised five kids, I believe I deserve a beer."

"It's not that. I've just never seen you drink casually."

"*You* raise five kids and see if there's room in your budget for indulgences. Then you can judge."

He wasn't judging. In fact, he liked seeing the softer side of the dragon. "Speaking of kids. I've been meaning to ask. Sam's property is in a nice area. Will it need to be sold?" *In other words, how did he afford it in the first place?*

The sudden sadness in his mother's eyes made him loathe the question, but he had to ask.

"Sam purchased the property in a tax sale, then worked with a local building contractor to bring the place up to code, although your brother did most of the work. He spent every spare moment he could on that house." The sorrow etched into her eyes and mouth deepened. "You should know your brother left the house to you."

"Me? Why me?"

"I think it was his way of tying you to Elkridge. Secretly, he was hoping you'd come home one day. You should know Camilla wanted to take over the loan payments before we found Sam's will. You might have gotten some backlash from her disappointment the past few days."

So that's why she's been a little testy. "I'll talk to her before I leave. The house is hers if she wants it. I don't need a house or anything other than family to bring me home."

His mother's hand covered his, just as Mara's final chord strummed. The crowd erupted with whistles and shouts of support.

"Thank you." Mara strummed her fingers along the strings, adjusting the pitch. "Thank you very much. This next song is one of my favorites. I think you'll understand why."

She closed her eyes and her body began to sway, her hand poised. The strings hummed along. Joey's body was ensnared by the rhythm as he tried to determine the tune. Then he knew. *Her parents.* The chorus to "One Moment More" filled the room. Mindy Smith would have been proud of Mara's rendition. Intense emotion made Mara's vocals gritty, especially when she pleaded for her parents not to go, to wait, to give her another moment more.

The image she created. The tender ache of loss.

He understood. *Sam.* He was gone.

The tender spot was still fresh. Did he believe he would see his brother again? His mother's hand reached for his under the table, as her other hand dabbed at her eyes with a crumpled handkerchief.

His sister wrapped an arm around his mother's shoulders while she reached for the tissue packet in her purse.

Joey leaned closer to his mother. "Love you, Ma."

She placed a hand on his cheek. "You're a good boy, Joey. A mother doesn't have favorites, but if I did, it would be you. You're the only one I didn't have to worry about. You always knew what you wanted, and you made a plan to get it."

Favorite? Was that true? All his life he'd struggled while watching his siblings get more than their fair share of attention. Until today, he'd resented the fact.

"But you're disappointed I'm not staying."

"Disappointed in you? No. I'm disappointed for us. You're a natural leader, Joey. People trust you. Look to you for guidance. This town needs someone like you."

"But I thought—"

"Always the thinker. You go, Joey. Be happy. All a mother wants is her children to be happy and healthy."

Mara's song drifted toward a slow conclusion. She couldn't see, but he swore the woman on the stage looked straight at him as she finished the last line.

The smart woman was right. Your parents seem proud of you not for the position or the title of your job, but the fact that you are giving back to your community. Go figure.

He had to leave. The ache of leaving family, leaving her, finally sank in.

The crowd grew silent. No one moved. Mesmerized, like he was. Looking at her. So beautiful. So brave and confident. The sexiest woman in the room with her fitted cotton shirt. Jeans hugged her slender figure. Maroon clogs hinged over the bottom rung of the chair, keeping the beat.

Finally, the crowd let her know how much her song meant. The roar of the place grew louder and louder, a few people even standing to show their appreciation.

God, he wished she could see the effect she had on people.

"Thank you," Mara said into the microphone. "I appreciate

you coming to hear me tonight. I have one more song before Jack kicks me off the stage."

Someone booed, and several people in the crowd laughed, and she lit the stage with her smile. The urge to take her somewhere to make love all night grew. But he couldn't go there. He was leaving tomorrow, and she'd think he just wanted sex. That's the last thing he'd want her to think about their special bond.

"Given this is my five-year anniversary, I can see my future a bit more clearly, and I'm looking forward to knowing there are blue skies ahead."

Strumming the opening notes to *I Can See Clearly Now*, he celebrated her song choice. *That's the way, Mara. Your rain is surely gone.*

"What are you smiling about?" Pia asked.

"Look around the room. I've only ever known one person who gives more than she takes. Look at her."

"That's just because you're in love with her."

He tore his gaze from Mara to look at Pia. "You may be right. I think I've loved her all my life."

"You're just now figuring that out, Joey?" his mother chastised, yet in a kind, teasing tone of voice. "I thought I raised you smarter than that."

When Mara's last song ended, he stood and kissed his mother on the cheek. "Thanks for coming." He let his sincerity soak in before he continued, "I'm going to see if Mara wants to walk home."

The looks he got from Pia and Franco he would accept because they were probably thinking the same thing. *He's a goner.*

Hanging back, he let the congratulators have their moment, because he wanted to steal all the rest of her moments. His intention had been to hang out at the bar, listen to the next band play, find more clues, but those ideas drifted away. The tired glaze starting to shutter her eyes made him change plans.

What if he changed his plans? Mara certainly didn't need him to prove anything. He'd already proven to himself that he was capable. He didn't need to prove his worth to anyone else.

At last he reached the front of the line. "You were amazing."

"I did it. I actually sang on stage." Mara reached out, and he placed a hand in hers. "You saying that means a lot."

"Hungry? You only ate a little."

It was only a little past nine, and he wanted to stay with her as long as possible. All night, if she'd let him just to hold her until he had to go.

"I asked Jack to make me a burger to go. I shouldn't have let my nerves consume all my energy. When the excitement wears off, I think I'll want to crash. It's best we say goodbye here."

Desperate to hold onto the moment, he loosened his grip finger by finger, letting go of the disappointment. "Next time you sing, it'll be easier." The conviction in his voice belied the depression that suddenly swamped him.

"I don't plan on there being a next time. I don't have a music sheet put together for any more sessions."

"Don't tell me you're going to do the one-and-done thing." The push of a strand of hair behind her ear, and her nervous laugh gave him insight. "Seriously? Music is part of who you are, Mara."

"Yes, but you and Kym are the only ones who know that. Let's keep it a secret among friends."

Friends? He didn't want to be her friend. Not true. He did, but he wanted to be much more. A sudden stir of activity across the room drew his attention.

Mara sensed the distraction. "What's going on?"

About to check, Joey paused when Kym came racing across the room and slid to a stop. "It's time."

"Are you ready to leave?" Mara tilted her head, a soft relief spreading across her face. "Good, me too."

"No! It's delivery time. You're going to be an aunt."

"Gina is not due for a couple more weeks." Mara stood and took a step back at the same time…and about fell off the stage. "Don't let them go yet. Please, help me get to Gina. And tell that knucklehead brother of mine to get the van."

Not liking the dismay in Mara's features, Joey decided to take over and lifted her into his arms. "Hang on tight." He plowed his way through bodies. "Coming through, folks."

Gina sat calm and cool while the world erupted around her. Joey stopped inches from the huffing and puffing woman gripping the sides of her chair and squinting her eyes. Mara tilted her head back, most likely wondering why they had stopped. He didn't want to explain they'd reached their destination because he'd have to let her go, and didn't want to. To have Mara's head inches from his chin, her body cradled in his arms, her arms wrapped around his neck felt amazing. So good, he hesitated another second before releasing her legs.

"Gina?" Mara reached out.

"I'm having a baby. Where the hell is the asshole who did this to me?"

CHAPTER SEVENTEEN

G ina took Mara's hand in a crushing grip.
"Tony will be here soon," Mara said gently. "You just
need to hold on."

She had no idea where Tony was, but she'd do or say whatever was necessary to keep Gina calm. The nearest hospital was
forty minutes away, thirty if Tony drove. She could feel the
heat of concerned bodies forming a semicircle around her
sister-in-law. "Breathe, Gina. You've got to breathe."

Mad Jack suddenly appeared at her side. "Gina? Describe
your contractions."

"Four, maybe five minutes. Sharp." Gina groaned.

Mad Jack, the town's search and rescue coordinator, carried
a first aid kit complete with blood pressure monitor and other
medical equipment. "Keep breathing. You're fine. I want to
make sure you're not just experiencing prodromal labor."

"English, Jack. Speak English." Gina's growl made Mara
wonder if she actually was fine. She didn't sound fine.

"Your doctor probably explained to you about first-timers.
You wouldn't want to travel all the way to Denver just to turn
around and come back home. That would be hard on Tony."

"Screw Tony."

"Honey, we already did that." Tony had picked the most inopportune moment to return and inject a bit of humor, but Mara had trouble stifling a snicker.

The squeak of Joey's shoe heightened her awareness of movement. "Hand me that beer mug, Gina," Joey said. "You don't need to be throwing things. You have plenty of time to bash Tony over the head later."

"Let's get you up and walking," Jack recommended, and Gina groaned again.

"I'm going to rip this place apart if we don't get moving toward the hospital."

"Yep, I'd say it's time to go," Jack agreed.

Gina didn't let go of Mara's hand, but eased off the stool to stand. "Oh, oh, oh, here comes another one."

Mara could feel the straining and tightening of Gina's muscles through the quivering tension of Gina's hand. Not knowing what to do to help gnawed at her patience. "Tony? We need to get Gina to the van."

Tony placed a hand on her shoulder to let her know where he was. She leaned in and whispered, "Gina? Don't kill my brother, even though I know you want to right now. And call me if you need me. I'll be waiting by the phone." She moved aside to let Tony take her place.

The center of activity moved away, leaving her behind, like a bit of debris floating to the ground after a windstorm. An intense sadness replaced the fearful joy. She couldn't go with them. She would be in the way. So many things she'd missed, and the birth of her nephew would be just another one to put on the pile.

A large, gentle hand landed on her lower back, soothing the raging stream of emotions. "Are you okay?" Joey's kind concern penetrated her dour reflections.

"My parents are going to miss the birth of their first grandbaby." She attempted to lighten the morose feeling with a smile but failed. "Don't mind me. It's been an emotional day."

"Let's get you some food and take you home."

"Kym's going to take me home." *You're too tempting.* "She should be around here somewhere." She listened for her friend's loud, high-pitched voice. It had disappeared.

"Jack won't let Tony drive. He's had too much to drink, so Kym's going to drive them to the hospital."

Great. My best friend gets to go, but not me. I swear someday I'm going to punch the Fate Faerie and give her a black eye. "I need to get my guitar."

She stretched her hands out in front of her and started toward the stage.

The roller coaster of life never seemed to end. Up one minute, with a loop-de-loop, then a spiral around and down. She should be used to the unsettling feeling by now. But she wasn't. The downward, belly-churning slide got faster and steeper every time.

Wrestling into her coat, she lifted her guitar and grabbed the dinner to-go bag. Joey eased the guitar from her hand, then escorted her to the door. The walk down the street with him leading the way settled her sadness. She embraced the silence. The night's sounds helped mollify her resentment about not going to the hospital. Mara had been prepared to stay behind and run the store until the moment when the decision became reality. She hadn't realized how much staying behind would hurt.

Joey led her across the street and then turned right. She slowed her normal pace to an almost- crawl, not wanting the evening to end, needing to postpone the unavoidable as long as possible. She lifted her face skyward. "The wind has picked up. That means the stars are out."

"Yes, they are. The Big Dipper is really bright tonight." Joey must have glanced her way because the pattern of his footsteps changed. He moved behind her and tilted her head back against his shoulder. "There," he whispered. "There's the northern star."

Mara could almost see the constellation. She'd looked at it so many times when she had her sight. The firm support of his body holding her, almost allowed her to let go. Lean on him. She was so tired of being self-sufficient. But in a few hours, he wasn't going to be available to prop her up. He might as well be on another planet.

"Thank you." She took a step out of his arms.

"My pleasure." He returned to her side. They walked a few minutes more before turning the corner into the alley. "Here we are. Just another few feet."

Another layer of disappointment heaped onto the pile. The time with him had come to an end.

"What time is your flight tomorrow?"

"Just after eight. I'll be leaving before the sun's up. I could come up for a few minutes."

"It's been a long, emotional day for me, and I'm tired. But I'm glad we got to spend time together. I think it's best to say good-bye now." She hoped the ache in her heart didn't suddenly show on her face. Keeping her secret hidden—the fact she didn't want him to leave, ever—drained the rest of her emotional reserves. She swallowed a couple of times, trying to stop the loneliness from choking her.

"Mara, if—"

"No," she reached a hand, aiming for his lips, but connected lightly with his jaw instead. "Oh sorry." She slid her hand down to his chest to feel his heart beat one last time. "You have to keep your promise. No strings attached. No regrets. Remember?"

"I should have never agreed. I'm going to miss you." His voice held a bit of a croak that hadn't been there before.

"I'll miss you too. Be sure to stop by the next time you're in town." She felt her brave slipping and quickly dug out the keys from her pocket to unlock the rear entrance door. Turning the key in the lock, she pushed the door open, not wanting to go in, but unable to find a reason to stand out in the cold night air.

"I put your guitar just inside the door. And here's your dinner." The edge of the paper bag nudged against the palm of her hand. "Where's Buddy?"

"I locked him in the apartment. Lately when he gets bored, he's been digging in the plants."

"Ah," Joey said.

The awkwardness choked off everything she wanted to say, but she had to say something. "Have a good life, Joey. Be kind to yourself," she finally managed.

Warm lips caressed her cheek, and the ache expanded.

"Mara, I—"

"Shhhh. Joey. Don't. Please, no what-ifs. I'm thankful for the time we shared. For the last few days, I haven't felt so blind. That's a wonderful gift."

"You're a beautiful woman, Mara. And you're more capable than most. I don't see you as blind. I only see your giant can-do spirit."

"I've gotta go," she managed through the choking heartache. "Have a good life, Joey."

No longer able to maintain her composure, she slipped inside and slowly closed and locked the door. Her dark world got darker. Insecurities lashed at her spirit, questioning, making her wonder whether anyone, ever, would love her.

She pulled her arms out of the sleeves, heaved her heavy wool coat up to hang on the hooks and then placed her keys on the rack by the back door. When she leaned over to retrieve her guitar case, she heard a sound.

"Who's there?" A silent alarm started ringing in her head.

"Hello, Daisy."

She froze. The nickname and C-range tenor tone she

recognized even through the slurred words. The hard *Z* in Daisy and the sharp tang of bourbon spelled danger.

Her laid-back and sometimes lazy ex-fiancé could get a bit too intense when he drank. Booze transformed stable into irrational and jealous. Add anger, and the unreasonable turned into dangerous.

"What are you doing here, Mark?" she asked while slowly moving toward the door, hoping she could get it unlocked before he stopped her. Maybe she could get to her purse and pepper spray. She took a step back, her shoulders pressing against the light switch, turning on the upstairs apartment lights. She prayed someone would see the light and investigate, since she didn't need light. She rarely touched the switch.

Suddenly, he blocked her path, ending her attempt. The stench of his breath combined with alcohol choked off her air. "Don't even try it."

"What do you want?" She turned her head away from his foul, rotten-egg smell before she gagged.

"I saw you with your new boyfriend." He leaned closer.

Mark dined on weakness and fear. She refused to feed his desires and willed her body to ease into a calmer state. "You're using. Drugs will kill you, Mark." Even though she did her best to stay neutral, she heard the disappointment in her voice. "You said you had a great marketing job lined up. The plan was to go to Los Angeles, make some good money and then get your college degree. What happened?"

"Enough questions." He pounded the wall behind her, and she flinched. He laughed, pleased by her involuntary reaction. "I came for cash."

The word *cash* shortened her breath. The hammering of her heartbeat in her ears beat like a clock ticking away seconds.

She'd placed the cash for tomorrow's flower delivery in a coffee can by the rear door. Thank God Mark didn't know the new procedure. If she'd purchased the fireproof safe Tony had recommended, the safe would have been open and the money already in Mark's pocket.

"I don't—"

"Don't play games." A hand tightened around her elbow and yanked. "I know you got cash. Just give it to me, then maybe you and I can have some fun, like old times. Would you like that?"

She shriveled away from his touch. "There's cash in the register," she hedged.

Mara grabbed a set of keys from the hooks and turned on the storefront lights, leaving the interior lights off, hoping a deputy or someone driving by might again question the lights and investigate. Thankfully, Mark didn't notice the change when she made her way from the work area to the register. Adrenaline exploded through her system. Her tongue had gone dry and made swallowing difficult.

Certain the one hundred dollars in small bills and change wouldn't be enough to buy a fix, she contemplated hitting him over the head with one of the larger vases. History had proved Mark's temper would get worse when he didn't get what he wanted.

Think, Mara, think.

Her chest thudding with frightened urgency, she opened the register drawer and took a step back, her other hand frantically searching for something large enough to crack his skull.

Stay calm, breathe.

Mark's low growl sounded just behind her. "I know you have more cash." He fisted her hair and yanked it, hard. Pain triggered her sharp gasp. "Don't mess with me, Mara. I'm not in the mood."

He shoved her into a table. Six-inch plants went crashing to the floor. Behind her, the sound of more inventory hitting the floor made her gasp. Fear paralyzed any additional response. She couldn't move.

"Tell me! Where's the cash?"

"You have it."

"You're lying." Loud crashes to the left and right sounded like bombs going off. "Keep this up and there'll be nothing left of your sweet little store."

Sensing movement, she threw up her hands to protect where her skull had been damaged on the back of her head. The doctor's warning echoed through her mind.

Another blow might kill you.

Protect your head—always.

"All right. All right. Stop. There's more money in the back."

"That's what I thought."

Mark gave her a hard shove, and she barely managed to stay on her feet. Another crash—this time glass shattering. The inventory. Minimal insurance. Her business. Gone. She asked herself why she hadn't just given him the money.

Because he would come back. Again. And again. Never stopping. I'm not his bank account. Not anymore.

Reaching the back room, she paused, thinking if only she could use her phone, call for help. But the backlight—cell phones had backlights. That would give her away.

"Stop stalling. I want the cash now." He sounded frantic. He shoved her forward and she stumbled, grabbing the counter just in time to avoid banging her forehead on the sharp, laminated edge.

Out of options, she reached for the coffee tin just when the rear door exploded off its hinges.

CHAPTER EIGHTEEN

After hitting the door at full speed, Joey felt searing pain roll down his arm and across his back, but he wouldn't think about that now. He only had one thing on his mind.

Save Mara.

The light from the alley made it easier to see the knife held to her throat.

Joey held his hands in front of him, showing the man he had no weapon, wishing for the Glock normally holstered on his hip.

The man was thin. Too thin, and the stench, the greasy matted hair and scruffy facial stubble told him the addict hadn't bothered to bathe recently.

"Easy. Deputies are on their way. Just put the knife down. You don't want to make this worse."

The thin man backed up. *Not good.* Joey moved away from the door, hoping the robber would do the easy, yet stupid thing, and go for the opening. The ploy worked. The guy started pulling Mara toward the door.

"Don't think I won't kill her."

"We don't have to go there. Put the knife down so we can talk."

Joey efficiently scanned the room, looking for potential weapons. When the drug addict's gaze shifted to the door, Joey's body automatically prepared to respond. The guy shoved Mara toward Joey, blocking his way, and escaped.

"Mara, you okay?"

She nodded, gulping. "Yes, go."

Joey raced to the alley but couldn't find any trace of the guy. He listened for a car, pounding footsteps, any noise to indicate the direction he'd gone. Nothing. Without a weapon, he wouldn't pursue the robber. Training discipline demanded no action. The guy's behavior, the clothing, all the clues indicated the guy wouldn't get far. Joey pulled his phone from his back pocket.

"Yes, this is Detective Gaccione again. I wanted to confirm there's been a robbery attempt at the Floral Shop on Main. The perp is about six feet tall, brown hair, wearing jeans and a dark-hooded sweatshirt."

"Joey?" Mara appeared in the doorway on her hands and knees. "Wait. I need to tell you."

"Stay where you are, Mara. There's glass everywhere."

"Tell the deputies they're looking for Mark Walters."

Mark Walters. The name filtered through his mind and several clues registered.

Son of Tom and Sarah Walters. The couple who'd been robbed during the funeral.

Was he also the guy stalking Mara?

Did Sam become a target because he investigated Mark for stealing from town members?

Could the murder, stalker and theft case possibly be solved?

"Yes, ma'am." Joey relayed. "I'm still here. The person you're looking for is Mark Walters. The situation here is secure. Thank you."

Joey shoved his phone in his back pocket. "We need to get you out of here."

"No." She stood up slowly, hands gripping the splintered doorframe with a determination that spelled out C.A.U.T.I.O.N.

"What do you mean, no?" *Woman, you damn near gave me a heart attack.* "This place is a mess. It's not safe."

"Joey, this is my home. My business. I'm not going anywhere. I need to understand the damage. I need to get the store cleaned up so I can open for business in the morning. We *can't* afford to be closed, even for half a day."

From the conviction in her voice, he would have assumed her unaffected, but then he saw her hands shake while rolling goose bumps spread up her arms. Then her facial muscles began to quiver.

Mara rotated with a whimper when she noticed the frenzied scratching at her apartment door. Anxiously waving her arms in front of her, she searched, reaching for any familiar object to navigate.

He caught up with her just as she reached the stairs. "Hold up."

She shoved at him. "Buddy!"

"Let me help. I'll get him. Just promise me you'll wait here and not move."

She grabbed the stair rail but went no farther. He raced up the stairs and opened the upper floor apartment door, catching the dog's collar before the seventy-pound animal could bolt past him. Buddy yanked his injured arm, triggering shards of intense pain slicing down his left side, halting his breath.

Everyone wants to protect Mara.

"Easy there, Buddy." *I can't lift you with my shoulder. Work with me here.* A couple of steps from the bottom, he released the dog's collar. Woman and dog immediately collapsed in each other's arms.

"Do you have a first aid kit?" Joey asked.

"I'm fine." She touched the nick on her neck from the guy's knife.

"There's blood on the stairs. I think Buddy ripped a nail trying to get to you. I think he bit the door handle as well."

"In the backpack by the door there's an emergency kit." Mara pulled the dog into her arms, searching his front limbs. Buddy whined in pain and squirmed, but she held him tight. She held her hand out for the supplies when Joey paused on the step below her.

"Mara, let me help," he murmured, taking her hand.

Her beautiful, blue, sightless eyes turned toward him. "Joey, I—"

"I know. It'll be okay."

"Joey." Her eyes opened wider. "I think Mark's the one who slashed your tires." She took a step. "I smelled spearmint that night when you went outside. I caught only a whiff, so the scent didn't completely register at the time. Mark chews spearmint gum, sometimes shoving stick after stick into his mouth. I bet if you look you'll find at least one wad of gum on your property."

"How do you know so much about this guy?"

"We were engaged."

Well, shit. "Good to know. I'll let the deputies handle the investigation. It's their job." *But will make damn sure they follow procedures.*

The sounds of sirens coming from the alley drew his attention.

He cupped a hand around her jaw. With his thumb, he rubbed off some dried blood. His heart ached when she leaned into his palm and closed her eyes, the physical connection clearly impacting her as much as him. "You're going to be okay."

Mara took a deep breath. "I know."

She gathered Buddy closer to her chest. Joey nestled beside her on the narrow bottom stair, studying her. Hair tumbled around her pale face. Spots of Buddy's blood covered her shirt and jeans. Her dog lifted his muzzle and licked Joey's face.

"Yes, I know, Buddy. You're going to be okay, too." Lifting a hand, he dished out plenty of pats to reassure the worried pooch.

Two deputies from the sheriff's department came through the door. Deputy Cunha introduced himself and Deputy Beaulieu, and gave him a cordial look when Joey flashed his badge. Little Napoleon, the guy with a slightly balding head and pursed lips, took a look around the shop.

Cunha whipped out a pad and pencil just as the paramedics arrived. Mara suffered through her medical exam as Napoleon hovered nearby listening as both Joey and Mara gave their statements.

"You say the intruder was Mark Walters. Are you certain?" Cunha asked.

Mara bristled. "Would you ask me that question if I wasn't blind? I have no doubt who held a knife to my throat. And I would be careful if I were you. He's desperate. He's looking for a fix. He needs money, and he only got what was in my register."

Joey wanted to ask how she knew so much about drug users, but he supposed most every small town across America had its fair share. "Do you know where this guy is?"

"Not yet. We've blocked the roads leading out of town. We believe he's still on foot. He won't get far," Cunha said, snapping his notebook shut and tucking away the pen. "I have enough for now. The deputy here will finish collecting evidence and take some pictures. Ma'am, you'll need to come to the station tomorrow to sign a statement since you can't approve it online. And you should find somewhere safe to stay tonight."

LYZ KELLEY

Buddy wriggled and stood. Mara pushed her foot forward, but a crunching noise made her pull back. She dropped her head into her hands. The blood on her hands from Buddy's feet smeared across her cheek while tears welled in her eyes.

"Mara, it's going to be all right." Joey promised with a conviction he hoped she could hold onto.

"Please don't make me leave. I don't want to stay some place I don't know, where I won't be able to find my way around or take care of Buddy."

The burn in his chest made him want to find Mark Walters and beat him raw for what he'd done, not only to his family, but Mara, and this town.

He put an arm around her shoulders. The shop might be a disaster zone, but he was finally beginning to understand. This building was her sanctuary. This number of steps to the sink. This number of blocks to the grocery store. This number of stairs to her bedroom. However, the back door now hung off broken hinges, and dozens of broken vases and potted plants lay scattered across the floor. Her apartment and store were no longer safe.

Her stubborn chin jutted, her spine straightened, her lips tightened. He turned his hand over to fold her tiny fingers in his. To get her out of the house, he'd probably have to pick her up and throw her over his shoulder, or worse, put her in hand-cuffs. At another time, under entirely different circumstances, handcuffs might be fun, but not now. She'd endured more than enough, and what she wanted was understandable and reasonable to a degree.

Her cold fingers grabbed his other hand. "Buddy needs to go out, but with the glass on the floor, he'll cut his feet."

"I'll carry Buddy so he can do his business, but with one non-negotiable condition. You let me call a couple of people to help secure your store. It's not safe for you to stay here."

"But—"

"I said non-negotiable."

"You've already done so much."

The deputy Joey had dubbed Napoleon spoke up. "I'll take the dog out. You're not going to lift much with that arm. You should get your shoulder looked at." Joey shot the little man a laser-pointed glare. "Just trying to be helpful," the officer added, and shrugged before zipping his jacket and bracing himself to lift the seventy-pound dog into his arms.

"What's wrong with your shoulder?" Mara asked, her hand reaching out and connecting with bruised and tender skin.

Joey sucked in a breath, unable to avoid an involuntary wince. "I ran into some trouble with a door. Seems it was locked, and I wanted to get inside. Please don't start fussing. I'll have someone take a look after I get a crew here to put this place in order. Just relax."

"Relax. Sure. My ex-fiancé just broke in, held me at knife-point, trashed the store and stole money I couldn't afford to lose. And I have a sister-in-law who's off delivering her first baby, and I can't be there because I'm blind. Relax, you say. I'll get right on that. See what I can do."

Buddy came bounding into the store, semi-favoring his right paw, and headed straight for Mara before anyone could stop him. Joey rechecked the dog's pads for additional cuts and glass and was relieved to find none.

"I'd better go get Buddy fed and see what I can do about his injured foot." Mara and her sad expression turned away. Her slow and steady footfall on the stairs to the apartment marked time to the rhythm of defeat. He waited at the bottom of the stairs until the upstairs door closed. Then he surrendered to the adrenaline depletion.

The two deputies stood in the smashed doorway. "Guys," Joey said, "thanks for coming."

Napoleon tapped on the door. "I've got an extra door in my garage from an unfinished basement." He studied the splin-

LYZ KELLEY

tered lock. "My wife's not going to miss tripping over the thing every time she walks in the garage. But I don't have a lock."

"Anything will help." He shook the deputies' hands before pulling the cell phone from his hip holster, wondering who he knew in town well enough, who, after ten years, might be willing to pick up a broom late on a Saturday night.

No one; that's who.

But it wasn't true. There was one person who could intimidate even a magpie into giving up its meal. Hitting his speed dial, he let the number ring.

"Hey, Ma. It's Joey. Need your help. Do you think Dad has a spare door lock lying around somewhere?"

With all his mother's interruptions, his three-minute story stretched to fifteen. In another twenty minutes, Franco arrived saying he couldn't find a spare lock. To Joey's amazement, word of Mara's need had spread like peanut butter on toast. All sorts of people showed up—people he knew, many he didn't.

Mara had called Tony to let him know what happened. Gina still hadn't delivered yet, and from the sounds of her progress, it would be a while.

Camilla and Kym arrived an hour later in the flower van, toting pizza, pasta and salad in containers that looked familiar —another gift from his ma.

At Kym's suggestion, Mara remained upstairs taking care of Buddy and soaking up some much-needed quiet time. Kym took command of the cleanup, since she had a good working knowledge of every inch of her friend's shop, while he and the others did the heavy lifting. Floors were swept, cabinets righted, doors repaired, and inventory salvaged.

Joey looked at the bottle of water in his hand. Every muscle ached, and his shoulder felt like someone had jabbed him with a hot poker. No way could he lift either arm high enough to take a sip of water from the plastic bottle.

"Are you going to hold that box in place with your butt all night?" Kym asked.

"I was considering it."

Kym kicked over a five-gallon bucket and sat next to him. "Got a question for you." She yanked on a pair of mittens and crossed her arms, holding off the shivers. The temperature in the store had dropped to barely above freezing since the door was busted. "We could have handled the cleanup. You didn't need to do this. Why are you still here?"

Kym, never one to be subtle, went straight for the jugular. *Why?* A question he'd been wrestling with since the first day he'd walked into this store.

"Ever heard the saying, 'protect and serve?' It's my job."

She pointed her half-inch lacquered nail, outlining the room. "This? This ain't no detective duty. You don't even work in this town. You went through a lot of hassle and expense to get your flight moved out another day. This, right here, is personal."

"What if it is?"

"I've known Mara since grade school. Me, I'm a cynical, bossy bitch. Have been since the age of two. That girl upstairs, she's an angel. Never had a bad word to say about nobody, even if they deserved it. She's got a giving heart. Gives you everything she's got until she's got no more. I don't want her to be hurt. She's been through enough."

Joey rubbed at the blister forming on his hand from sweeping, carrying and stacking. "I know she's too good for me. But when I'm with her, it's like I'm back on the soccer field. I've got the ball, and I'm heading for the net. There's no one else. Just me and the goalie. Two people. Wanting a victory." He rocked back on the stack of boxes. "I get what you're saying. I'll leave her be."

"Most guys need a brick upside the head, but I think, in your case, you need a whole house of bricks to flatten you. Did you know Mara's had a serious crush on you since seventh grade?"

"Really? I had no idea. I just thought—"

"Do me a favor, and don't think. You're bad at it. Just get your cute little rump up those stairs."

He heaved a massive sigh and straightened. "I can't stay. She knows that. So what could I say to make this situation better?"

"The shape you're in, you wouldn't need to say a thing. Knowing her, she'd take pity on your sorry ass and have you bundled up on the couch in eight minutes, tops. Besides, the bad guy is still out there, Tony's at the hospital, and she might like to have a friend around. Especially someone with a nice, big, bruised shoulder to lean on."

Joey never could figure out how Mara and Kym connected. They were as different as a Ford and Chevy. Somehow, though, the two had become each other's support system, even with the notion Kym's support came with some jagged edges. "It's late. I'll walk you to your car since it's probably still at Mad Jack's. Then I'll see about climbing those stairs."

"If you do decide to do some climbing, make sure you have some long-term intentions. Mara's loyal. She's liked you for a long time, and I get a feeling she'll wait if you give her a good reason. Just remember, my two older brothers and six cousins live within a days' drive of this place and will kick your ass if you act like a jerk."

Joey gave a quick nod. "Roger that."

CHAPTER NINETEEN

Mara closed her apartment door after being banished from the ground floor. She felt so useless, so bleak, a sinkhole of unhappiness opened in her chest. First the baby's arrival, now this. There were days she considered herself capable. Today wasn't one of them.

Kym had arrived about an hour after she had told Tony about the store and Mark. Tony had threatened to leave the hospital, but she wouldn't let him, which was most likely the reason Kym had arrived. Her friend had been up and down the stairs at least eighteen times, asking where display tables went, or if she could store the spilled dirt in a five-gallon bucket, or whether she should create a sign to sell the damaged flowers at a discount. Mara wanted to help, but no one would let her.

With the silence came feelings of abandonment and claustrophobia, strangling her air supply.

"Come on, Buddy, we need to go down and figure out where they put everything."

Her hand skimmed the wall on the way down the steep stairwell, keeping Buddy behind her. When she reached the bottom step, she searched the floor tentatively with her foot.

"So far, so good. I think it's safe."

Sliding her feet along the linoleum tile, she let Buddy pass and take the lead. She felt along the store's outer wall, surprised to encounter a solid door. She then made her way to the sink. Her mat, scissors, and knives had been returned to their proper places. Stacked buckets lined the far walls, ready for tomorrow's delivery, a delivery she luckily could afford since Mark hadn't gotten his hands on the coffee can money. The shelf above her head normally containing various shapes and sizes of vases was empty. She made a mental note to tell the deputies to update their case file with the damaged items. Hearing footsteps in the alley, she called Buddy to her, pulled a knife from the magnet board, crouched down, and pulled the dog behind a stack of buckets.

The door opened behind her. "Go away. I don't have anything you want."

"I wouldn't be so sure about that."

Her emotions pulled in opposite directions. She experienced relief for recognizing the voice and aggravation over the humor layered on top of the words. "I find nothing funny about this situation."

"If you want to defend yourself, I'm going to have to teach you to use a knife correctly." Joey closed the door behind him and slid a chain into place. "I didn't mean to scare you."

The difference between not meaning to and doing seemed a blurry line. He sounded despondent, which made her pause. "You're still here. I thought you might have gone back to your brother's house. You must be exhausted. Can I get you anything?"

"A carpenter and locksmith are coming to fix your rear door in a few hours. The best we could manage was drilling new holes for a chain guard. If you have a sleeping bag or couch I could crash on for a few hours, I would appreciate it."

You can share my bed. The idea buzzed around her head like a bee around a flower.

"Did they catch Mark?"

"Not yet."

Damn you, Mark. She let out a long, frustrated breath and decided to remember the positive aspect of this mess. If Mark hadn't tried to rob her, the yummy-catchy-monkey would already be headed for the airport.

"You would be the type to take the floor when there's an empty bed upstairs." *Her bed* again came to mind. "I can throw fresh sheets on my bed while you take a shower if you'd like. I'll take the fold-out in my office. Tony has a change of clothes upstairs. I'm sure he wouldn't mind you borrowing them."

At least the G-rated offer seemed decent. Her mother wouldn't have to do a flip-flop in her grave for a severe breach of courtesy. She sensed his hesitation. Envisioning his conscience and his body having a standoff with neither side willing to fire the first shot, she figured she'd better negotiate a cease-fire. "It's no trouble," she added.

"May I ask you a somewhat awkward question?" His croaking tone, the rustling of his clothes and the shuffle of his feet gave her the impression the question might strangle him if he didn't ask whatever he wanted to know and quickly. "I mean, you don't have to answer if you don't want to."

"If I can...I'll answer."

"Did you have a crush on me in high school?"

When she saw Kym next, she'd smack her with a dozen rose branches. Unable to prevent flames from heating her cheeks, she turned to place the knife above the sink and washed her hands, starting the count to a thousand to avoid the humiliation.

"Mara?" A warm, gentle hand landed on her shoulder.

If the cat she'd had as a kid could stick his head behind a curtain and pretend to be invisible, why couldn't she? She reached for the towel, but used it to dry her hands rather than giving into the urge to put the piece of cotton over her head. "To answer your question, I did. But so did half the freshman class. So you see, having a crush was no big deal."

His hand dropped. "Half the class? Who knew?"

She pushed past him to make her way upstairs. "I'll change those sheets now."

Joey said something to Buddy, but spoke too softly for her to hear. Both followed her up the stairs.

Shame added twenty pounds of iron to her boiled wool slippers. Why couldn't she admit going all googly-eyed the first time Joey had walked past her hall locker? He looked so dang yummy she almost dropped her books at his feet. The way he felt, she bet he still looked just as good.

Entering the kitchen, she released a frazzled breath and pointed down the hall. "The bathroom's the first door on the left and my room is on the right. There are shampoo and towels under the sink. I'll bag some ice for your shoulder."

And I would be happy to help scrub your back if you'd like.

Saying it out loud would have taken courage.

After the day she'd had her courage reserves were empty.

JOEY PROPPED his hand on the nearest wall to lock his knees so he wouldn't fall over. He swore under his breath, encouraging his fatigued muscles to be overachievers. "Just a change of clothes would be appreciated."

He didn't turn or move because it would hurt, and the hardwood under his feet would leave him with some impressive bruises if his knees decided not to hold.

"You sure you don't want a shower?"

"If you would just show me where I can lie down and then push me over, I'd appreciate the help. Right now, I can't bend over to get my shoes off, much less get undressed."

"You lie down in your condition, and you're likely never to get up again. You need an ice pack first, then a hot shower. I can help."

"I think I'd rather curl into a ball on the floor and roll into the bedroom."

"What's your problem, Gaccione? It's not like I'm going to see anything."

He lifted his Saint Michael's medallion to his lips, kissed the gold disk, and groaned a prayer, just in case the Higher-up was listening. No way was he signing up for ten extra Hail Mary's for pushing her into something she didn't want.

"See if you can make the fifteen steps to the bathroom," she encouraged. "I'll find something to ease the pain."

The pain from his injury suddenly locked his shoulder blades together, his breathing reduced to small hitches of air. He couldn't breathe without pain slicing across his body. "Ah, not sure I can make it to the bathroom. How about I sit at the table?"

He managed the steps necessary to land on the oak spindle-backed chair, missing the small round table by a couple inches. Mara hurried back to check on him, bottle in hand. "Read this. Make sure the label says diazepam."

She held the bottle an inch away from his nose, making his eyes cross. He pushed her arm back. "Yep, that's the right stuff."

"I'll get you an ice bag first, then we can worry about a shower. You shouldn't take these meds yet. You might pass out in the bathtub."

Why couldn't he just take one now to knock his pathetic self out and avoid dying of embarrassment? He was twenty-eight, not sixty-eight. Mara wrapped a damp kitchen towel around the zippered bag and placed the ice on his shoulder. A loathsome sissy-hiss escaped him.

"Why didn't you let the paramedics check you out?" Her accusatory tone made him wince.

"My shoulder didn't hurt this much at the time."

"Of course it didn't. At the time, you had a gallon of adrenaline pounding through your veins. Since I can't see, you need to tell me whether an emergency room visit is warranted."

"It isn't," came out of his mouth way too quickly, and Mara's lips took on that determined little pooch. *Damn.* "Look. I've had a lot worse. Like you said, ice pack, hot shower, and some rest will fix me right up. I'll even take one of your muscle relaxers, which I never take, if you drop the emergency room bit. I'll be fine."

The silent moments ticked on as she debated. "Fine. But if your shoulder isn't better in the morning, you're going to get X-rays to make sure you didn't break anything."

Nothing was broken. He'd already been there and done that... and been sidelined for the soccer season for the privilege.

"Are you numb yet? Ready for a shower?"

He closed his eyes, dreading the pain of standing. "Sure," he said, and gritted his teeth in preparation.

Mara extended her hand. With a tug, a pull and a bit of jostling back and forth, he made it to the bathroom and plopped down on the toilet, only to have Mara kneel and attack his shoelaces moments later. Buddy sat in the doorway with a look of poor-guy empathy.

She hesitated before aiming for his belt buckle.

"You want to go there? 'Cause I'm game if you are." The timbre of his voice deepened, becoming soft, yet carnal.

Her hands slowly retreated. *That's what I thought.* Disappointment added another layer of ache to his already bruised body.

She pushed to her feet. "Go ahead and make jokes, but if

you're not in the shower in five minutes, I'm going to come help. I learned what it's like after having my legs smashed. Painful and humbling months of therapy taught me not to be so proud."

Guilt set in before she rounded the corner and abandoned him to his pride. Appearing helpless wasn't something he accepted easily, but his body refused to respond the way his sixteen-year-old body had—practically a rubber band, snapping back into shape instantly.

"You doing okay?"

"Yep. No need to worry."

Without an option, he started at the top and worked his way down, leaving a heap of clothes on the bathroom floor. After twenty minutes of heated bliss, he rotated the tap, and wondered if crawling to the bedroom might be a better alternative. He braced himself and, inch by inch, lifted one foot out of the tub, then the other until both feet were steady on the tiled floor. Slowly, he wrapped the towel around his waist, securing the cloth around his midsection. If his sergeant saw his sorry-ass condition, he'd be placed on physical fitness duty for three months.

The bed called oh-so-sweetly, but just as he got to the door, she was there with her hand outstretched and on a collision course he couldn't avoid.

Her small hand slid down his torso. The feather-light touch caressed his senses. He focused on holding onto his towel.

Mara pulled her hand back. "I…um…did the clothes I left not fit?"

"I figured if I had to get up in the night, dealing with only a towel would be easier."

Stupid. Real stupid. Buddy could have come up with something better than that pitiful excuse. He winced, not from pain, but from the awkwardness.

"I put the pills and a glass of water on the nightstand. After you get settled, I'll put your clothes on the chair just inside the door, in case you change your mind."

She had changed into nightclothes, and he caught a view of the lettering below. Her oversized T-shirt said, *When one is blind, the truth is heard.*

His body had heard the truth, even if his brain was a little slow. He wanted her. No one else, ever.

He let out a slow breath. "Just get me to the door, and I should be good from there."

"Put your arm over my shoulder," Mara said. "We'll take it slow."

She walked. He hobbled. They tipped into the wall. He cringed. Eventually, he managed to make the twenty feet to the first bedroom.

Her room was neat, a queen bed in the middle surrounded by an oak dresser and nightstand. With the blinds and drapes open, he could see the handmade quilt and pictures of her family lining her dresser. There were even pictures hanging on her wall and a television sitting on top of a stand…odd, given the fact she couldn't see.

Joey turned, and his weight tilted him toward the bed. Mara released him just as he landed. "Do you keep any weapons in the house? A gun maybe?"

"No. Can you imagine me with a gun? I just might shoot Tony." She straightened. "Gaccione, I know you detective types have an overprotective gene buried somewhere in your body, but I don't need your testosterone directed at me. I'm a bit old for a babysitter." She backed up two steps and bumped into the doorframe. "I turned the electric blanket on and put some sports cream on the nightstand, next to the muscle relaxers, just in case. Can I get you anything else?"

"I'm good, thanks."

Good. Good seemed a relative term. If Mara didn't have

that headstrong, I-don't-need-anyone, ornery look on her face, he might be good.

"Unless." His word seemed to stretch into almost a question. "Unless?"

"I wouldn't mind some company."

Those blue eyes he'd come to love stared, unblinking. "I'm assuming you mean to continue where we left off the other night. It's a tempting offer, but I'm not sure you're in any condition for company."

"You could be on top." *It would hurt like hell, but I would be in heaven.*

"A few minutes ago you couldn't even move. Take your pain meds, Joey. That's what you need right now. Besides, I can't. I'm sorry."

"Good night, then."

His disappointment didn't stop her from backing out of the room. When she disappeared, a whole new kind of ache wrapped around his heart and squeezed.

He looked at the medicine bottle, knowing nothing would ease the heartbreak kind of ache.

Besides, he couldn't take the pills anyway. He needed to stay alert—protect her—there was a killer on the loose.

CHAPTER TWENTY

I *can't,* rolled around in Mara's mind.

She lay on her back. Face pointed at the ceiling. Sleep evading her desperate need to rest. Minutes passed, then an hour.

Images of a hot Colorado day ten years prior ran and re-ran in her head. The heat index had soared above a hundred degrees, unusual for late summer. The high school soccer team decided to take their shirts off after practice. Her cheerleading squad was practicing their routine and got the fifty-yard-line view. Coach Leanamen ruined the heavenly, picture-perfect scene when he swore he'd have every one of the boys suspended if they didn't put their shirts back on before he counted to ten.

But that center-seat view was nothing compared to the smooth skin she had experienced personally. Her hand opened and closed, remembering.

Her mind raced back several dozen hours and contemplated toned thighs and quad muscles that supported an adorable, athletic rump. Mara rolled onto her side, hoping reality would stop her from pursuing any more impractical ideas.

Joey probably had several interests in Seattle. Maybe some cute district attorney, or a warrant officer? Who knew? He still wasn't a great talker. Besides, what did it matter? Time spent on the impractical and excuses were just a waste of precious energy.

Joey, while exciting, definitely fell into the impractical category.

When the night air turned chilly, she pulled the comforter up under her chin. She spelled the word *sleep* over and over and over again in her mind, willing her body and mind into slumber so she could avoid thinking about the man in the next room. On the eighteenth spelling, a shout made Buddy jump to his feet. He whined. His whiskered nose nudged her chin.

"I heard it. It's okay."

When another loud shout disturbed the quiet, she pushed the blanket aside and made her way to her bedroom door.

"Sam!" Joey shouted. "Hold on, Bro."

The anguish in his voice made her worry. She pushed the door open. Muffled sobs came from the bed. "Someone help him," Joey pleaded to some hallucination.

Mara's legs bumped the edge of the mattress. Not hesitating, she climbed on the bed. "Joey, you're dreaming."

A hand encircled her wrist. "Call for help. He's bleeding to death."

"Joey. You're dreaming," she said with empathy, knowing the horrific nightmares of the past could seem so real.

She reached a tentative hand forward, her fingers encountering his face. His jaw muscles tensed under her touch. Her fingers came away wet with his tears.

"Mara?"

"You were calling for Sam."

He pulled her fingers from his face. "I've had the same

nightmare over and over and over again. I can't get it out of my head."

"Do you want to talk about it?"

"No."

The vigor of his refusal meant not even a can opener could open that topic easily. Mara sat back on her heels, trying to think of a way to broach the subject. He had to talk to someone. Maybe if he knew he wasn't alone.

She settled on the edge of the bed. "After my parents died, I had nightmares for months." She fisted her hand for courage. "In one, the car was rotating through the air in slow motion. The car stopped. Suspended. I kept waiting to crash, but the car never hit the ground. In another one, I could see my parents in the front seat. I kept trying to get them to say something. They just continued to stare out the mangled window. Sometimes I wouldn't sleep for days. I was so afraid to dream."

Joey rolled to his side. "I've seen a lot of bad stuff—stabbings, gang turf wars, bodies burned beyond recognition, child abuse. But this...this is something different. It's like he's jumping right out of the crime scene photographs to tell me something."

"Losing family hurts more. It's personal."

He threaded his fingers through hers. "It's not just that."

The dog nudged her leg to get attention. "It's okay, Buddy. He's all right." She stroked fingers through the dog's fur and pulled gently on his soft, floppy ear before turning back to Joey. "It's hard losing family. If you don't want to talk to me, Buddy's a halfway decent listener," she said to provide a hopefully helpful grain of levity. "He'd probably prefer to share a man's point of view rather than listening to me chatter on about flowers and inventory lists."

Joey puffed out a thin stream of air, indicating he appreciated her attempt to lighten his mood. His thumb drew circles in her palm. "There have been so many times I wanted to drive to the airport, leave, and bury myself in work. I truly miss him." His words were slurred. "Everywhere I look, there's something to remind me of him. Staying in his place nearly gutted me. His favorite pair of boots, the picture of us from three years ago in Vegas, his favorite drinking chair, and the half-bottle of single malt scotch. Did you know this morning they hung a line-of-duty plaque honoring his death at the station?"

"I didn't know." She pulled his hand into hers and began to draw words with her finger on the palm.

"How am I supposed to go back to my life when everything I've done, I've done so that my family would see I was better than him? Better educated with a better job. All those long hours of studying and working—none of it matters. I wanted to make my dad proud, and why? I don't need his approval. I never did. I just wanted someone to believe in me. The unit back in Seattle—they've got my back."

"I believe in you." Mara crawled farther onto the bed and leaned back against the headboard and attempted to drag the grieving man into her arms, before he helped. "Give into the pain, Joey. Don't hold on to the regret anymore. Let the grief go."

Threading his soft hair through her fingers, she started to sing one of the songs she'd been working on for several weeks. The song had never sounded right until the rawness of anger, sorrow and vulnerability of the last eighteen hours caught up and sank in. Eventually, the arms circling around her waist grew heavy. Wave after wave of sobs tore at her heart. His emotions stirred her own. The demons from her past shook the walls of the cages where she'd banished them.

She could empathize. Returning to Elkridge after the accident hadn't been easy. After the first thirty days, two aunts, an uncle, and a handful of cousins went back to their normal lives and left her and Tony to figure out how to move forward without any of the skills needed to make the right decisions. At

LYZ KELLEY

least Joey had a family to support him, and she'd be there for him if he let her in.

In her lap, Joey's head became heavier. Then he said, "When I was sixteen, I used to sneak into the church balcony on Thursdays to listen to you sing. The sound of your voice always touched my soul. Tonight, your singing took me back. Tonight, I realized I loved you even then."

Her heart paused at the sound of those three gigantic, earthshaking words.

Without a full dose of painkillers circulating through his body, she'd bet he never would have dropped the L-word.

He didn't really mean it. The past several days had been emotional for him. That was all.

But the sentiment was lovely to hear. Maybe she should sing *his* song. The one she'd pulled out of her old files and dusted off. Even if she sang, he wouldn't remember. Not with the drugs in his system.

Pulling the covers over his bare shoulders, she let the melody drift into the night, allowing him to fall further and further into an easy sleep. When the song finished, she lifted his arm to slip quietly away, only to have both arms wrap more securely around her waist.

She understood what being alone in the dark felt like. The isolation. The abandonment. The need to cling to something solid.

Her head dropped back against the headboard. "Well, Buddy, guess I'm stuck here." She pulled the comforter higher across his shoulder.

"How am I ever going to let him get on that plane without getting on my knees and begging him to stay?"

224

Joey had no intention of missing the most beautiful blessing he'd ever been granted just to get up and let a carpenter and locksmith fix a door. He'd learned his lesson the first time. A cute and mussed Mara waking in his arms was an unlikely and extraordinary event.

He remembered how she'd come to be in the same bed, but the reason she'd come didn't matter. The erotic and romantic implication was just too hard to pass up.

Buddy circled the edge of the bed, jiggling the mattress before flopping onto the floor.

Mara brushed a tuft of hair off her face and grumbled, "Buddy, give me five more minutes, and I'll let you out."

A slow reluctance pushed Joey toward the self-sacrificing ledge. "How about you sleep and I let him out? But you have to promise me you won't get up this time."

Mara bolted upright. "Joey?"

A laugh rumbled from his belly. "I hope you don't make a habit of waking up with strange men in your bed. Of course it's me."

Her instantly relaxed body felt as pliable as putty. He pulled her back under the covers to keep her warm.

"You were shouting in your sleep, probably from taking the meds. I came to check on you. I must have fallen asleep."

"I didn't take any meds. Mark's not in custody, and I didn't want to take the risk."

A funny expression crossed her face as memories of the night started clicking into place. She'd held him. Comforted him. She smelled like lavender. He buried his nose in the crook of her neck to breathe her in. Trained to control his body, his emotions, and use cool judgment, he decided to abandon reason and let his lips connect with her soft skin.

"Joey?"

"Please, Mara. Let me just have a little taste."

To his surprise, she turned toward him. "Only if I also get to sample."

Her lips connected with his chest and worked up.

"Ah, Mara. Vixen behavior has consequences. The result of which you'll be able to witness in a moment if you keep going."

"You don't always have to be in control, Joey. I wonder what Joey Gaccione's like when he lets go?"

Mara's teeth sank into his skin gently and he hissed. "Mara, are you sure about this?"

"I know I've been sending mixed messages. I'm just scared," she said a bit sheepishly. "Yesterday reminded me again how easily life can change."

"I get that." He placed a finger under her chin and beckoned her to his lips. "Come here. Don't be frightened."

"Yes, Detective."

His lips brushed her cheek and then the edge of her jaw. "I hope you're not in a hurry." His hand slipped under her T-shirt and palmed her breast, which fit his hand perfectly.

Her stomach muscles trembled. She pulled the towel from around his waist and found *him*. He gasped and slid his other hand up so he could cup both breasts and her erect nipples in retaliation, but the sensation was anything but punishing.

Her T-shirt disappeared faster than Buddy made it to his bowl for dinner. Joey threw the covers back and lifted up on his elbow. "Let me look at you."

He placed his hand between her breasts and circled each mound, then continued downward until reaching her flat stomach. His right fingers moved over her ankles, then began sliding up her legs, stopping at each scar. He leaned in and kissed the six and eight-inch scars on each leg, then lay beside her when his back and arm began to spasm.

"My shoulder is still not in the best shape."

"It's okay. Maybe some other time."

Refusing to allow her to misread intentions, he pulled her over on top of him. "That doesn't mean I can't take my time." He cupped both breasts.

His hands trembled, yearning for something other than a fifteen-minute romp. The contrast between bed-bouncing sex and the tender, loving embrace narrowed. He wanted both. Now.

"Mara, I want to feel you around me." His hands circled her waist and pulled her closer.

"Maybe if I leave a lasting impression, you'll think about coming back."

"You've already left a lasting impression."

He'd already been thinking about coming back. In fact, he'd been thinking about not leaving. The more he thought about it, the more Mara had been right. He could make a difference in the community. He could bring some expertise to the local department, and he could be around for his family and Mara. Sure, he was part of the Seattle team, but there were a dozen more cops wanting to fill his slot. Elkridge had no one—well, no one that was qualified.

From the moment he walked into the flower shop, something had changed. He didn't recognize the emptiness he'd felt for years until he was in her presence. She made him laugh, question his life, and invited him to enjoy simple things like holding hands. He wanted to make her understand, but expressing how he felt seemed impossible. But he had to try.

"Sam and I took a road trip the summer after I graduated. We were camping in Steamboat under the summer sky. I remember feeling like my life was perfect. I had a full-ride scholarship to school to play soccer, and life was mine to have. Then I got to school and was almost cut from the team. My grades sucked. I put all my efforts into improving. After I finally graduated, I just got on the treadmill of life. Not until I saw you and my family did I realize how much had changed. You reminded me of who I was back then. Who I want to be again."

She placed her palms on his chest. "I like who I am when you're around. I feel strong and sexy. I don't feel blind."

Joey traced a finger over her lips. "You are sexy. Mara Dijocomo, would you like me to beg?"

"A grown man pleading? What would the guys back in Washington say?"

"To hell with them. It's just you and me, and I want you." He pulled his finger straight down her chest. "I want you bad. And if I can figure out where my wallet is, we might be able to enjoy each other before the locksmith shows up to fix your door."

"I should tell you, I never went off the pill to regulate my periods, so I'm good."

Yes you are. He was clean, but he wouldn't be irresponsible. He spotted his clothes neatly stacked on the chair, rolled her to his side, and carefully reached for his wallet, his muscles still smarting a bit. He dropped the foil-wrapped packets on the nightstand and settled back into bed.

"Now, where were we?"

Joey slid his hands up and over her breasts. He narrowed

the gap between their lips to replace his imaginary images of her with the vivid realities of her body. She kissed him back, climbing over him on hands and knees, then slowly, slowly, slowly lowered to snuggle her body against him, connecting, stimulating, caressing.

His plan to take his time exploring each body part didn't last. When chemistry and nature took over, his brain ceased functioning. He slid a hand between her legs and found her already wet and waiting, waiting for him. He let out a groan and reached for a condom. Sliding the protection into place, he reached for her hips, and pain raced up his arm.

To hell with my shoulder. For her, he'd ignore the pain.

He adjusted her position atop him and thrust up, pulling her down at the same time. She threw her head back, arched, and lifted slightly before encircling him more deeply, then repeated the motion. Their twin gasps of pure delight floated into the room. He pulled on her hips, controlling her thrusts, not wanting the pleasure to end too soon, but when she moved, rocking to meet his thrust, he decided the heck with waiting.

"Oh, God, Mara. You feel so good."

"Please, Joey. Please." Her words released on a sigh.

With every thrust she took him higher, climbing to the top of the cliff, so high he was ready to take off.

His hands spread around her small waist, and he groaned her name when her muscles tightened around him. When she threw her head back and her body pulsated around him, he swore he'd never seen anything more beautiful—then one more thrust, and another, and he followed her right off the tip of the peak, catching her when she collapsed on his chest, wrapping his arms around her protectively. "I think you just crushed every fantasy I've had so far." He lifted his head to kiss her shoulder.

A soft sniffle caught his attention.

He rolled and tucked her into his side. "Did I hurt you? If I hurt you—"

"You didn't hurt me. I just never thought...I didn't think. Would you make love to me again?"

Not another word was needed. Words weren't required, for the urgency had disappeared and the sweet, slow, dance had begun again. A soft pink hue crept into the room from the early morning sunrise, and he watched her body arch and bend and reach for him again and again.

He skimmed his hand down between her legs, his thumb applying pressure in the right spot. She turned and applied lips and tongue to his nipple, her teeth erotically scraping the edges.

His focus and determination intensified.

"There. There. Don't stop!" Mara inched her way up his body.

He nibbled on her lips while her body vibrated beneath his hand. Kissing her eyes, cheeks and neck, he continued to stroke while her ecstasy stretched to new heights.

Her mouth opened slightly. "Joey," she whispered.

He cupped her breast while he hovered over her core. She lifted her legs for him to thrust forward, to lock their bodies together. Her fingers entwined with his.

Finally, when his back couldn't move any longer, he rolled, pulling her into his arms, folding her body into his. Protecting. Cherishing.

"You're so beautiful and delicate and so intense and fiery. Mara Dijocomo, you're a surprise."

She was a marvel mixed with trouble. Not just the sexual kind. The get-fired-from-your-job kind. Because he seriously could stay here, with her, forever.

At the moment, releasing the woman in his arms seemed impossible.

CHAPTER TWENTY-TWO

"I'm going to beat you until you're a bloody pulp." Tony's anger preceded him into Mara's bedroom. "If you're sleeping with her, you had better be thinking about buying a ring."

"I can explain." Joey moved to shield Mara with his body. "... I think."

"No, you won't," Mara said, climbing over Joey and, pulling a sheet with her. "There's nothing to explain. How did you get in here?"

"With difficulty. I left you a message three hours ago to tell you you're an aunt. When I couldn't get hold of you, Gina refused to let me stay at the hospital. She was worried."

I'm an aunt. "Are Gina and baby okay?"

"Both are fine. Little Anthony is a strappin' seven pounds, eight ounces and twenty-one inches long. I left them sleeping. I just came to check on you, take a shower, and get some different clothes. I'm going back in a few hours to pick them up." The exhaustion in his voice, and the fact that he'd needed to leave his wife to check on her, made her feel guilty. "By the way, two guys were hanging out by the front door drinking coffee. They were here to fix the rear door, so I put them to work. But a broken door doesn't explain why this monkey is in your bed."

"And he doesn't need to. You might say thank you. Did you look around downstairs? The shop's wreckage wouldn't have been cleaned up if it weren't for Joey. Speaking of wreckage, how are you?"

"I think Gina broke my hand during delivery, but everything else, luckily, is intact. Ask me again in about four hours, after I've gotten some sleep."

The tension in the room and the glorious ache of her body made her light-headed.

"Buddy needs to go out. Tony, would you take him?"

"Why's Buddy got a bandage on his foot?"

"I'll explain later. First I'm going to make breakfast for all of us. You can shower and eat here if you like, since I know you have no food at the house, and you won't let this go. If we're going to discuss it, at least let's talk about it with clothes on and maybe full stomachs."

Buddy, upon hearing the word *out*, started up his usual tail-thumping, body-wiggling routine, then joyfully followed Tony down the hall.

"That wasn't the alarm I was hoping for this morning." She said a little prayer, hoping Joey didn't regret the indiscretion. "Do you know where my pajamas went?"

"Let me get them for you." The bed shifted when he got up.

A moment later, a wad of cotton landed in her lap. She dressed in clumsy silence. Sore muscles reminded her of what Joey's callused hands could do when his fingers homed in on spots of intense erotic sensitivity. She didn't mind the soreness. In fact, she hoped the ache would last as a blissful memory of what Gaccione could do when he took her body into his protective custody.

"How are your back and shoulder?" Mara asked, trying to break the awkward moment.

"I'm fine."

Fine. What is that supposed to mean?

"Give me five minutes in the bathroom, then it's yours. Don't worry about Tony. I'll make him some pancakes. Maple syrup always puts him in a better mood."

"Mara, I want to explain something."

"Whatever you're going to say, don't."

She didn't want to hear about regret or disappointment, or any other excuse he'd come up with in the last five minutes. Explaining he'd made a mistake after loving her into oblivion not only wasn't required, it was unwelcome.

"Kym told me you changed your flight. You should check with the airlines to get your seat assignment for tomorrow," she said, keeping her voice light and airy to hide the hurt.

"I would rather find out if Walters is in custody."

She pointed in the direction of the nightstand. "The phone's over there if you want to call. I'll start breakfast." She walked down the hall, hoping to avoid hearing what she wasn't ready to accept.

"I'll just be a minute," Joey said more formally, more detached but kindly, more *I'm going to leave tomorrow, and we shouldn't have gone there.*

Mara's feet shuffled along the wood floor until she reached the kitchen. Her fingers gripped the tiled counter and dug in. No way would she cry. Not in front of Tony. Not in front of Joey. Not going to happen.

Buddy came bustling into the kitchen. The heavy clomp up the stairs could only be Tony.

"Want some pancakes?" She turned toward the door. "I'll make berry compote, unless you want syrup."

"I want to know why you and Gaccione were in bed in the buff."

She grabbed a pan from the skillet rack. "You may want to know, but you being curious doesn't mean I have to tell you anything. One of these days you're going to have to accept that, while you're still my big brother, I'm no longer a little girl."

"We'll see about that. I'm desperate for some coffee." A kitchen cabinet above the counter opened and the rich, bitter smell of French roast made her stomach churn.

"I know what you're up to, and it's not going to work. Joey is permanently off the discussion list. However, you, the baby, and caffeine we can talk about."

"Got any milk?"

"There's a new carton on the top shelf." The noise from the lower floor penetrated through the stairwell door. "How does the store look? My impression is Joey, Kym and the team they assembled did a nice job getting everything put back together."

"You said Joey was off-topic."

"What about me?" Joey asked, entering the kitchen.

Mara's heart squeezed at the sound of his voice. Gone was the tenderness, the passion, the softness. "Tony was just saying what an awesome job you did cleaning up the store. Weren't you, Tony?" If the 'be gracious' hint wasn't big enough, she'd hit him over the head with a large skillet, the one she conveniently held in her hand.

"Yeah, man, thanks. Want some coffee?"

"Don't have time. We have to go down to the station."

The word *we* made her forget what she'd reached for in the pantry. "We?"

"They found Mark. I'd like you to come down to the station with me."

A cup slammed against the kitchen counter so hard she flinched.

"Mara's not going. Mark messed her up enough the first time. She doesn't need to go through that again." Tony's heavy-handed, big-brother protectiveness had become chin-hair-pulling tiresome.

"Mara doesn't need to worry about Mark anymore. He OD'd last night. His dad found him this morning. Mara, if you're up for it, I'd like to take you through his place to see if we can double-confirm he's been the person following you."

"What do you mean following her?" Tony stepped in front of her.

"Tony. Stop. I didn't want to worry you."

"So, what are you going to do? Ask her to sniff him?" Tony's sarcasm held a full heap of anger.

"Something like that."

Tony took another step and Mara reached to pull Tony back and placed her body between the two chest-beating hulks. "That's enough. Both of you." Turning to Joey, she let the agitation in her stomach settle. "Poor Mr. and Mrs. Walters. They must be devastated. Do I have time to shower?"

"I'll wait."

Tony gripped her arm. "Mara, come to your senses. Don't do this. There's nothing to be gained by going. Kym told me you gave your statement last night. Don't get involved."

All the reasons not to help rolled into a perfect floral bundle, all pretty and perfect, but only one beautiful, thorny reason to go remained—Joey needed answers, and she wanted to know whether Mark was the person who'd followed her into the grocery store. In her heart, the decision had already been made.

"I'll be okay. You need to let me live my life, and learn to trust me." She patted Tony on the cheek and turned to Joey. "Give me twenty minutes, and I'll be ready." If this was her last chance to help Joey find a path to his happiness, and her to find peace of mind, then she couldn't let the opportunity pass.

CHAPTER TWENTY-THREE

Mara fumbled for the door handle and exited Joey's SUV. Her hand automatically dropped to where Buddy's head would have been, but he hadn't come along for the ride. She craved the comfort of combing her fingers through his fur, especially having spent the last several hours at the station reviewing the event sequence. She missed her constant companion, but Joey would take care of her. She had no doubt.

"There are several police cars here." Joey placed his hand on the small of her back to move her sideways so he could close the car door. "Ernie Barker is heading our way. You might remember him from school."

She clutched her walking stick under her arm and allowed Joey to escort her forward.

"Ernie," Joey greeted the deputy. "Thanks for allowing us to take a look."

"What is she doing here?" Annoyance, and possibly a bit of denigration, added a nasty undertone to the deputy's question.

"Someone's been following and harassing her. I'd like to

make sure Mark was the person stalking her. She's got a good nose. Let her see if she can ID the smell."

"You're joking. Right?" Ernie puffed out the question on a chuckle.

"It's very irritating when people talk about me as if I'm deaf." Mara stepped into the conversation. "I can hear perfectly well, and would like to try. Mark isn't the type to do laundry every week, so there should be a residual smell."

"I don't know about this." Ernie released a skeptical huff, "but I guess she should know what her ex smells like."

Mara winced at the hostility in Ernie's statement, just as Joey stiffened.

Mara's nose flared. "Hmm. Mint, possibly cumin and vanilla, a little cardamom, and an overtone of bergamot and sandalwood. Very common. Jean Paul Gaultier cologne perhaps, Ernie? Yet...the vanilla is too pronounced. I'm thinking an Asian knockoff, but close."

"That's unbelievable."

"Bacon, eggs, and I bet hash browns for breakfast, but only because I smell ketchup."

Joey's chuckle gave permission for a victory smile to crease the corners of her mouth.

"Okay. I'll allow her in, but don't let her touch anything. Joey, you know the drill. Get some gloves from one of the deputies inside. Oh, and I should tell you, that truck over there matches the tire prints at Sam's place, and we found several wads of gum, just like you said."

"Good work, Ernie. Thank your guys for the follow up."

Mara inwardly laughed at the lack of Joey's sincerity. She extended her arm sideways to make sure Joey was still standing close. "Thanks, Ernie."

She wrapped her fingers around Joey's bicep, feeling the warmth and appreciating the comfort.

Joey helped her climb the steep steps of the mobile home trailer.

"Stay close. There's a lot of trash on the floor. I think the best place to start is in the bedroom and then work our way to the front."

At the smell of rotting food, she covered her nose and mouth with one hand. The buzzing insects made her glad she couldn't see. *Mark. What happened to you?* Gone was the neat, fearless boy who laughed easily and had dreams of starting a marketing firm. He'd gone to L.A. to make it big. Big wasn't what he achieved.

"Do you know how long he's been in town?" she asked Joey.

He leaned closer. "Not yet. Mark called his dad last night to say he was sorry. His cell phone happened to have one of those trackers and allowed deputies to trace the call to this mobile home. Unfortunately, he was found too late. When I called earlier, Ernie told me they found his mom's diamond bracelet, so I guess we know who robbed the Walters' house during the funeral."

The news stopped her breath. "The Mark I knew had a temper when he drank, but he wouldn't have stolen anything. Something in L.A. must have changed him."

"Stay here. Let me get you one of his shirts."

The snap of latex and the squeak of a floorboard was followed by a sense of bitter cold air. What sounded like pine needles tapped against a window, created a picture in her mind. She sensed movement.

"Here, take a sniff of this shirt."

Overtones of human musk combined with mint, and some-thing else—something sour, almost rancid, like cat pee or vinegar—surrounded her, then undertones of pizza and possibly motor oil. Her stomach lurched and her throat closed off.

No cigarettes.

"It wasn't him. He's not who was stalking me."

"Are you sure?"

"Positive. The man following me into the grocery store smelled like cigarettes, licorice and marijuana. Mark sliced your tires, but he's not the one who was following me."

"I'll make sure to have all the shoes here bagged and tested for prints to see if they match any from the cabin."

Mara hated hearing the disappointment, but she didn't want to give any of the deputies false hope. "I also don't think he shot Sam, either. The facts don't line up."

"What are you talking about? Mark meets the profile." The agitation in Joey's tone caused her to proceed more cautiously.

"Does he? Mark didn't like guns. He hated when my dad talked about hunting. Whoever shot Sam was an expert shot and based on the fact you told me the car door left only a narrow gap for the shooter to hit his target."

"Sometimes people change, Mara."

"I know that, but I'm still not convinced Mark is Sam's killer."

"Let's get you out of here. Would you mind waiting in the car for a bit?" Joey's distancing politeness in his voice seemed wrong on many levels. "Here, take my arm."

"You don't believe me." Mara pulled her arm back.

"It's not a matter of not believing you. I've been doing investigative work for a long time, Mara."

"Then, if you are as good a detective as you believe, look at the facts. I know you want to believe you've caught Sam's killer. It would be mighty convenient if Mark were the thief-stalker-killer all wrapped up in one. But then what happens when this town lets its guard down and the bad-guys are still out there?"

He guided her hand to his elbow and dodged her question. Her frustration made her feet grow roots and twine around the floorboards. "I'm not going anywhere until you tell me you will at least look at the facts again."

"I'm looking at the facts right now. There are two rifles, a handgun, and enough ammunition in this place to rob a bank. The ammunition is the correct caliber. I'm sure there are more firearms hidden, but that's just what I see."

"Fine. There are weapons. Over thirty percent of Coloradans own guns. I suggest you dig deeper. Find out who owns this place, because for me, it's not adding up. Mark might have made bad choices. Most likely someone in L.A. dangled dollars in front of him, and he was too naïve to know the dollars came at a price. He's not a murderer. Time may prove me wrong, but my gut tells me he's not your guy."

Joey led her through a narrow corridor to the front door and then to the rental car. "We'll let the deputies determine whether or not he killed Sam."

"So now you trust the deputies to do a proper investigation?"

"What is it you want me to say? That you're right? Fine. You're right."

Sheer sympathy for Joey sobered her thoughts. She stopped and turned to him. "I don't want to be right. More than anything, I wish...I..."

He leaned closer to her ear. "I wish you could have seen Ernie's face when you told him what cologne he was wearing. It reminded me of a guy soliciting a prostitute caught with his pants around his ankles."

"Let's just hope Ernie does a proper investigation this time. Otherwise, he's going to look like one of those middle-aged idiots who can't keep his do-dads in his pants."

"Do-dads?"

His light chuckle made heat stream from her chest, up her neck and across her cheeks to her ears. "You know what I mean."

He opened the car door for her. "About this morning."

Mara's fingers tightened around the door handle. "Let's not complicate things and, instead, focus on one thing at a time. And, if you don't mind, I'd like to find some food. I never did get to make those pancakes."

"Food. Right. I don't suppose a smashed protein bar sounds appetizing. I have one in my computer bag, but I'm warning you, the bar could have been in there awhile."

Mara waved her hand in front of her face to get rid of the thought and scrunched her nose. "I was thinking more in the lines of banana cream pie."

Laughter released the blazing tension. "I like the way you think. Will you be all right for a second? I just want to follow up with Ernie."

"Stop worrying about me. Tony does enough worrying and suffering for everyone."

He planted a quick peck on her cheek, and shut the car door. A surge of fear gripped her body. Her stalker was still out there. Was he watching her now? Laughing? What was she going to do? Joey wasn't going to be around to protect her.

He was leaving.

She was no longer safe.

More importantly, what the heck was she going to tell Tony?

CHAPTER TWENTY-FOUR

Joey opened the car, slid behind the wheel and leaned into Mara. "I'm tempted to kiss you right now." Joey brushed his lips over the tip of her ear.

"Not here," Mara hissed. "You have no idea what it's like having an entire town who have decided to take Tony and I under their protection."

"It can't be that bad."

"Think of your parents times fifty. I have to live with these people after you leave tomorrow." She turned to fasten her seatbelt.

Tomorrow. He didn't want to think about tomorrow when she was right beside him today. Not letting her outmaneuver him, Joey put a finger under her chin and softly guided her head towards him. "Then where?"

"You are tenacious, Gaccione."

When she shivered, he put the keys in the ignition to turn on the heat. "Tenacious. That's a mighty fine word, and yes, madam, I am."

"I don't think we should complicate things."

"What's so complicated? It's just you and me. I was hoping

we could talk about next steps."

"You're joking, right?" Mara shifted toward him. "Your boss wants you back in Seattle. Besides, what would your mother say?"

"My mother happens to be a fan of yours. She even came to hear you sing," he countered with such vehemence, he hoped she got the message.

The theme from *American Gigolo* began playing, then grew louder, and louder, and louder.

"Answer your phone."

"I'd rather talk about us."

"Answer your phone, Joey," Mara insisted.

"Hey, Ma," Joey sighed, wanting to bang his head on the steering wheel. "Dinner celebration? I don't think—yes, Ma. Six o'clock. I'll ask. Ma, I said I'll ask. I don't know if she has any food allergies. Geez. Enough, already. Okay. 'Bye."

He dropped his phone into the middle console and then gripped the steering wheel until his knuckles turned white. "My mother would like to extend you an invitation to come to the restaurant tonight. I should warn you. She won't take no for an answer."

"I heard the word celebration. Your mom must think you found Sam's killer."

His hands tightened around the steering wheel. "I'm not so sure."

"The rumor mill is more efficient than you think. Joey, I'm scared people are going to let their guard down. Not be as careful."

That old gut swirling action started again. "Sometimes it's a good thing to be oblivious."

"It's not good to live stupid. I heard something about six o'clock. When is that? I've lost track of time today."

"It's a bit past three now."

She tipped her head at a ten-degree angle, an angle saying

I'm thinking, and stared straight ahead. He wished he could read thoughts the way she read smells.

"I bet my not coming to dinner would be easier, less complicated, and would require less explanation. We're two smart people. We should be able to generate a feasible excuse your mom will accept."

"I would rather you come." Joey reached over and threaded his fingers through hers. "However, my family can be over-whelming. I'm not sure who will be at More Than Meatballs, maybe us plus my parents, or the whole mob. The way I figure it, you can be properly reintroduced to the family tonight, or the next time I'm in town. S'up to you."

"When's that? Ten years from now?"

"I was thinking a little bit sooner than that. The fact is, I like Buddy, and I think he likes me. I'm hoping to find out if you're okay with having another male in your life. Buddy and I are both loyal. I, however, promise not to chew on your shoes, wake you at five o'clock in the morning to go out, or knock your mom's vase on the floor with my tail. Sure, our relation-ship will be long distance," *for now*, "but I promise to call, and schedule some real vacation time this coming summer. What do you say?"

"I'm not sure this is a good idea. Long-distance relation-ships with no future plans are difficult. I'm not the typical girl you'd bring home to Mom."

Or marry, he heard her think but not say. No, she sure wasn't. Who wanted ordinary when spirited, determined and courageous was available?

"It's not like my family doesn't know you. Both my parents invited you to dinner. The invitation's genuine. Tell you what, I'll drop you off so you can change if you want, and I'll pick you up around five-thirty. If you're uncomfortable once we're there, just tell me, and I'll walk you home. The restaurant is only a couple of blocks from your store. How's that sound?"

Her face puckered in thought. The urge to persuade, and the inclination to avoid pushing his preference, battled against each other until finally her head turned toward him. "I'd like to go, but I want to make sure I won't be an embarrassment."

"You are never an embarrassment. At least not to me."

"Dinner would give me the chance to make another bouquet for your mom."

"So you'll go?" Joey leaned in and planted a kiss on her cheek.

Her hand lifted and caressed the spot. "You know, Joey, I figured you as a perfectionist. The type of guy who never considered an A-paper or a five-minute mile or three perfect bull's-eyes good enough. I have to tell you, that kiss was rather lame."

"Is that so? I thought you didn't want people to see us kiss."

"I changed my mind."

"Then, Ms. Dijocomo, I suggest you bring your face closer and prepare yourself."

Mara went still. Pensive. Curious. Anticipating. She leaned in. He smiled just before his lips touched hers. He tasted. He savored. He deepened the kiss. When he forced his lips from hers, he opened his eyes to an expression of wonderment.

"And what do you think now?" he asked.

"I think you need to practice."

"Practice?" He savored the taste on his lips.

"Yep, a lot."

"I think you're right. It's going to take a great deal of practice. I think we should start now."

He leaned in, but her hand pressed against his chest. "I think you need to get me home so we can get to the restaurant on time."

He released a pithy sigh. He'd rather be kissing Mara than eating, or just about anything else—like getting on the plane in less than twenty-four hours.

CHAPTER TWENTY-FIVE

Mara preceded Joey through the door of his family's restaurant and stopped just inside.

The warmth of his hand pressed against the small of her back sent a sizzling spark up her spine, overloading the signals in her brain. The realization that she and Joey seemed to be on a real meet-the-parents type date tugged on her like a whirling, up-and-down amusement park ride, titillating, yet nerve-racking, all at the same time.

She automatically reached for Buddy before remembering she'd again given him the day off. The dog seemed exhausted from the past day's events, and she could always use walking stick practice. Mara worked to calm her fluttering heart and held a large bundle of flowers in front of her, like a shield, yet at the same time offering peace.

"It's going to be okay, I promise," he whispered. He weaved through the open tables to the back room just off the kitchen, reserved for special occasions or family dinners. "Hello-oo, we're here."

A honey-bee hum of voices from the back room migrated toward them like a swarm. Shouts of "Uncle Joey!"

preceded the pounding of several pairs of little feet. Joey stepped slightly ahead of Mara to ward off the gathering ambush.

"Ma, you remember Mara." Joey reached back to put a comforting hand between Mara's shoulder blades and eased her forward a bit.

"Welcome. Welcome. Look at you. You're all grown up. And so beautiful."

Optimism pressed Mara to lean in. "I—"

"We came to hear you sing the other night." Mrs. Gaccione's scaling tone, climbing higher and higher, kept up the pace with her words. "You touched my heart."

"Well, I—"

"And you brought my favorite flowers. How lovely." His mother hauled Mara into a hug, and she felt like a beloved stuffed toy being squeezed by a two-year-old. Her arms splayed, and she didn't know exactly what to do. His mother released her and turned to him. "Joey, didn't I teach you better manners? Take her coat and get her something to drink, and don't you dare leave her alone with your sisters, or they'll talk her ear off."

She laughed, trying to figure out what to do next. Her forehead creased in concentration as the family presented themselves one-by-one.

"Dad." Joey's body turned.

"Well done, son. I knew you would do it. You found your brother's killer."

Joey's body stiffened, and he coughed out his trepidation. "Dad, all the evidence hasn't been processed. There's still a possibility Mark isn't the killer."

"We will know soon enough." While Mr. Gaccione's words had appeared perfectly civil, a tacit displeasure rumbled through the room. "Come. Let's sit down."

Mara squeezed his hand, hoping to provide some support.

"I almost forgot." Joey reached for the package he'd hidden in the inside of his coat. "This is for you, Ma."

"For me?" The ripping of wrapping paper sounded like a child opening a Christmas present. "Oh, my. A sexy hot-pink apron. Look, girls. Are those little flowers? Thank you, Joey. I needed a new apron."

"Well done." Pia whispered over her shoulder into Joey's ear.

"Let's find you a place to sit," Joey suggested. "Can I get you something? Looks like dinner is going to be buffet style."

Mara placed her hand on his arm. "Water would be nice."

"I'll get it," Sophia offered.

Mara turned her head. "Thank you, Sophia. That's very kind of you."

"I don't know how you identify people so easily." The amazement in his voice gave her a sweet feeling of satisfaction.

He escorted her to the far side of the table. Walking past the food, Mara heard Anna, Joey's youngest sister, giggling with her silly friends, but couldn't quite catch the conversation.

"Ready for circus hour at the Gacciones'?" he asked, guiding her hand to the nearest chair.

"Sounds wonderful. And the smell, it's heavenly." She tucked the folded stick under her arm and let him lead her forward.

"Let's get some food."

Camilla, and possibly Franco were engaged in a heated debate about Mark's parents. She turned slightly. "I wish people wouldn't be so hard on the Walters. They had nothing to do with how Mark turned out."

"You just never know about people."

She disliked the skepticism in his voice. "They were good to Tony and me after my parents died. The Mark I knew was different. Something in L.A. changed him."

"Probably drugs."

"Probably." Obviously, a good-paying job and marriage had been way too much responsibility for Mark.

After the accident, she'd been barely conscious, bandaged from head to toe, with tubes coming out of every limb and the pain meter fluctuating between a seven and nine—a nine only because she didn't want to admit what a ten felt like—when Mark entered her hospital room.

She'd grabbed onto the dear sound of his voice like a lifeline for a fraction of a second that then bled away when he told her about the L.A. job. He stayed a generous fifteen minutes to ask her to give him back the engagement ring, and loan him her apartment key so he could get his favorite hoodie. At least she hadn't married him before discovering his inability to handle sickness. Which, she realized later, also meant it was highly unlikely that he'd be able to stick around through health, either.

Joey placed a thick china plate into her hands. The hand on her back pressed in, inviting her to move forward. "Would you like some salad?"

"Yes, please." The turmoil growing in her stomach intensified. "I know you and your family want Mark to be the killer, but in my heart—"

"Yes, I know. I provided Ernie with the information you gave me. It will be up to him to follow up." Her plate suddenly became heavier. "Blue cheese? Balsamic? Or Italian?"

"Balsamic." Thoughts whirled around and around in her head, dissecting the intent of his reaction. But his apparent indifference, or at least lack of interest, didn't sit well. "So, you're washing your hands of the investigation?"

"I didn't say that. Fettuccine Alfredo? Chicken parmesan? Penne Bolognese? Or lasagna?"

"Fettuccine. Then what are you saying?"

"I'm saying I still have no jurisdiction here. I'm lucky the authorities let me do as much investigating as they did. The sheriff's office needs to handle this."

"I see." She wrestled to find patience because his reasons sounded more like excuses.

"Look. I came home to bury my brother. That's all. Like I said I'm too close to this one. I can't be impartial. Besides, nothing I ever do is going to satisfy my parents. I did the best I could."

A marble of guilt stuck midway down her windpipe. Not able to quite breathe or swallow, she gripped her plate harder and reached for Joey's sleeve. "You did a lot for us. I'm being insensitive. I'm sorry. I wasn't thinking. I—"

"Mara, it's fine. Really. Your water is already at the table. Let's enjoy the meal my mom worked so hard to cook." The irritation in his voice heaped on an additional shovel of guilt.

"It sure does smell good," she responded, hoping to turn the conversation toward a benign topic.

A warm hand again touched the small of her back. "Turn ninety degrees left. Your seat is to the right."

She took a tentative step forward, then another, following his lead, homing in on the subtle shifts of his fingers directing her left or right. A dozen or so steps later, he touched her arm. Chair legs scraped across the floor, and her plate disappeared from her hands.

"Would you mind describing where the bathrooms are so I can wash my hands?" she asked while extending her walking stick.

"They're just behind you. Turn right down the hall fifteen feet, and the bathrooms are the second door on the left."

"Great. I'll be back in a minute."

She stepped and tapped, stepped and tapped, feeling her way down the hall to the second entrance. Entering, she found her way to the third of three stalls. In the process of locking the stall door, she heard the bathroom door open.

"Come on, hook me up on a date with your brother. He is so yummy," a female voice whined while sensually expanding *yummy* into a word twelve inches long.

"Eewwwww. He's an idiot. Why would you want a date with him?"

Mara recognized Anna Gaccione's voice. Joey's little sister drew out her vowels in a similar manner.

"You're just eew-ing because he's your brother. Take a good look, sister-girl. Your brother is hot. I'd let him strip search me in a heart-pumping minute."

"Did you see him with that Dijocomo girl? How pathetic." Anna's disdain topped the snark charts. "Maybe he feels sorry for her since her dad's bank account was wiped out. But who does she think she is, coming in here with her arm wrapped around my brother like she's some model hanging off the arm of a billionaire? She deserves to be put in her place."

Deciding she didn't need to go to the bathroom after all, Mara opened the stall door. She would have given anything to be able to see. Given anything to stop the women's opinions from hurting.

She extended her stick. "You're wrong, Anna. I know my place. I also know no one should have to bury half their family. And no one should have to listen to scorn from those who have more, or less. And yes, the cost to pin my body together was extremely high, but you know what? I'm going to be fine. You know why I know that? Because I don't need to prove anything to you or anyone else in this town." She took a step toward the door and then turned back. "And tell your friend if she wants Joey, she better hurry and put on her big-girl panties and act fast because he's leaving tomorrow. She doesn't need to use you to get to your brother."

Mara opened the door with such force the heavy metal handle bounced off the back wall.

Home. I need to get home.

The cruelty of Anna's words, the pain of hearing them—*how pathetic!*—reverberated in her mind, making it hard to breathe.

No. No, I'm not pathetic. Just blind. Not pathetic.

She retraced her steps past the kitchen to the main dining room, then stumbled through people, chairs and tables, working through the complex maze to find the front door. She didn't apologize for stepping on toes or bumping into bodies. She couldn't. Her pride wouldn't let her. The remaining shreds of her dignity wouldn't allow her to give in.

I'm not pathetic. I'm not.

Exiting the restaurant, she turned right, knowing her store was just four blocks down the street, somewhere. The temperature had dropped, but she wouldn't stop. She wouldn't return for her coat. She wouldn't go back. Only forward. Just one step at a time.

Forward. Only forward.

Keep going. One step. That's it.

Footsteps raced behind her, forcing her to concentrate on the ground beneath her feet, and the vibration and sound when she tapped her pole.

Step, *tap*. Step, *tap*. Step, *tap*.

"Mara? Stop. Where are you going?" Joey's concern blasted through the hurt.

"Home." She took a step but found her way blocked. *Please, let me go.* She moved left, then right, fighting for every inch of ground. "Please, I need to get home."

The vulnerability in her voice made her cringe. She rejected the frail emotion. Those women couldn't win. She pushed forward again with more determination.

"Mara. Please." A jacket warmed by body heat surrounded her shoulders. "What happened in that bathroom?"

His plea drained the fight from her like water draining from a bathtub.

"Joey. Don't you get it? You keep treating me like I haven't changed. But I have. My family's money is gone. Medical bills, burial costs, paying off Tony's and my college loans. It's all gone. The only things we have left are the flower shop and the two-bedroom house Tony purchased with the proceeds from our parents' home. Everyone in Elkridge knows I'm not the person I used to be but you. I'm blind. I'm not pathetic. And I don't need anyone to tell me what I've lost. I have to live with my parents' death and disability every day."

"No one said you were pathetic."

Your sister did. "Go back to your family. Celebrate tonight. You're leaving tomorrow."

"Mara, don't go. Not like this."

"Let me go, Joey. Live the best life you can." She took a step around him, stopped and turned. "Joey. I know you believe people thought more highly of Sam than you. But it's not true. You're an amazing man. Find what makes you happy, because that's what I'm going to do."

It took everything she had to lift her chin, push her shoulders back, and pretend life hadn't just taken another slice out of her soul.

She wouldn't cry. No, she wouldn't.

At least not until she'd found her apartment, and spent the rest of the night trying to convince herself that she hadn't just lost the one chance she had to be happy with someone who accepted her for who, not what she was.

CHAPTER TWENTY-SIX

Joey watched Mara struggle, his heart wrenching every time she stumbled, came dangerously close to the edge of the walkway or reached out a hand to study and negotiate an obstacle. He followed her until she was safely home, but at enough of a distance that she was unaware of his presence.

He'd done this to her.

He'd brought her to the restaurant.

He'd promised her she'd be safe. And look what he'd done. Anger lit a fuse straight to his core. He wanted to explode. Damn his family. Damn them for taking the one sparkle of light in his life and dousing the flame.

He yanked open the door of the restaurant and scanned the back room. He shot straight for the one person he knew without a doubt had caused this mess. After all, he'd noticed Anna and her friend head toward the restrooms a few moments after Mara disappeared down the hall.

"I would like to talk to you. Outside. Now."

Anna's eyes flared, then eased, looking around. Seeing heads turn their way, she was sure her brother wouldn't cause a scene, especially in front of their dad. But the old Joey didn't exist. He wasn't that shy, quiet guy anymore.

"I'm busy," she said. A sisterly taunt, but haughtier.

"Joey. Stop hassling your sister."

"Stay out of this, Dad." He said without taking his eyes off Anna.

"Joey!"

He whipped his head towards his dad. "I said stay out of this." He took a step into Anna, so that she had to tilt her head back to see him. "What happened in the bathroom?"

He noticed his sister's two friends had gathered around to provide an audience. Her smug expression told him she would take advantage of his innate courtesy, but she didn't know him. Not anymore.

"Why Joey, you know girls tinkle in the bathroom."

Her girlfriends laughed at her petty little joke. He didn't find her sarcasm the least bit funny. Drug lords. Prostitution rings. Pedophiles. He'd helped bust them all. Being outmaneuvered by a spoiled brat wasn't going to happen.

"I'm giving you till the count of three. If you don't tell me what I want to know, I'm going to throw you over my shoulder, toss your sorry butt in the wet food dumpster and close the lid until you tell me."

"You wouldn't dare."

He took a step closer, his breath mixing with hers. "Try me."

"Joey, Anna, in the kitchen, *now!*" His mother's authoritarian voice broke the tension for only a second.

Anna, sensing a victory, seized the opportunity, her lips revealing her white teeth in a contemptuous smile. "Mother's waiting."

He itched to haul her up off the ground and shake some sense into her delinquent head. Instead, he gritted his teeth, and calmly replied, "Lead the way."

He followed his sister down the narrow hall, through the

swinging door, and into the prep station. Just inside the doors, he stopped, assessing where the knives, pots, and pans were stored. Today wouldn't be the first time a family member threatened to cut off another family member's body part.

"What's this about?" His mother's rigid tone left no room for lies. "Anna?"

"Why me? He started it."

"Somehow I doubt that." His mother's brow raised in an old, familiar arch. The one advising everyone that she'd heard too many excuses, lies, stories and wanted the truth.

Anna studied her French-manicured nail tip, then put it in her mouth to nibble nervously.

"I'm waiting, Anna."

Anna pointed one of her manicured nails at his chest. "He should have known better than to bring that Dijocomo girl here. She doesn't fit in. Besides, I didn't know she was in the bathroom. It's too bad she had to hear the truth."

"It is too bad." His mother held up a hand asking for Joey's silence. "And I understand why Joey took exception. But I just buried a son. I will not have my other children fighting. Do you understand me?" She looked first at Anna, then him, to secure agreement.

His childhood resentment and the justified reasons for leaving Elkridge dropped into a heaping pile, one, by one, by one. The mound kept growing into what seemed like a month's worth of smelly, stinky laundry. His animosity intensified until he saw a shift in his mother's eyes and her body drooped.

Since when had she become so brittle? The dragon of the family appeared to have run out of fire.

In a matter of seconds, his perceptions shifted. Through more adult eyes, he saw his mother as a woman responsible for raising five children. He observed the tired soul. The burden. The heartbreak of losing one too early. He saw her not from the perspective of a rebellious teen, but from a man's point of view, a man who might be responsible for raising a child some-day. He released the lifelong resentment and inhaled long-overdue healing air.

"It's a fair request," Joey said. "I will honor Sam. There will be no more discussion of this tonight." He took a step back. "I'll say my good-byes to the family. I have a plane to catch in the morning."

He turned, but his mother's hand on his arm stopped him. The somber look in her emotion-filled eyes made him turn back to hear what she had to say.

"Anna. You have always been my baby. Always will be. But I indulged you. Spoiled you. You got away with more than all your other siblings combined. I still believe that someday you'll grow into the woman you have the potential to be."

Anna's mouth dropped open to reveal devastated aston-ishment.

"I agree when you said Mara Dijocomo doesn't fit in. She's been through more than anyone can imagine, but she's managed to keep her courage and pride. I've always tried teaching you kids that money doesn't separate people, it's how you face your challenges that defines you. Mara has always been one to face her challenges head-on, never once complain-ing. And to address your point, I seriously doubt she will ever 'fit in.' She's extraordinary. A true one-of-a-kind. I would hope that every Gaccione member would be open to learning from her example, accepting and supporting her in this community. Elkridge is our community. I've been feeding this Elkridge family for close to thirty years. It's time you learned who butters your bread, young lady."

"But her eavesdropping wasn't my fault."

"You, young lady, shouldn't have thought, much less expressed that type of nastiness. I can only assume by your actions that your words were mean and cruel and spiteful. So tomorrow you're going to apologize to Miss Dijocomo."

"Oh, no I'm not."

His mother's chest heaved with a deep breath. "Okay. I respect your choice."

The smugness on Anna's face became so sugary sweet that Joey wanted to renew his threat, just to reveal her true stench. Anna pushed past him toward the door, but his mother almost snarled, "Anna, I'm not finished."

His sibling turned back reluctantly.

"Now, respect my position. If you do not apologize within the next twenty-four hours, your father and I will not sign for your car loan, and my wedding dress, the dress you've coveted since you were six, will be given away to someone who deserves to wear it. I have tried to raise my children to be respectful. Obviously, I've failed somewhere along the line."

"But—"

"No, Anna. No buts. Not this time. You're old enough to know what's right and wrong. You were wrong. You know it. I can see the guilt in your eyes."

"I hate you." Anna shoved the kitchen door so hard, Joey had to catch it on the backswing. He released the metal, letting the door slowly swing shut.

"And you." His mother pointed at him. "I heard what you've been up to."

"What have I been up to, Ma?" he asked, his exhaustion squashing his ability to react to her ire.

Her eyes mellowed, her expression wise. "You've been doing the right things, that's what. Meeting with the deputies. Investigating on your own. Catching a killer."

"Ma—"

"Let me finish. The way you've been treating Mara, that makes a momma plumped-up proud. You're a good man, Joey. I've been waiting a long time to tell you. But you never came home, and forgive your old Ma, it's not something I can say over the phone. I figured I'd better make good use of this moment because I'm afraid you'll leave again before I get the chance to tell you. Your father and I are proud of you. I wanted to say it. So that you hear it. So that you know it."

She lifted the edge of her white cotton apron and dabbed the cloth under one eye, then the next.

The little boy buried deep inside the man had desperately needed to hear the rarely granted accolade. Joey took the remaining two steps to bridge the gap and folded his mother in his arms. "I love you, Ma. Maybe I haven't told you so you understand, either. You and Dad gave me the skills to make a good life for myself. I just didn't realize to what extent until now."

His mother's breath hitched before her arms wrapped around him a bit tighter. He stood and held the woman who'd just lost her oldest son. The woman, wife and mother who reflected on life and her shortcomings. The woman he realized he didn't know very well and should take the time to know better.

For the first time in his life, he looked at his mother not as the disciplinarian, the negotiator, the teacher, but as the woman who had sacrificed a good part of her life to put food on the table, a roof over her family's heads, and provide opportunities for a better life for each of her children. The enraged bitterness of being so controlled in his youth began to dissipate, and left behind a gentler understanding of the family matriarch.

He looked out of the round kitchen window. "Where did Dad go?"

"Who knows? You know your father doesn't deal well with family matters. Don't judge him too hard, Joey."

"Judge him? I think you have the judgment part the wrong way around. Nothing I ever did was good enough."

"That's not true."

He couldn't stop an incredulous eyebrow from lifting. "Really?"

"What can I say? Your father has just never learned to love, or be loved. His parents were farmers who worked from sunup to sundown. The boys were in the field. The girls were in the kitchen. His family had little time for love."

"It's hereditary. That's his excuse. Is that what you're saying? That I'm going to beat my kids with belts, refuse to listen, and demand each get a college education with no support from the family? Ma, I'm not the one who barely graduated from high school. I'm also not the one who hides his liquor in the shed out back and thinks the family doesn't know."

His mother's eyes grew wide with hurt.

"I'm sorry. I didn't mean it." Joey crossed his arms and looked at his feet, struggling to button down his resentment.

"Yes you did," the defiance in her voice came through. "You've always spoken the truth. So I'm going to do the same." His pint-sized mother seemed to grow inches taller while he watched. "Your father works too much, he drinks, and he hides his feelings. He's difficult to read. So are you. Both of you have found jobs allowing an escape from the domestic world. You both can find any excuse to work and never come home. You're more like him than you realize."

No. I'm. Not. I'm nothing like that man.

His mother lifted her hand to his cheek and gave him a gentle pat. "You need to tell people in your life how you feel. Start with Mara. Go to her. You've watched that girl for a long time, Joey, and don't you roll your eyes. A mother sees things, even when you don't think she's watching. I'm thinking maybe you've been watching, possibly avoiding for too long. Do yourself a favor. Let her go and move on. Or take her hand and explore. Because, if there is one thing I've learned, there's only do or not do. There are no half-ways in life. And life is too short for regrets."

I've already got regrets. Enormous ones. Like not appreciating you more.

"I'm leaving tomorrow, Ma, and you raised me to not start something I can't finish. Watch over Mara for me, and I'll promise to do everything possible to avoid repeating history. But be warned. When I open up, you might not like what I have to say."

The softening of her shoulders gave him pause. "All I've ever wanted for my children is a healthy, independent life. Whether you want to believe it or not, your dad and I just wanted to give you a solid foundation. A good education. An understanding of how far a dollar stretches. Life isn't going to be all puppies and kittens, Joey. You have to work at making a happy life."

"And all this time I thought you weren't sentimental."

"When you become a father, Joey, you'll understand the genuine love and absolute terror of raising a child. It will change you. Your life will no longer be your own."

He uncrossed his arms and let her conviction circulate through his soul. "I resented you and Dad. Nothing I did was ever good enough."

"That's not true. You were always hard on yourself and just never heard the kudos. Oh, my Joey. Always so serious."

An awkward silence extended between them. Previous perceptions worked their way into a new form.

"I'd better go say my good-byes." Joey took a step to leave, then paused. "One more thing." His mother drew in a heavy, uneasy breath as if bracing for what he would say next. He admonished himself for the thoughtless choice of words, and thought carefully before he continued. "About Sam's case. I don't think Mark Walters killed Sam." He ran his hand over his head, then squeezed the base of his neck. "The details and timelines don't work."

"What are you saying?"

"The killer is still out there."

His mother placed a hand on his chest. "I can see in your eyes there's something more. Tell me."

"Something doesn't add up. My gut tells me Sam stumbled onto something big, too big, and he got himself killed. If Dad finds out, I'm afraid he might push the wrong buttons and make himself a target. We might want to put this behind us, at least for a while, before someone else gets hurt."

"Your father isn't going to like this."

Joey managed a dry puff of humor. "Why do you think I told you first and not him?"

"Joey Gaccione, I didn't raise a coward."

"No, no, Ma, you didn't. You raised a very intelligent man, one who knows not to light a firecracker while he's holding it, or tell his father something he absolutely does not want to hear."

"Then you go work your case in Seattle. I'll manage."

He had no doubt she would manage. The woman had a backbone of steel.

"No. I'll go find Dad. I just need to figure out how to get him to listen for once."

That's if I can find him.

He needed to find a way to get through to his dad the seriousness of the danger, because if he didn't, he just might have another murder to investigate.

His chest hollowed with sudden awareness. *I bet I know where he is.*

CHAPTER TWENTY-SEVEN

An hour later, Joey slid onto the stool at Mad Jack's bar. "I figured I'd find you here."

His father's bloodshot eyes turned slowly in his direction, took a few moments to focus, then squinted with disapproval.

"What are you doing here? You're s'pose to be with your mother." The whiskey-saturated statements tumbled out in one jumbled slur.

Joey glanced at the sports channel replaying the week's highlights, then the waitress clearing the tables for the night. His dad, the last patron in the place, sat cemented to the barstool. Jack closely monitored the activity, but remained at the other end of the counter washing dishes. He appeared ready to cash out for the night.

"You left without telling anyone where you were going." Joey monitored his father's movements. "The family's worried. Have you had enough?"

"Don't you start with me, boy."

Joey motioned to Jack, and the man he'd known since he could see over the bar came to stand in front of him, a drying towel and glass in his hands. "What'll it be?"

"Two coffees, black."

"I don't want any of that shit. Bugger off."

"No can do, Dad." His jaw clamped shut, preventing him from giving the man his unadorned, completely honest opinion, words he might regret if he had a moment to consider what he so eagerly wanted to say.

"What are you going to do? Huh? Force me? Come on, try it. I dare you—you little piss-ant. I'd squash you like the worthless bug you are. You didn't think I'd hear?"

"Hear what, Dad."

"I heard you didn't catch your brother's killer after all."

The agony of keeping his emotions tucked inside suddenly became too much, and he allowed his neck muscles to ease, his head to drop, and his hands to curl into tight fists.

Same old crap, just a different year.

Exhaustion from hearing the repetitive, worn-out commentary of his dad's opinion of him sank deep under his skin. He didn't want to fight. The adolescent fear had evaporated. In its place, he'd cultivated a mature sense of pity.

"Okay, Dad. You have a choice. You can drink some coffee, then I'll take you home. Or I'll have Jack cut you off, and we can sit here all night so you can continue to tell me what a worthless piece of crap I am."

"Jack's not going to cut me off. I just buried my son, for fuck's sake. In fact, pour me another double."

Joey's gaze connected with the old biker. He'd never known Jack to be anything other than a smart man, and Jack proved it by setting two cups of hot coffee on the old wooden bar, along with a bowl of creamer and some sugar.

The bartender's action spiked his father's temper to flaming hot, causing him to turn his laser-focused anger at Joey. "You're a pompous piece of shit. Why couldn't you be more like your brother?" His father's spittle and liquored breath landed on Joey's cheek, and he wrestled with the desire to fight back.

That's what his father wanted. A fight. An outlet for his rage, the intense rage that had been burning red hot for too many years.

"Antonio," Jack warned.

"It's okay, Jack," Joey said with a sigh. "He hasn't managed to say anything new for years."

A scowl tightened his dad's brows and mouth. "Why did you come back, anyways? Huh? Why?"

Good question. He'd asked himself the same thing a thousand times before getting on the plane. He hadn't come home out of obligation. The family ties had worn thin over the years. Had he come back to avoid more regrets? To find closure, possibly reconnect? Or was returning home his way of figuring out why he'd left in the first place?

"I don't know, Dad. It just seemed the right time—shitty circumstances, but the right time."

"What type of crap answer is that?"

"An honest one."

"An honest one…wah-wah-wah."

The sarcasm hit a raw nerve. He swallowed the vile taste of despair, let guilt seep into his bones, and strengthened his resolve to not let the liquor-saturated man before him push him to the edge. Never again. Never again would he allow another person to demoralize and degrade him until he believed the rhetoric. The drunk before him wouldn't qualify as a decent man, much less a father.

"Come on, Dad." He put a hand on his father's back and pushed up from his stool. "You can sober up at Sam's place." *Because there's no way you're going to lay a hand on Mom. Not while I'm here.*

Why she hadn't left him years ago, Joey had never understood.

"Don't touch me." His dad went to shove his arm away but missed and lost his balance, landing hard on the cement floor.

His eyes turned black with embittered animosity. "Look what you made me do."

The man rolled to his knees and slowly stood before taking a swaying step and another swing. His massive fist connected with Joey's jaw, and the pain exploded in his head, whipping his upper body to the side. His mind numbed and his body reacted by releasing years of pent-up wrath. His body whipped back, fingers bunched into a steel ball, picking up speed, connecting with his father's face. Surprise registered briefly in his father's eyes before they rolled up, his body losing the battle to remain vertical and toppling backwards like a felled tree.

Joey didn't reach out. Didn't try to break the fall. Just watched. A heavy sigh escaped as he shook the pain from his hand. *Well, crap.*

"I've been waiting for one of you boys to knock some sense into your old man."

Joey's gaze met Jack's. "Hitting him wasn't something I planned, but I can't say he didn't deserve some form of payback after all these years."

Jack chuckled with empathy. "Planned or not, I don't think many people would've gotten in your way. Some might even cheer you on. Let me get a bag of ice for your hand."

"Much appreciated."

Pain rocketed up and down his arm while he lowered to the barstool and checked to make sure he hadn't broken a finger. First his shoulder, now his face and hand. He glanced at the man on the floor, the adrenaline-induced numbness slowly winding down and easing into a throbbing agony.

He took a slow breath and let the events of the day seep in and register.

For too many years he'd been on the move, ducking and weaving like a fighter in the ring, trying to dance out of the way to avoid a bloodbath. Years of avoiding bloodshed had made him realize he could only dodge, crouch and bow to his father for so long before he became too tired to fight. Exhausted, he had to put an end to the abuse, and with a single punch, he'd taken a stand.

"Here you go." Jack passed him a clear bag of ice.

Lifting the bag, Joey placed the ice pack over his lower jaw and closed his eyes against the pain. "I suppose I should get him to Sam's place so I can keep an eye on him. I expect he'll be a bear come morning. Would you mind helping me get him to the car?"

Jack peered over the bar top. "You can leave him there if you want."

Tempting. "Thanks, but I think we need to have a conversation, and he needs to be sober for it. It'll be my last chance before heading to the airport. If he wakes up in this bar, he's liable to start in again. What do I owe you?"

"Why don't you have one of your sisters bring some leftovers over tomorrow, and we'll call today a wash?"

Small town kindness. He'd missed the hospitality. Sure, people in Seattle were friendly, but the Northwest goodwill only extended so far.

"Sounds good. Got a wheelbarrow so I can wheel his sorry ass out of here?"

"Just so you know, I'm sorry to see you go. I was hoping you were going to stay." A slow, humor-filled smirk settled across the bartender's face. "Give me five, and we'll figure something out."

Joey nodded, ignoring Jack's praise.

Then a realization began expanding like the sun's rays coming over the mountain ridge just before dawn.

This town hadn't changed.

He had. Mara had.

He promised her he'd protect her, yet all he'd done was put her in awkward situations with his family and break her heart.

He'd never forget the pain on her face. The best thing he could do for her was to leave her be.

The past week, he'd busted up his body but that didn't compare to his heart.

His body would mend.

His heart was a totally different matter.

CHAPTER TWENTY-EIGHT

Ouch! The biting sting of a fresh cut shot up Mara's hand and wrist while disappointment hunkered in as she contemplated just how many vases could be broken.

She rushed to the counter and shoved her fingers under the cold water while reaching for the first aid kit.

Anxiety and frustration over now needing to deal with an international vendor and possible insurance claim, she dropped the emergency box, and the contents scattered across the counter.

Really? What else can go wrong today?

While she was hunting for a bandage, the front doorbell sounded.

"I'll be with you in a minute," she said, trying hard to push the pain aside so she could sound pleasant and welcoming.

"Just me," Kym called back. "I came by to see how your dinner went with Joey."

Mara patted the counter, searching for the correct Band-Aid size.

"What happened?" Kym asked, accompanied by a snap and pop of bubble gum.

"The vases arrived broken."

"No way. That sucks."

"Especially since I don't have the time or money to replace them in time for Easter. I should have never ordered them from China. The time. The risk." Mara carefully wrapped the plastic strip around her finger, disposed of the extra paper, taking a few extra minutes to gather and shove the emergency supplies into the box.

The front door sounded again. "Be with you in a minute," Mara called and tucked the emergency kit back where the box belonged.

"Take your time," came the response.

The female voice, the elongated vowels, the sweet, lyrical tone, made her drop her head and cringe.

"What's wrong?"

Mara took a long, deep inhale to calm the queasy feeling beginning to rumble in her stomach. "It's Anna. Her parents probably sent her to apologize, but I don't want to deal with it today."

"No. I will deal with it. No one is going to call you pathetic."

Mara grabbed Kym before she could move. "No. You. Won't. You will smile and be nice to my customer." Mara stepped through the doorway into the front room, forcing her customer-friendly smile into place. "Good afternoon, Anna. How may I help you?"

Shuffling footsteps stalled and then approached the counter. "How did you know it was me?"

"It's complicated. Are you here for some flowers?"

"Actually, you left so quickly last night you forgot your coat, and didn't get any dinner. That's my fault. I shouldn't have said those things." At the clink of metal buttons on the counter, Mara reached for the familiar wool fabric. Joey's coat was still on her bed. Last night, she'd clung to the fabric doused with his scent as the hurt and pain absorbed into the torrent of tears.

"My sisters and I packed you some meals. They all can be frozen, except the tiramisu."

The rustling of bags and the quiver in Anna's voice gave Mara the impression Anna was uneasy and possibly feeling a tinge of genuine regret.

"That's mighty kind of you to bring the food," Kym stepped from the back room. "Mighty kind." The tightness in her friend's voice spelled trouble. Just for once, Mara wished people she loved would allow her to handle her problems.

"Anna, you remember Kym. She owns the salon next door." Mara pushed the residual animosity aside with an exhale.

"I think you did my nails for prom."

"Most likely. I think I did just about everyone's nails for prom."

Mara pulled the closest oversized bag of food across the counter hoping to draw Kym's attention away from Anna. "This is a lot of food. I appreciate you bringing it over. And, Anna, I understand why you said what you did. I know what people around town are saying. I do."

"Let's be clear. I said those things out of jealousy because you lived in a big house, had nice clothes, and drove a car. My sisters and I shared a room. I never had new clothes and had to make the best out of patched hand-me-downs. I couldn't even make the cheerleading squad."

"Maybe, you should have practiced more." Kym purred.

Tension rolled like a ball of string across the tiled floor, getting more tangled as it went.

"That's just the thing." Mara hugged her coat to her chest. "Anna almost made the squad. I sat on the judging panel, and you were one slot away from making the team. You should have tried again your sophomore year."

"My point." Kym pushed her agenda again.

"Kym," Mara warned, "I'm sure Anna knows anything can

be achieved with practice. Nothing, and I mean nothing, is easy for me. In school, I felt like a dork half the time."

"You were a dork, but we all loved you anyway."

"Speak for yourself." Mara laughed, then Kym joined in, followed closely by Anna. Mara loved the expanding harmonic sound, because it had a thread of forgiveness, provided a sense of peace, and began to bind the women together.

"My friends call me a dork all the time. We're more alike than I thought," Anna admitted.

The way Anna's explanation crumpled together almost as a single word made Mara suspect admitting the similarities must have been excruciating. The tension again expanded, and Mara contemplated ways to calm Anna's uneasiness.

"I should get back to sorting out the mess in the back. I can't believe all my vases arrived broken."

"Can I help?" Anna offered.

"I have an idea." Kym's nasally tone grew tight. "Why don't you two go check the order, while I put away all this food. All of the vases can't be broken."

"If they are, maybe Anna will want them. Are you still doing those fun mosaics?"

"How did you remember?"

"Are you kidding? Your artwork is amazing. Maybe you can use the broken pieces on new projects. The shipper certainly won't want them back. If you're willing, I can sell your art in the store. We just need to keep the items small because space is limited. A little extra cash never hurts."

"Really? That would be great." The excitement in Anna's voice generated a warm, buzzy elation. "I've been looking for a part-time job, but employment in college towns is hard to find."

"You could do some sample pieces to see how they sell before fully committing."

"Yolo, right?"

That's right. You only live once.

Anna's enthusiasm was contagious.

"What are you going to do when you graduate this spring?" Mara asked. "Business, right?"

"Entrepreneurial business design, actually."

The reluctance in Anna's voice made her wish she hadn't been so nosy. "Don't you hate those vexing questions? I do. After I found out I wouldn't get my eyesight back, people kept pushing to discover what was next. I never knew the answer. The way I figured it, I didn't have a choice but to take one day at a time."

"I don't mind you asking. It's just no one knows. I got a call and accepted a job in Denver this morning."

"That sounds wonderful." Mara took a step closer. "But somehow I don't think you're excited about it."

"No, I am. It's with one of the biggest marketing firms in town."

"But...?"

"But I know my parents want me to come home and help with the restaurant."

Parental expectations. Joey seemed to have a similar problem. Mara perceived her parents had a list full of expectations. College, a job at a big CPA firm, marriage, grandkids. She envisioned her mom and dad designing her destiny and putting her life into a perfect picture frame. Too bad the frame was shattered before the picture was completed.

"Are you sure that's what your parents want? Sometimes, a conversation is needed just to be sure we know what's-what."

"You might be right about perceptions and conversations. I should talk to them. My starting salary is great. I'll be able to pay off my student loans faster because the last thing I want is debt hanging over my head."

"That's the right attitude. Maybe I'll even hire you to figure out how to make my business run more efficiently."

Anna fell silent again, and provided a reason for Mara to open that invisible door a bit wider. "Or if you have ideas now, I would love to hear them."

For the next ten minutes, Anna rattled off a number of articulated ideas, each one better than the last, about managing the inventory and catering to commercial clients rather than just the public.

"I don't know, Anna."

"What's not to know? Anna's ideas are amazing." Kym said on her way down the back stairs. "I mean really, amazing."

"You think so?"

"I know so. Ideas like these are exactly what could help make this business sing."

Every time Gina, Tony or Kym mentioned a new idea Mara squirmed. *Maybe it's me, and my insecurities that are preventing this business from being profitable.*

Anna's sudden insight hurt. "Hearing your great advice makes me realize I don't have all the skills I need to run a successful business. My mom ran this shop as a hobby, and to get out of the house while my dad worked. The business wasn't set up as a moneymaker, but we have to make a profit. This business is all Tony and I have. We have to make this work."

"Have you considered doing something else?"

Something else? "Like what?"

"Really?" Kym piped in. "How about accepting Jake's offer to sing, or Karly's offer to train dogs? You can do anything if you practice."

Oh, she so wanted to stick her tongue out at Kym, but managed to control the urge.

Doing something different had crossed her mind, but her blindness created limitations. Singing and songwriting had come to mind, but she was no Taylor Swift.

"I've worked in this shop since junior high, and even before then. Arranging flowers is what I know. After the accident, learning to walk the streets of Elkridge took me almost a year. Even though I've lived here all my life except for the semester I went to college, I had to learn how to get around, how to do the basics. When you can't see, life limits your options. So I'm determined to make this business work."

Anna's hand landed on her forearm. "You can do it. You make fabulous arrangements."

"It's not hard. You just have to know the configurations."

"Seems hard."

Mara noted the apprehension again, and figured maybe a demonstration might help. "You know, Anna, if you focus your mind on your goals, you can do just about anything. Let me show you." She stood and pulled some supplies off the shelves. "Can you hand me one of those vases?"

Cold glass touched her outstretched hand, and she closed her fingers around the object. "Ah, this is one of the smaller, shallow pots. So we're going to use a one-three-five configuration. See those buckets of flowers over there? I want you to pick out one snapdragon bunch, three mums or daisies, and five stems of greens that are in the smaller buckets, and bring them to me. There are labels with the flower names on the side of the buckets to guide you."

Mara listened to the hesitant footsteps while she centered the bowl on the worktable and prepared the jar with water-soaked floral foam, securing the green circle with floral tape to the bottom of the jar, then placed fresh moss on top, tucking the greenery into the sides.

"Here you go."

Mara accepted the flowers from Anna and spread them on the countertop. "Great. Now I'll show you the secret to making great arrangements." She felt the flower stems, selecting the thickest one. "Take your snapdragon, and freshen the stalk by cutting off the end at an angle. This will help the flower absorb water. Place the single stem in the center, like this." She pushed the stem gently into the foam. "Do the same with your next three flowers, placing them at two, six and ten o'clock." Using touch, she selected a stalk of mums and placed the separate bunches. "Then take your five greenery stems, placing them at one, three, five, seven, and nine o'clock. *Voila!* You have an arrangement. Just water using a flower nutrient additive, and your flowers should last a week or more."

"You make flower arranging look so easy."

"You make business management sound easy. All I have to do is remember to let the flowers do the work." *It's websites and social media and business plans that give me the hives.* "Take the flowers home, Anna. Enjoy them."

The small, thrilled gasp made Mara gather her caution flags and put them away.

"You know, I've been in a panic." Anna admitted. "Next Monday, I have to turn in an idea for my senior cornerstone project. Every senior has to pick a business and write a paper on how we would improve business operations. My friends started their papers weeks ago. So far, I haven't been able to think of anything other than my parent's restaurant. Which would be stick-a-finger-down-my-throat boring."

The passion tumbling out paused briefly. Then, hesitantly, Anna asked, "Would you be willing to collaborate on my paper? I don't know the flower industry, but I'm willing to learn, and like you said, I already have some ideas we could work on together. I could use the school library to review market statistics and demographics."

Mara silently groaned. "I wouldn't want to trouble you."

Kym nudged her in the side. "Yes you would. Take her offer. She has some great ideas, and it's a win-win for you and her."

"Well, if you wouldn't mind." Mara worked to ease the apprehension building.

"Mind? This is going to be great. I'm going home right now to start the research. I've got so many ideas."

"Oh...okay." The click of excited footsteps followed by the front doorbell ringing made her wonder what she just had agreed to. Mara stood in the middle of her shop perplexed.

"That wasn't so bad, was it?" The smugness in Kym's voice she could also do without today.

"What are you up to, Kym Zhang."

"Oh, I don't know." The sweetness in her friend's voice made her brace for impact. "I bet Anna will come up with some good ideas so you don't have to work so hard. You could have the time to train dogs, which you love. Or, sing. Imagine that. A fulfilling life. Seeing my best friend happy, a spectacular thought."

"I'm happy."

"As a rock."

"Why are you here? Don't you have customers or something?"

"I'm here because you're in love with Joey and he got on an airplane today. So I came to make sure you were all right. I didn't expect miss fancy pants to stop by, but turns out a Gaccione had already crashed your pity-party. Come on. Admit it."

"I wasn't feeling sorry for myself."

The tinkle of broken glass made her turn. "Careful. Don't cut yourself."

"Don't change the subject. You were nose deep in self-pity, but it's okay if you don't want to admit it. How about I unpack. You stack. What do you say?"

"I guess I say, thank you." Mara held out her arms. "Come here you. I need a hug."

"See, told you. No pity-parties without including me, because I give great hugs." Kym wrapped her arms around Mara's shoulders.

After a few seconds Mara pulled back. "Do you think Joey will ever come back for a visit?"

"I certainly wouldn't hold my breath. It took him ten years to come back the first time."

"You're right. I thought for sure he'd stay in Elkridge."

"You've got a business to run. You have no time to think about men."

Kym was right.

She needed to move on.

Now if she could just get her heart to oblige.

CHAPTER TWENTY-NINE

"Let's not talk about this during Gina's baby shower." Mara turned her back on Tony, and headed to the kitchen to find Kym and the party supplies.

The air smelled sickly sweet with a bitter undertone. If she ate one more cupcake, cake pop, or drank one more cup of coffee, Kym might need to pull her down from the ceiling. The sound of Tony's footsteps following her a bit too closely made her skin tighten.

"If not now, when?"

How about never?

"What's up with you two?" The snippy in Kym's question made Mara pause. "You've been at each other all day."

"I just don't want to talk finances. I understand the pizza shop is closing, and that means Gina's out of a job. But can we not talk business for just *one* day?"

"I'm talking survival here. How do you think Gina and I are going to be able to pay a mortgage, put food on the table and raise a baby on my income?" Tony challenged.

First you could eat at home more. "I've been thinking about that, so I've—"

"How about we let Gina come to work at the flower shop. We could set up a crib in the back room, and she could help you with the store. That way you wouldn't be in the store alone anymore."

And, you wouldn't worry so much. The overload of caffeine and sugar made her stomach ache. "We were barely making it on three incomes. How do you suggest we make it on less?"

"Well...."

"Why don't you tell him about Anna's plan?" Kym interrupted. "She had some good ideas."

"Anna? Who's Anna," Tony asked.

"Joey's sister. The one who's getting her business degree." Mara pushed the plate of extra cupcakes aside and went in search of the party supplies.

"The one who said all those nasty things about you? And don't scrunch your face at me. That little snot should get her butt kicked."

"How did you hear...never mind. This town is way, way, way too small." Mara sighed, wishing Tony didn't solve all his problems with anger and reached forward finding the bags she and Kym prepared for the party. "Anna came to apologize, and, while she was here, she offered to put together a business plan for us. Tony, I wish you would give people more of a chance. She sounded like she really was sorry...didn't she Kym."

"She did." Kym took the bags from her hand. "Let me help."

"So are you going to tell me about Anna's plan, or not?"

"Actually, no. I have a different idea." Mara folded her arms across her stomach fisting her hands to hold in the jitters zinging though her arms and chest. "What if I turn Blooms over to you and Gina to run? Both of you have good ideas and want to expand, but I've been reluctant to make the necessary changes because I've been afraid."

"Afraid. I've never known you to be scared of anything."

Tony took a step closer, his hand landing on her arm. "Why didn't you say something?"

"I didn't want to be a burden." Mara felt a sting at the back of her eyes. She turned away to gain her composure. "I also didn't want anyone to see that I wasn't capable of running the shop. Gina and Anna both have great ideas, but implementing them would be a challenge—for me anyway."

"You can do it." Both Kym and Tony said simultaneously.

"That's just the point. I don't want to." Mara bit her lip. Here was her chance. Now or never. "I called Karly yesterday to ask if I could work for her."

"You did what?" The shock in Tony's voice hit her like a hundred-mile-an-hour baseball to the chest. "You don't need to find another job."

"You don't understand. I want to work with Karly. She needs the help, and she offered to let me keep all the money I make from obedience classes and training service dogs. In return, I would assist at the shelter and help with adoption days. It's something I love, and it would provide an opportunity for you and Gina to make the changes you want to make."

"Who would do the flower arrangements?"

"Gina could do the arranging. I could train her. Since I'd still be living in the apartment, I could step in when needed." Mara let out a long stream of air. "I wanted to discuss all these changes with Gina present. It's a big decision, and I wanted her to be involved."

"I say yes." The excitement in Gina's voice blared into the kitchen and provided Mara some relief. "And, your nephew agrees. Anthony just smiled. Mara, do you want to hold him?"

Mara held out her arms to accept the precious bundle. "I'm glad you like the idea." She said to all in general. "You should also know, Jack stopped by to give me my check. Over two-hundred bucks—just for singing."

Kym wrapped an arm around her shoulder. "I told you, you'd be great."

"Jack extended his offer again, but I said no."

"What? Why would you do that?" Kym's chastise made her smile.

"Because, I told him I'd only do twice a month. I need time to practice and get my song list put together." She shifted her nephew in her arms. "I know the payoff won't be that much going forward, but I'd be getting paid for doing something I'd do for free."

Kym gave a tug on her hair. "Brat."

"Look at that." Gina cooed over her adorable baby. "Little Tony is giving you a high-five."

"Oh, God," Tony groaned. "There are too many women in this kitchen. I'll be out back with the guys drinking a beer."

As the footsteps disappeared, Gina started to giggle, then Kym, before she joined in.

Family. This was her family.

She reached to find the contentment deep inside, but couldn't find a thread, and understood why—Joey.

He wasn't here.

She missed him.

Every day, she wanted to pick up the phone and call, but she couldn't.

Instinctively, she understood he needed to find his own way home.

While he had been in town, she'd hoped to show him he was needed in Elkridge. His family needed him. She needed him. Somehow, the love of family and friends wasn't enough to bring him back. She wasn't enough.

Mara couldn't blame him. After all, who would want the burden of a blind person?

A bitter acceptance fell into place, and she pulled her

nephew closer. "Hey little man. I'm going to spoil you rotten. Yes, I am." She leaned in to kiss his forehead.

At least going forward, she'd have puppies and babies in her life.

Unfortunately, none of them would be hers.

CHAPTER THIRTY

Joey reread the case memo on his desk for the sixth time without comprehending a single sentence.

The past nine days had seemed like an eternity.

The moment he dropped the pen on his desk, his hand moved automatically to the phone handset, then withdrew.

What are you doing? Call her.

He lifted the receiver and dialed before he lost the nerve again.

"Hello?"

He closed his eyes and let her voice soothe the deeply embedded loneliness that had hit him as soon as his feet touched the airport ramp.

"Mara, it's Joey." The silence on the other end of the line did nothing for his confidence. "Are you there?"

"I'm here."

He allowed her voice to remove his doubts. She was still there, a lifeline on the other end of the phone. He'd never realized how bleak his world had become until Mara wasn't in his life providing a ray of sunshine.

"How's Seattle?" she asked finally.

"It's okay. It's been raining every day since I got here, and I've been crazy busy."

Busy because he needed to catch up, but more importantly, because he didn't want to return to his empty apartment. The once masculine, yet modern, chic steel metal, grays and creams seemed sterile and gloomy.

"I miss you," she admitted softly. Suddenly, his lungs opened and he could breathe again. "I think the deputies miss the extra set of hands as well. At least that's the scuttlebutt at the Café. You made a good impression while you were here."

I hope you miss me more. "That's why I called. Mom told me there was another break-in."

"Yep. The Bainbridge sisters were robbed at gunpoint. People are scared. Elkridge doesn't know how to deal with this. It used to be big news when people got lost on the ridge, the road flooded out or a bear ate some trash. Not anymore."

Jesus Christ. "Are the sisters okay?"

"They have minor cuts and some bruising from being tied up and left for ten hours. A nosy neighbor found them after he got suspicious when they didn't pick up their mail. They're okay. Just shaken up."

The violence was escalating. And instinct told him the crimes were going to get worse. "Any arrests?"

"Nope. Not yet." There was a pause. "Your mom stopped by yesterday."

He felt a smile creep across his face in concert with the lift of an eyebrow in wonderment. "What did she want?"

"She asked if I would be willing to supply flowers for the tables at the restaurant. She said something about needing to start supporting the people of Elkridge. She mentioned canceling contracts with vendors and using local suppliers."

"Did she?" His smile expanded. "That's good. I hope more stores in Elkridge decide to do the same."

"Anna also came by to apologize and offered to help Tony

and me with a business plan. She sent me a draft outline yesterday. Tony converted the document to my reader. She's got some great ideas, many of them I think we can implement. She's very talented."

He sat back in his chair, not knowing what to say.

"Joey, if you're calling to check on me about, well, you know…"

"Are you having regrets?"

"None. I told you before I wouldn't." The truth was reassuring. "Do you have regrets?"

Only one. "No," he finally managed. "Well, maybe. The only regret I have is not coming home sooner." *And staying.*

"Next time, don't wait so long between trips." She sighed. "Joey, it's nice to hear your voice, but I'm late for an appointment."

Frustration carved a chunk out of each syllable. "Take care of yourself. Call anytime. 'Bye."

The click of the phone interrupted him just as he was about to tell her he didn't want to be gone at all.

As he hung up, movement across the room caught his attention. Two official-looking men in blue suits entered his boss's office. All sorts of people visited, from the DA to other public officials, but this time, he recognized one of them as his buddy from the Joint Task Force Office. Chuck gave him a look that said, *we need to talk.*

A few minutes later, a "Gaccione!" shout rang out from across the cubicles. "My office," his boss demanded.

Everyone in the squad room turned around and looked at him. He could hear the snide remarks now. What had Boy Wonder done to get his butt in a sling? His feet dragged a bit while he tried to get his head around what the visit meant.

"Take a seat," his boss suggested as he closed the door behind him.

Joey assessed the one man he didn't know—the emotionless

stare, the red power tie, the erect posture. The man had an invisible FBI pin attached to his suit's breast pocket.

"These gentlemen would like to ask you a few questions." The way his boss sat back in his chair and crossed his arms gave him the impression his mentor wasn't happy.

He didn't bother telling his friend he'd met Chuck years ago and had spoken to him last week. Turning slightly, he grabbed the back of the chair to keep from crossing his arms, a sure indicator of defensiveness. A slow, deep breath helped maintain his usual heart rate. "What can I help you with, gentlemen?"

"I'm Special Agent Bantner."

"Joey...Joe, it's Joe Gaccione."

"You called me about a week ago. At the time you called, I was not at liberty to inform you I'm in charge of a special joint FBI and DEA taskforce. We've checked your security clearance and received permission to inform you we know who killed your brother, and it wasn't Mark Walters."

Joey sucked in a gallon full of air. "Have you arrested the man?" he asked, even though the man's body language had provided the answer. Yet he needed to hear the words.

"Unfortunately, no. I'm going to ask for your patience and cooperation in the matter. Your brother's killer is a pawn in a much larger case, and we've only recently managed to place someone on the inside. We can't risk bringing the man to justice yet, for reasons I'm sure you can guess, but I promise, he will be charged and convicted."

Sacrificing one for the greater good. He hated the thought, but accepted it.

"How long?"

"A year, maybe two," Bantner offered, not pretending to mistake the question. A quiet respect for the man began to form.

"It's big, isn't it? Whatever's happening in Elkridge is big, and my brother just happened to push a little too hard, or be in the wrong place at the wrong time."

Chuck stepped closer. "When you called, you said you'd been asked to run for Sheriff."

"Is there a reason you didn't accept the offer?" Bantner asked.

Yes, and it's none of your damn business. "I get the impression you're about to ask me to reconsider."

Bantner looked around the room. "As a matter of fact, yes. We need someone in place we can trust and call on if needed— be part of the team. Your assignment would be a promotion of sorts."

"You mean you need someone in place to keep a lid on the drug issues while you work the sex trafficking angle." His eyes connected and held Bantner's direct stare. "Am I wrong?"

"At this moment, I can't answer your question. It's classified."

"Well then, since we're not going to have *this* conversation, you didn't hear me suggest you check into the pharmacy records and find out who's purchasing prenatal vitamins, or get a surveillance camera into the local grocery store to ID the guy purchasing feminine products. He's about six-foot-two, brown hair, drinks, smokes and possibly rolls his own cigarettes with a strain of marijuana with licorice accents." *And I have shell casings, a marijuana joint and a pile of other evidence I'm keeping in a safety deposit box, for now, until I know whom to trust.*

Bantner turned to Joey's boss. "How fast can we get this man to Denver?"

The belligerent straightening of his boss's shoulders made him take a step forward to avoid the brewing confrontation. "I need to go, sir. Based on this visit, I can only assume my family and everyone I love is in real danger. I'm not a hothead—you know that. Someone needs to protect the residents of that small town. If not me, who? Small-town deputies don't know how to handle big crime. Someone else is going to get killed if they don't get the proper training. Someone in that town is dirty, I just don't know who, and maybe these guys can flush that person out."

His boss pointed at Bantner. "If anything happens to Gaccione, I'm going to hold you two personally responsible."

"Before I accept your offer," Joey took a deep breath, "I have two conditions." He turned to face the suits. "I need funds to update the electronics in the cars, and I want body cams and armor for each deputy. I'll find the funds for training, but I want the deputies protected."

"And the second?" The question was asked without hesitation.

"I need a contact, someone who will warn me if I'm getting too close. I don't plan on taking a bullet."

Bantner extended his hand. "Your requests are fair. After you become sheriff, you'll receive paperwork to apply for special grant monies for developing rural counties. My suggestion is not to ignore that paperwork. In the packet, you'll find a contact number."

Joey extended his hand to Chuck with gratitude. "Thank you." He also shook hands with Bantner.

"Watch your back," Chuck suggested. "Colorado has some great skiing. Never know, I might come out for a visit."

"You're welcome anytime. A visit from an old college friend, perhaps?"

A slow, shrewd acknowledgement crossed Chuck's face before the two men funneled out of the office and shut the door behind them. Joey sank slowly into the visitor chair. His boss and mentor rolled his shoulders back.

"You sure about this?"

Joey tapped his fingers on his knee. A combination of excitement and caution crashed into his chest. "You've put together a talented team, and I've had the privilege of serving among some of the best. The Elkridge department needs train- ing, discipline, and leadership. If they can't handle petty theft, how are they going to handle something big? Recently, I've discovered that Elkridge will always be my home. Those people are my family. I couldn't live with the fact I knew what was coming and did nothing to help them prepare."

His boss steepled his fingers in front of his face. "Then I suggest your mother has become critically ill, and you need to leave immediately under the guise of the Family Medical Leave Act. After your twelve weeks are up, you can submit your resignation. How's that sound?"

"It sounds like I need to finish writing my reports. Thank you, sir."

"Gaccione, it's been my pleasure. If you ever change your mind, you have a place in my organization."

Joey nodded and walked toward the door, knowing nothing would change his mind.

The choice felt right.

Unfortunately, he'd need to learn to keep secrets. Keeping information from his family would be easy. Mara? Not so much.

CHAPTER THIRTY-ONE

Nothing had changed. Mara still missed Joey every minute of every day.

His absence left a hollow space that echoed throughout the day, always there, never absent, and intruding into everything she did. She'd tried shutting off the feelings. Not calling him had been the toughest of all.

He'd left her a cryptic voice message a few days earlier when she was training Gina and couldn't get to the phone fast enough. Late at night, lying in bed, she could play the recorded message over and over and over, just to hear his voice. He sounded busy and tired.

She traced the leaves of a violet with her fingers, checking for dead leaves and feeling the soil to determine if the potted plant needed watering. As she leaned over to lift the watering can, the store's bell sounded.

"Good morning. Please let me know if there's anything I can help you with."

The customer didn't respond. She took a deep inhale, checking for the smell of cigarettes or alcohol. Then she heard it. That faint little squeak. The one she desperately longed to hear, but hadn't believed she'd hear, at least in the near future.

She slowly stood and held her breath, making sure the noise wasn't just a hopeful inventiveness.

"Are you here for a bouquet for your mom? Or are you considering a plant this time?"

"You're truly amazing. I'm not here to make a purchase." The light humor in the tenor voice seemed promising. "In fact, I'm here to see if the shop owner would take a walk with me."

Her heart's pitter-patter was so loud in her ears she almost didn't hear him ask her to take a walk. A confetti-tossing excitement burst out of her heart and filled her.

"We'll have to wait. Gina took my nephew to the pediatrician, and Tony's out delivering flowers," she managed in a calm and collected voice. "He should be back any minute."

The squeak moved closer and closer, until she could savor the familiar scents that eased her soul.

"I just called him. He said he'll be here in ten. And he said not to wait." His gentle fingers wrapped around hers.

"Joey what are you doing here?"

"I figured another ten years was a bit too long. Plus, I had some unfinished business in town."

Sam's killer. He just couldn't let his brother's death go. Instinct had told her he'd be back, just not so soon.

"Where's Buddy?" he asked.

At the mention of his name, Buddy came through the doorway. Joey squatted and waited for the dog. "Hey, Buddy. Missed you, big guy. Ready to take a walk?"

You missed my dog, but not me? She choked out a laugh at Buddy's thrilled response, his claws *tap-tapping* on the floor. "Now you've done it. You said the W-A-L-K word. I'll get his halter."

Mara took the necessary steps to retrieve Buddy's harness

and her coat and prepared for a journey. "You never said where we're going."

"It's a surprise."

Her heart pounded with trepidation. She didn't like surprises. People didn't understand that when you're blind, newness was a bit scary. Joey, however, she would follow to the end of the trail and back.

He led her to the front door.

"Can you flip the 'open' sign?" she asked.

"Got it. Here we are on Main Street. Right?"

"Yes. Thank you." The sarcasm in her voice expanded. "I think I know where our business is located." If the muscles in her eyes would allow her to roll them, she would. "What are you up to?"

"You'll understand in a few minutes. Just trust me."

Trust him? That she did. Joey led her around the corner and up the hill, past the grocery store and post office, then right.

"Do you know where we are?" he asked.

"Cherry Street. Up ahead are the municipal buildings and the city park. To the left are houses."

"You're amazing. Come with me. I want to show you something."

A gate opened and Joey tugged at her arm. She drew a deep breath and took a leap of faith to follow him. She could feel the excitement in his twitching muscles. He practically sizzled with anticipation while he helped her climb three stairs and then escorted her through an open doorway. Her clogs clunked on what sounded like wood flooring.

"Joey?"

He took her by the hand. "I wanted to show you this house. Here's the living room," he tugged again on her hand, "and through here is the kitchen. It's small, just the way you like it. You said you like to be able to touch everything. The kitchen doesn't have much cabinet space, but I can add more storage, eventually."

"Cabinets. For what? I don't understand."

"Neither did I until I went back to Seattle. I want to come home, Mara. To stay."

"But what about your career?"

"I called the mayor. He said the sheriff position might still be open. The people of Elkridge will hold a special election soon, but I could fill an interim position until then."

"So you've come home to find Sam's killer."

"No. Well, yes. I've come home to protect this town and the people I care for, but we're not here because of Sam."

She turned around. The echo of her footsteps filled the space. "This house is empty. Is this Martha Bishop's home? Someone from out of town made the purchase," she whispered, putting clues together like flowers in a bouquet. "It's you. You bought this house."

"Yes." His admission was delivered almost as a whisper.

"Four bedrooms is a mighty big house." She couldn't breathe. Should she dare hope he might not be thinking of living alone?

"Mara?" He took her hand and pressed her palm to his chest. "Do you feel that?"

"The beat of your heart?" The strong *lub-dub, lub-dub* pulsed under her fingers, easing her breath, helping her fall into the same steady pattern.

"Not just the beat, but the ache. Knowing I wanted to be with you, but I couldn't because you were here and I was in Seattle. You said no strings, but that doesn't work for me. I'm more of a long-term type of guy."

Tears spilled over onto her cheeks, her chest tightened, and she suddenly was completely certain she couldn't love Joey any more than she did at that moment.

"So you want me?" she asked, wanting him so much to say

yes. Yes, he wanted her, even as broken as she was, he wanted her.

"No, Mara."

Her world stopped and tilted. Despair swamped her until his chin came to rest on the top of her head.

"I don't just want you. I need you. You're my oxygen. You fill me. I bought this house for us, because your apartment is too small for us, and the kids I want to have with you. Marry me, Mara. Make me the happiest man in Elkridge."

"Did you just ask me to marry you?"

"I know the proposal is unexpected and not very romantic, but I feel like I've waited for you all my life. I don't want to be apart anymore. I promise I'll be the most romantic guy on this planet going forward. And before you ask, I'll add being romantic to my list of things to practice. Please say yes."

The events of the past weeks came flooding back, sweeping away a response. The joy of the previous moment crashed into the wall of responsibilities, and her heart wrenched. "Oh, Joey. I'm not sure I can accept your offer."

"Why not?" he asked, not able to keep the confused hurt from filling the empty room.

"It's not you. Really. It's just...I don't want to be a burden to anyone. With all the changes that have happened in the last several weeks, Anna got me thinking."

"Anna? What does my sister have to do with us?"

She rested her hand on his chest again and felt his tension. "When we were talking about the flower shop, she asked if I'd ever considered doing something else. At the time I dismissed the question, most likely out of fear. After the accident, I took over the flower shop because arranging flowers was the only job I felt I could do at the time. Anna reminded me that we only live once."

"I don't get what your flower shop has to do with us."

"It doesn't. It has to do with me. A couple of days ago, we

had a family meeting, and I officially turned the flower shop management over to my brother. With all of Anna's great ideas, I'm sure Tony and Gina will do fine."

Joey took a step back and began pacing around the room. "Does that mean you're leaving Elkridge?"

Leave? Laughter bubbled in her throat. "No. I can't leave. I know where I belong, and it's here, in Elkridge."

"Then what are you going to do?"

"I'm going to do something different. Jack's offered to let me sing at the pub, and I'm going to start a dog training business. With Karly's help, I'm going to expand the class schedule at Helper Shelter. There's a demand for more classes, and it's something I love doing. Besides, there's a shortage of trained guide dogs to help people like me."

All of a sudden, arms circled her waist, and her feet left the ground. "Really? That's wonderful news."

Joey spun her in circles to the point she couldn't contain her laughter. Even Buddy joined in the frenzy and let out a rare but exuberant bark. When Joey finally set her back on her feet, she hung onto his arms for balance.

"From your reaction, I take it you don't think it's odd that I'll be singing in a pub."

"No, why would I?"

'Cause my parents would be appalled. "It might hurt your chances of getting elected. You know how this town is."

"I do, and I don't care. I'll handle the election. I want to marry you, Mara Dijocomo. It's that simple."

"Joey, are you sure?"

"Yes, I'm sure. You make me laugh. You say what you mean. I don't have anything to prove when I'm with you, yet, you inspire me to be a better person."

She turned her head and placed an ear against his chest, needing to feel his heat, hear his heartbeat. Tears welled and trickled down her face, soaking into his flannel shirt.

"Shhh, it's okay. If you don't want to get married now, I'll wait. But I'm warning you—I won't give up. You and I are meant to be together. I've waited a long time to be with you. I'll wait until you're ready. Please don't cry."

Her hands skimmed up his body to find his face. "You don't understand. These are tears of joy, not of pain." The melancholy of the previous moments evaporated. "Do you really want to have kids? What will your family think?"

He grabbed her by the wrist and kissed the sensitive skin. "My mother might have concerns—for you, that is. After all, if I get elected sheriff, you might have some doubt about marrying a town official. I'll probably be working long hours and gone sometimes, plus there will be things I can't share. Would you have a problem with that?"

"Serving and protecting people is part of who you are. You're really good at it. This town needs you." She clutched his shirt. "Did you really buy this house?"

"We needed a bigger bed and a kitchen that fits two grownups, but yes, I bought this house for us. My salary will be considerably lower, but we can budget. I don't have much to offer, but I wanted to find a place that made you feel safe, and makes you happy, especially since I'll be gone a lot. The house is within walking distance of pretty much everything in this town. There's a yard out back. You could grow flowers or herbs or anything else you want. That reminds me."

He pulled her with him and placed her hand on the back door knob. "Open the door, slowly."

She twisted the cold metal and cracked the door, but the door was shoved open and bumped against her forehead. Chaos erupted, with dogs barking and Joey rubbing her head. She became disoriented.

He pulled her against his chest. "That didn't work so well. Let's try this again. Lean forward and reach out your hand."

She reached out her fingers and felt a coarse, sandpapery

texture and snatched her hand back. She thought for a moment before reaching out again and squatting in front of the exuberant obstacle. "Gus?"

A wiry, fuzzy mass pushed against her and flopped at her feet. She tilted her head up. "You adopted Gus?"

"I figure he's so ugly, no one else will adopt him. He's a good dog, one of the best scent hounds around, and he adores you and will protect you when I'm not here. Maybe he can be your first student."

Her chest tightened and a burst of laughter escaped as she stood and turned into his arms.

"Mara...there's one more thing. You might not be happy with me, but...um..."

His muscles tightened and contracted, giving her an uneasiness signal. "What is it? Talk to me."

"Well you know that girl Brianne you talked about? The one who blames herself for the accident?"

"Yes," the word elongated with concern. "What about her?"

"I did some checking with the State. Brianne's a little older than Sophia, but quiet and seems into the same things as my niece. Changing foster homes every few months isn't a healthy way to grow up. You said you were the only one she connected to."

"Because of the accident, she believes we have a connection somehow. And she's right. She lost her entire family. I can understand how that feels."

"I was thinking she might fit nicely into the family. We meet the criteria of foster parents. All we need to do is complete coursework and an assessment. I figured if we both watched our spending, we could afford—"

Mara squealed and jumped into his arms, wrapping both legs and arms around him. "I love you, Joey Gaccione. You're the kindest and most wonderful man."

He sucked in a breath of air. "Is that a yes?"

"You might have regrets when I hold you to the romantic and kissing part. Even a blind girl has standards," she said, trying to make him laugh.

"Is that so?" He lifted her higher to capture her lips for a long, slow, beguiling kiss. She poured all her dreams and wishes and heat into the kiss, hoping he understood what he'd just given her.

"Mmm. Practice." She pressed her nose against his skin and inhaled. "We definitely need a lot of practice. Like every-day-for-the-rest-of-my-life kind of practice."

His laughter filled the kitchen.

"Like I said, a woman after my own heart. I love you, Mara, and I don't care what you do, as long as I can come home to you every night. I think I've loved you from the first moment I saw you."

His fervor and sincerity took a moment to absorb. The fear of being alone forever began to dissolve. His large family and Tony and Gina would be there. Joey had come home, back to family, back to her, to stay.

Joey placed a finger under her chin and lifted. "So, Ms. Dijocomo, is that a yes?"

She hadn't realized he needed her to say the words. He'd become her every thought. His memory had been with her every morning when she made her coffee and every afternoon when she was doing chores. And his memory had been with her every night, invading her dreams, holding her and making love to her over and over again. How could he not know?

She curled into his body. "I've dreamed of finding someone who would want to be with me. I'm blind, and some days I can't walk so well."

"Mara—"

"Please let me finish." She placed her forehead on his chest and then lifted her chin so he could clearly hear her response. "And then you came along. You never treated me like I was different. You never treated me like I was broken, handicapped or helpless. And for that reason, I fell in love with you, Joey. I want to build a life together. The answer is yes."

"Yes?"

"Yes!"

Joey lifted Mara and swung her around, their laughter lifting and expanding into a perfect harmony, before he set her gently back down. He cupped her face and kissed her nose, eyes, and chin until she giggled. Then the moment stilled.

"Ummm, Joey? You mentioned kids. Do you think we can start practicing soon? Because I think we need to practice—a lot."

I'm so glad you could join Mara and Joey on their journey to their happily ever after.

Those of you who have read my books or been part of my newsletter have heard my explanation for why Authors never see their Star Ratings requested by Amazon, so thank you for allowing me to share the information once again.

When Amazon asks a reader to "Rate this book" on their Kindle, Amazon is the only one to see these ratings.

I'm left clueless about how you feel about this book. Your input matters.

Book reviews help me decide what kind of books I write. Plus, the more people who leave an review, the more likely Amazon is to move a book up in the rankings? Written reviews help other readers find and love a series.

Please continue to rate the book on your Kindle or reader

as this helps Amazon, but take an extra moment to pop over to the review section and leave a few words!

Seriously, a few words like, "great story," is enough.

If you have not read my Elkridge Series or the Lonely Ridge Collection, and have no idea why authors keep asking you as a reader to take a few minutes to leave even a couple of word reviews, here's the break down of how reviews work in this crazy business.

Reviews (not ratings) help authors qualify for advertising opportunities. Without triple digit reviews, an author may miss out on these valuable opportunities. And with only a "star rating" the author has little chance of participating in specific promotions, which means authors continue to struggle, and many talented writers give up writing altogether.

Readers aren't the only ones who use reviews to help make purchasing decisions. Producers and directors use your reviews when looking for new projects.

This is why I'm asking for your help.

A few kind words make such a massive difference to me. Your words give me the encouragement I need to continue writing because honestly, I write my books for you, and I'd like to keep delivering the types of stories you want to read.

And, yes, every book in a series needs reviews, not just the first book. Even if a book has been out for awhile, a fresh review can breathe new life into a book.

So, please take a few minutes to leave a short review. Even a couple of words will brighten my day.

Lastly. Thank you for reading this book. I hope to see you again soon. Cheers!

More Books By
Lyz Kelley

Elkridge Series

BLINDED
ABANDONED
ORPHANED
RESCUED
UNMISTAKEN
ATONEMENT
BITTERSWEET

DO YOU WANT A FREE BOOK?

I've got a present for my readers, your very own ebook exclusive: *Regrets, the prequel to BLINDED* when you sign up for my newsletter.

Click here to start falling in love today!

DEDICATION

For Sam, for the best brother and friend, a little sister could have.
1959 – 1983
May you rest in peace.

AUTHOR NOTES

Dear Readers,

For some, there is a point in a person's life where there is a complete and utter moment of clarity. I was a week from graduating high school when my first moment came. My mother and I got a phone call from a hospital in Maryland that my brother, Sam, a US Naval Corpsman, had died. That single moment changed me. Changed how I looked at and lived my life. When a Navy detail showed up the next morning, my emotions closed inward, and I was thrown into an all-consuming numbness.

For me, personally, I wanted to re-explore those few months of trying to hold onto the past, knowing everything in my life was going to be different from that day forward. My best friend was gone, and he wouldn't be coming back.

I hope you enjoyed reading Joey and Mara's story, their struggle to adjust to their new lives, and finding a satisfying comfort in each other's arms.

~Lyz

ACKNOWLEDGMENTS

FOR BLINDED

A book is hardly ever written by a single person. To make the story as strong and rewarding as possible, it's written by a tribe of special people.

My sincere appreciation goes to Jeannine for helping me see that Mara's and Joey's story needed to be told. To Margie Lawson, the book whisperer. To Amy, Rachelle, Mineela, Sue, and Lori, my gracious beta readers, who were brave enough to provide constructive suggestions for improvement.

Faith Freewoman and Zoe Dawson, my amazing editors, who pushed me to put the emotion on the page and worked tirelessly to make the best book possible. For Shelby Reed and Carol Agnew, who crossed every T and dotted every I. To Rogenna Brewer, who created a great cover for my story. To VFRW, Lalala's and the GIAMers for pushing me every step of the way. You have my sincere appreciation.

And, to Special Agent Michael Bantner who answered my

endless stream of questions about FBI, DEA, and local procedures. I'm honored you gave me permission to use your name in my books, and hopefully I created a good-looking character just as you requested. For the readers, know this character is completely fictional and in no way can measure up to the real Special Agent Bantner.

Last but not least, to my husband Mike for accompanying me to Ft. Logan National Cemetery and encouraging me to write when there were so many perceived obstacles in my way.

You all have my sincere gratitude.

~ Lyz

THANK YOU FOR READING: BLINDED

Award-winning author Lyz Kelley mixes a little bit of heart, healing, humanity, happiness, honor, hope, and honor in all her books that are written especially for you.

She's is a total disaster in the kitchen, a compulsive neat freak, a tea snob, and adores writing about and falling in love with everyday heroes.

Please also consider leaving a review on Amazon and/or Goodreads. Reviews help readers find new books to read, and authors find their footing.

You can also find Lyz on Facebook and Twitter for news, contests, giveaways, and more exciting stuff!

COPYRIGHT

Belvitri
Services

Cover Art: Covers by Megan Parker

30185561R00197

Made in the USA
San Bernardino, CA
22 March 2019